英倫文化

Learning GEPT
with British Culture

學全民英檢

GEPT

中級 聽力+閱讀

Dr Michael Ayers
(Clinical Scientist, King's College Hospital NHS Foundation Trust)
英國國民保健信託基金會倫敦國王學院醫院 臨床醫學儀器科學家

This book that you have in your hands right now was devised and written by my dear friend Ann.

I first met Ann in Taiwan in 2014. At that point in time, Ann was considering studying English literature in my home country, the UK. Even at this early point in our friendship, I saw in her a level of enthusiasm for the English language that is rare amongst those that teach it.

Later that year, Ann travelled to Southampton, a city in the South of England, to commence her studies. In a class dominated by native English speakers, it was testament to her dedication and passion that Ann not only persevered in her studies, but excelled in a way that impressed both her tutors and myself. I read many of Ann's essays. Each one reflected in it the qualities that had initially brought Ann to the UK and that led her to receive her Masters degree the following year.

After a year back in Taiwan, Ann returned to the UK for a trip in early 2017. Together, we visited many places that have now become the inspiration for much of the content in this book.

This book is different from other language learning books that you may have read. It does not focus on the details or formal linguistic rules that can often discourage learners. Instead this book provides scenarios that encourage readers to think about the English language in a more intuitive sense, in the way that you would learn your native language when growing up.

It is my hope that readers of this book find it as entertaining to read as I did. It is my wish that this book can instil in others a love of the English language and of learning it that Ann always shows.

Dr Michael Ayers

李豪英文 高雄鴻揚盛世升大學

鴻揚教育集團 李豪 總經理 / 英文首席

在英語教學這塊領域奔波、走跳數年，歷經學校與補教界的磨練，中級英檢這個區塊一直是國高中學生求學路上的必經關卡。我與作者大學同班四年，深知作者專注於教育的精神，這本書絕對是一本正在準備英檢考試的孩子們可以參考的工具書籍。內容簡單明瞭不複雜，圖片以作者遊歷各國的親身體驗，完整生活化呈現。題目難易適中，精簡扼要又犀利的點出重點。再者，無論從模擬試題的編排結構、解答到文法的細膩解析，除了為本書畫龍點睛，也深刻的表達出作者的用心、細心及耐心——所謂教學三大心和教學態度。

教育無他，唯愛與榜樣。知名藝術家李國修曾說過：「一生只要做好一件事情就功德圓滿。」這是我一路走來銘記在心的座右銘，我看到同學——也就是作者在書中投入的熱忱和用心做好一件事的付出讓我非常感動，因為她不僅完美了演繹這句話，也造福了所有迷惘中的孩子們，替他們指點迷津。因此我由衷、真心的希望大家不要錯過，在此敬祝大家考試順順利利。

自序

學語文沒有捷徑，除了一些天賦外，勤勞是必備的要素。身在台灣受教育的我，在出國念書之前，發覺想要營造英文的學習環境是很困難的，畢竟我們的生活環境周遭，不是國語就是台語，英文僅能從書中學習到再加上在地文化的影響下，所謂的台式英文就此產生。而現在資訊發達，學語言有很多的管道及方式，只要找到合適自己的方法，學英文就能變有趣！

在我的教學生涯中，學生們總喜歡詢問有關句子該怎麼說，或是詞語的正確說法，舉例來說，「孝順」兩個字在我們的文化當中其實是一個簡單的概念；但是在西方文化中並沒有這兩個字的說法，更沒有孝順這個概念，當然不是指西方人不孝順或是不善待自己的父母或家人，而是對於孝順這個概念，東西方的文化觀念不同。學英文或是其他語言，除了勤背單字和句子的用法之外，該語言的背景文化也是我們需要學習的重點。因此，此書除了幫助正在學習英文的讀者熟悉英文考試，也會與讀者們分享英國文化與英式英文詞語的介紹。除此之外，我的英國朋友們還幫忙錄製了本書的聽力部分，與我們平常聽到的美式發音有些不同，讀者們可以欣賞到英式英文的迷人之處。

Ann
in London, UK.

目錄

Section One：Listening　聽力練習與講解

Listening Module 1 聽力模擬測驗

Listening Module 2 聽力模擬測驗

Section Two：Reading　閱讀練習與講解

Reading Module 1 閱讀模擬測驗

Reading Module 2 閱讀模擬測驗

Section One：Listening
聽力練習與講解

全民英檢第一部分為聽力測驗，這個測驗涵蓋三種測驗方式：看圖辨義、問答、簡短對話，滿分為 120 分，最低成績不得低於 72 分。通過此項測驗即表示能聽懂一般會話，並能大致聽懂公共場合的廣播、氣象預報及廣告等等，同時也能聽懂簡易的產品介紹及操作說明，或是外籍人士的對話及詢問。

Ann 的小叮嚀

做聽力測驗時必須非常專注，因為不會重複播放，如果播放當中你不小心卡在一個題目或是一句話，那麼思緒就容易受到影響，甚至可能突然腦袋一片空白。尤其聽力測驗都在考試的第一部分，注意不要喝太多水分（例如水或是咖啡），也不要吃太飽（因為吃太飽容易想睡），考聽力測驗時精神才能專注。此外，適當的 taking notes（邊聽邊記錄重點或關鍵字，例如時間或數字）能幫助選擇正確的答案。

全民英檢中級的聽力內容大致如下：

	Content	Questions
Part 1	Picture Listening	15
Part 2	Q & A	15
Part 3	Short Talks	15

第一部分的聽力測驗著重在看圖辨義，首先觀察圖片內容，在聽到「題目」之後，以 5 W (what, where, who, why when) 和 1 H (how) 找到合適的答案。在開始我們的課程之前，先來一些有趣的聽力練習吧！

▶▶ **Let's come some interesting listening!!**

A Questions 1-2

1. A B C D
   ☐ ☐ ☐ ☐
2. A B C D
   ☐ ☐ ☐ ☐

B Questions 3-4

3. A B C D
   ☐ ☐ ☐ ☐
4. A B C D
   ☐ ☐ ☐ ☐

C Questions 5-6

5. A B C D
   ☐ ☐ ☐ ☐

6. A B C D
   ☐ ☐ ☐ ☐

D Questions 7-8

7. A B C D
   ☐ ☐ ☐ ☐

8. A B C D
   ☐ ☐ ☐ ☐

E **Questions 9-10**

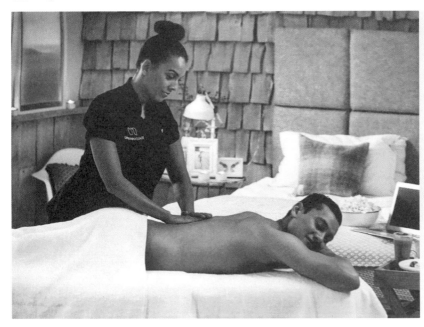

9. A B C D
☐ ☐ ☐ ☐

10. A B C D
☐ ☐ ☐ ☐

F **Questions 11-12**

11. A B C D
☐ ☐ ☐ ☐

12. A B C D
☐ ☐ ☐ ☐

G Questions 13-14

13. A B C D
☐ ☐ ☐ ☐

14. A B C D
☐ ☐ ☐ ☐

H Questions 15-16

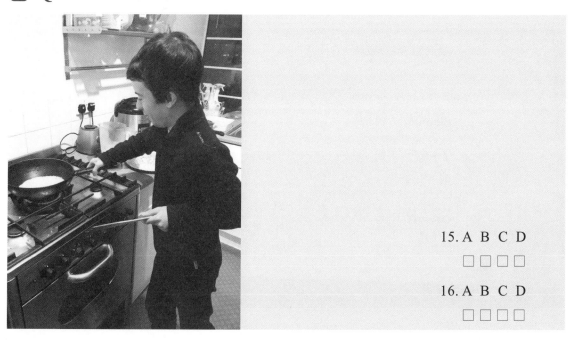

15. A B C D
☐ ☐ ☐ ☐

16. A B C D
☐ ☐ ☐ ☐

I Questions 17-18

17. A B C D
    ☐ ☐ ☐ ☐

18. A B C D
    ☐ ☐ ☐ ☐

J Questions 19-20

19. A B C D
    ☐ ☐ ☐ ☐

20. A B C D
    ☐ ☐ ☐ ☐

Judge not from appearances.

人不可貌相，海水不可斗量。

A

照片中,很顯然就是一台巴士,因此,最有可能出現的問題會和交通工具有關,或者是和地點有關,例如在哪一個城市、國家或地區(大都市 city/metropolis (n.);市區/urban area (n.) 或是郊區 suburb),所以當看到此圖時,可以先想好可能會出現的問題。

1. Look at picture A. What is driving on the road?

   (A) A cat
   (B) A factory
   (C) A bus
   (D) A post office

1. 請看 A 圖。何者在路上行駛?

   (A) 貓
   (B) 工廠
   (C) 巴士
   (D) 郵局

2. Look at picture A again. Where do you think this picture was taken?

   (A) In the city
   (B) At the airport
   (C) At the theatre
   (D) In the hospital

2. 再看 A 圖。你認為這張照片是在哪裡拍的?

   (A) 在城市中
   (B) 在機場
   (C) 在電影院
   (D) 在醫院

Ann's notes

先將圖中人事物及地點看清楚後,是不是覺得答題沒那麼困難了呢?眼尖的同學們,或許看到照片中的雙層巴士就已經猜到拍攝地點在哪裡了,當然,這是英國最常見的紅色雙層巴士,而且也是倫敦的代表。拍照的地點就在 Victoria Coach Station(維多莉亞客運總站),National Express(全國快車客運公司)可是留學生的最愛呢!Ann 在英國留學的時候還辦過 young persons card(一年 10 英鎊),這張卡超好用的,搭一兩次車的折扣,就可以賺回 10 英鎊的辦卡費用了!

B

Ann's reminder

照片 B 中，非常清楚的題幹重點就是「機場」（where/place）、「飛機」（what/transportation or transport [英式英文用法]）、「旅客」（who/ passengers 旅客），這三個 W 極可能出現在題目中，播放錄音時，要特別注意這幾個問題。

3. Look at picture B. What is in the picture?

   (A) A plane
   (B) A bird
   (C) A train
   (D) A tank

3. 請看 B 圖。照片中為何物？

   (A) 飛機
   (B) 小鳥
   (C) 火車
   (D) 坦克車

4. Look at picture B again. What will be inside?

   (A) Vehicles
   (B) Passengers
   (C) Houses
   (D) Aliens

4. 再看 B 圖。物體中會有什麼？

   (A) 車輛
   (B) 旅客
   (C) 房子
   (D) 外星人

Ann's notes

像這樣的圖片，物體清晰，因此很容易可以判定這張照片一定跟機場、遊客、搭飛機、交通工具等有關。因此，在聽力練習或是考試時，要必備這些基本的單字喔！（Ann 在前面有提過，背單字、擁有高單字量讓你在聽力練習或是考試中，會減少很多臨場壓力喔！）照片中的 easy Jet 是歐洲（隸屬英國的航空公司）的廉價航空，Ann 當時搭乘 easy Jet 從英國倫敦出發去西班牙旅行，來回機票不到台幣 1500 元呢！早起的鳥兒有蟲吃，只要先規劃好旅行時間，提早買機票，歐洲有許多廉航都是物美價廉的呢！同時，遇到的機長不一定會是英文母語人士，因此在飛機上常常遇到印度口音的機長廣播，是非常好的英文聽力訓練。語言是用來溝通的，所以有機會多聽不同的英文口音腔調，可以了解到更多不同的文化喔！

5. What is shown inside the circle?

    (A) A microwave

    (B) A hinge

    (C) A sandwich

    (D) A bottle

5. 畫圈中為何物？

    (A) 微波爐

    (B) 鉸鍊

    (C) 三明治

    (D) 瓶子

6. Look at picture C again. What is shown in the picture?

    (A) A door

    (B) A tablet

    (C) A window

    (D) A computer

6. 再看 C 圖。照片中顯示的是什麼？

    (A) 門

    (B) 桌子

    (C) 窗戶

    (D) 電腦

Ann's notes

C 圖第一個題目就問到「畫圈」中的東西是什麼，很多人可能不知道門鉸鍊的英文是什麼，聽完全部選項是不是很容易找出正確答案呢？因為微波爐（microwave）、三明治（sandwich）跟瓶子（bottle）都是基礎單字，刪除這三個答案之後，就可以猜出正確答案是 hinge (n.) 鉸鍊 / 鉸鍊轉動 / 樞紐 / 中心。第二個題目就更簡單啦！很顯然地，這就是一道門。

7. Where are these people?

    (A) At the airport
    (B) At the train station
    (C) At the department store
    (D) At the theatre

7. 這些人正在哪裡？

    (A) 機場
    (B) 火車站
    (C) 百貨公司
    (D) 戲院

8. Look at the picture again. What are the people doing?

    (A) They are walking.
    (B) They are buying something.
    (C) They are waiting for a train.
    (D) They are doing house chores.

8. 再看這個圖。他們正在做什麼？

    (A) 他們在正走路。
    (B) 他們正在購物。
    (C) 他們正在等火車。
    (D) 他們在做家事。

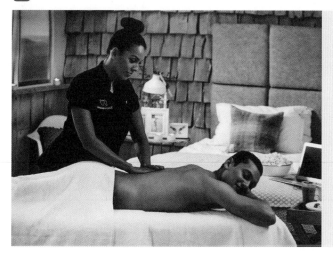

Ann's reminder

圖片 E 看起來就是很舒服的按摩服務。圖片中有兩個人（who = the client/customer 客戶 / 客人，the rubber 按摩師 [rub (v.) 摩擦 / 按摩]），此外，在這裡會做的相關事情（what）一定跟按摩有關，所以一定要留意跟按摩有關的詞彙。

9. What is the woman doing?

   (A) She is rubbing.

   (B) She is acting.

   (C) She is writing a scientific article.

   (D) She is reading a book.

9. 這位女士正在做什麼？

   (A) 她正在按摩。

   (B) 她在在表演。

   (C) 她正在攥寫一篇科學文章。

   (D) 她正在閱讀一本書。

10. Look at the picture again. What is the man doing?

   (A) He is sending a message to his mum.

   (B) He is enjoying a massage.

   (C) He is watching a film.

   (D) He is eating popcorn.

10. 再看此圖。這位男士正在做什麼？

   (A) 他正在傳訊息給他媽媽。

   (B) 他在享受著舒服按摩。

   (C) 他正在看電影。

   (D) 他正在吃爆米花。

Ann's notes

這兩個題目需要注意單字拼音及發音。因為 massage (v. n.) 按摩和 message (v. n.) 訊息的拼音相似，但發音不同，大家可以注意錄音檔唸的 massage 和 message 的差異。另外，除了 massage 這個字，rub (v.) 也是按摩的意思。

F

Ann's reminder

F 圖片就是一個 object（物件），它可以是地方（where=place），也可以有其他問題的發展，例如誰會去那裡（who=people, tourists）或是去那裡可以做什麼（what）。

11. Where is this?

    (A) A factory

    (B) A business building

    (C) A castle

    (D) A school

11. 這裡是哪裡？

    (A) 工廠

    (B) 商業大樓

    (C) 城堡

    (D) 學校

12. Look at the picture again. Ann is going to this place. What can she do there?

    (A) She can study in the school.

    (B) She can go sightseeing.

    (C) She can climb the mountain.

    (D) She can go cycling.

12. 再看此圖。Ann 正要去這個地方。她可以在那裡做什麼事情？

    (A) 她在學校讀書。

    (B) 她可以去觀光。

    (C) 她可以爬山。

    (D) 她可以騎腳踏車。

Ann's notes

這張照片是英國溫莎城堡（Winsor Castle）一隅，也是目前英國女王伊麗莎白二世的住所。Buckingham Palace「白金漢宮」是官邸，她本人最喜歡住在溫莎城堡。也許 Buckingham Palace 就像是她的辦公室，當然大家都不想 24 小時待在上班的地方，女王也是人，她也想度假休息囉！溫莎城堡有對外開放參觀，但女王住的房間或是正在用的場所是不能參觀的。女王如果不在溫莎城堡時，許多交誼廳或是晉見重要人物及國家元首的地方都會開放給民眾參觀，Ann 就走訪了溫莎城堡，感受一下：如果是 Princess Ann 的話，好像真的很 royal family 吧！

圖片 G 是一張菜單（menu），所以詢問圖片為何（what）就是最簡單的問題，除此之外，詢問這張菜單相關的問題或地點（where）的題型也非常容易出現，抑或是人們去那裡做什麼（what）。

13. What is this?

    (A) A train timetable

    (B) A book

    (C) An airplane ticket

    (D) A menu

13. 這是什麼？

    (A) 火車時刻表

    (B) 書

    (C) 機票

    (D) 菜單

14. Look at the picture again. Where will you find this?

    (A) In a restaurant

    (B) In the play ground

    (C) At the airport

    (D) In a book shop

14. 再看此圖。哪裡可以找到這個東西？

    (A) 餐廳

    (B) 遊樂園

    (C) 機場

    (D) 書店

Ann's notes

這是一張內容清楚、並載有很多資訊的菜單。除了餐廳名稱（Horse & Groom）之外，還可以看出餐廳位於 Windsor（倫敦近郊），此外，黑框下方的小字 AD.1719 顯示這間餐廳從 18 世紀便開始營業（1719 年便有營業的文字紀錄，實際的開業時間甚至可能更早）。由此可知，這是一間歷史悠久的餐廳。菜單中的 Chef's Specials（主廚推薦）也可能會是考試重點之一。所以一張菜單可以衍生出不同的題目，取決於英文考試的難易度。

H

Ann's reminder

H 圖片，可以觀察到有一個人（who=the man）在廚房（where=kitchen）裡面煮飯（what=cooking）。

15. What is the man doing?

    (A) He is playing video games.

    (B) He is singing a song.

    (C) He is cooking.

    (D) He is watching a film.

15. 這位男士在正做什麼？

    (A) 他在打電玩遊戲。

    (B) 他在唱歌。

    (C) 他在烹飪。

    (D) 他在看電影。

16. Look at the picture again. Where was this photo taken?

    (A) In the kitchen

    (B) In the bathroom

    (C) In the living room

    (D) At the bus stop

16. 再看此圖。這張照片在哪裡拍的？

    (A) 廚房

    (B) 浴室

    (C) 客廳

    (D) 公車站

Ann's notes

圖片 H，可以聯想到的是 what= cooking or cooking (food), where= in the kitchen，所以從圖片中先去猜想可能會問的問題，有了心理準備後，聽力的題目一播放，就可以找到最合適的答案了。

I

17. What is this?

    (A) A train

    (B) A ship

    (C) A small mountain stream

    (D) A ball

17. 這是什麼？

    (A) 火車

    (B) 船

    (C) 小溪流

    (D) 球

18. Look at the picture again. What time of
day do you think the photo was taken?

    (A) At lunch time

    (B) In the afternoon

    (C) In the evening

    (D) At dawn

18. 再看此圖。你覺得這張照片是什麼
時候拍攝的？

    (A) 午餐時間

    (B) 下午

    (C) 晚上

    (D) 清晨

Ann's reminder

圖片 J 是一張門票，如果對音樂劇熟悉的人，應該很快會注意到劇名 Mamma Mia，這是一齣很有名的音樂劇，也曾經被翻拍成電影。如果不清楚音樂劇背景也沒關係，門票上方有一行黑底字 Novello Theatre，因此可以判斷這是一張劇院的票。門票上面所有的資訊都可能成為考題，例如：what day 星期幾、what date 幾月幾號、what time 幾點幾分、where 位置地點（grand circle, B14）等。還有一點值得注意的是，英式英文跟美式英文拼字稍有不同，在這裡 theatre 是英式的劇院，而美式拼法則是 theater。

19. What do you think this is?

   (A) An essay

   (B) A ticket to a musical

   (C) A train ticket

   (D) A flight ticket

19. 你認為這是什麼？

   (A) 一篇散文

   (B) 一張音樂劇的門票

   (C) 一張火車票

   (D) 一張機票

20. Look at the picture again. Where can Michael take this ticket?

   (A) To the bookshop

   (B) To the museum

   (C) To the theatre

   (D) To a car maintenance shop

20. 再看此圖。Michael 可以在哪裡買到這張票？

   (A) 書店

   (B) 博物館

   (C) 劇院 (theatre 英式英文拼字 / theater 美式英文拼字)

   (D) 車子保養廠

Ann's notes

19 題題目很單純地問這是什麼（票），很容易就可以選出適當的答案。第 20 題則問 Michael 可以在哪裡買到這張票？我們可以預測答案應該是在劇院或是網路訂票。而 A 選項書店，似乎也很合理，但也不是所有的書店都有售票的服務。在國外，書店就是賣書，頂多設置有咖啡廳讓人一邊看書一邊品嚐咖啡。而 B 跟 D 很明顯不可能是正確答案，所以本題讓人比較難以判斷的就是選項 A 跟 C 了。但謹記一點，在考試中，必須選一個最適合的答案。即使我們覺得在書店買到音樂劇門票似乎恰當或者合理，但 C 選項比起 A 又更適合，所以該題還是應該選 C 為正解。

以上的練習，是否有了一些概念了呢？

Let's move on our important parts at the test.

▶▶ Part 1：Picture Listening 看圖辨義

Ann 的小叮嚀

試題上有幾幅圖畫，每一圖畫約 1~3 個描述該圖的題目，每題播放題目以及四個英語敘述，選出符合圖示與問題的答案。

Example：Q1 and Q2

1. A B C D
   ☐ ☐ ☐ ☐
2. A B C D
   ☐ ☐ ☐ ☐

1. What are they doing?
   (A) They are watching TV.
   (B) They are shopping for clothes.
   (C) They are cooking dinner.
   (D) They are reading a newspaper.

2. Please look the picture again. Where are the people ?
   (A) In the department store
   (B) At a car showroom
   (C) In a factory
   (D) At the movie theater

1. 他們正在做什麼？
   (A) 他們在正看電視。
   (B) 他們正在買衣服。
   (C) 他們正在煮晚餐。
   (D) 他們正在閱讀報紙。

2. 再看此圖。這幾個人在哪裡？
   (A) 百貨公司
   (B) 車展場
   (C) 工廠
   (D) 電影院

Ann's notes

我們可以判斷圖中應該為購買衣服的地方,三個人在服飾專櫃前討論購物,所以大概可以得知問題一定跟 shopping 有關。圖片中他們應該在討論買衣服。所以,必須注意 shopping、clothes、department store 或是 shopping mall 這類型的關鍵字。

牛刀小試

Part 1：看圖辨義

A Q1 and Q2

1. A B C D
   ☐ ☐ ☐ ☐
2. A B C D
   ☐ ☐ ☐ ☐

B Q3 and Q4

3. A B C D
   ☐ ☐ ☐ ☐
4. A B C D
   ☐ ☐ ☐ ☐

C Q5 and Q6

Weather Warning Report　　　January 18, 2017

City	Temperature	Chance of Rain	Visibility
London	7°C	30%	6.4 km
Cambridge	5°C	50%	6.4 km
Oxford	8°C	60%	6.4 km
Southampton	8°C	50%	11.3 km
Exeter	7°C	20%	16.1 km
Bath	9°C	40%	12.9 km
Visibility:5-10 km/moderate 10-15 km/good 16 m +/very good			

5. A B C D
☐ ☐ ☐ ☐

6. A B C D
☐ ☐ ☐ ☐

D Q7 and Q8

BBC One TV Programming

Time	Program	Type
1300-1400	Sherlock Series 4:3 The Final Problem	Detective
1400-1600	Let It Shine Episode 2	Musical
1600-1700	Not Going Out Series 8:1 Romance	Romance
1700-1800	Death in Paradise Series 6:Episode 2	Science

7. A B C D
☐ ☐ ☐ ☐

8. A B C D
☐ ☐ ☐ ☐

E Q9、Q10 and Q11

Time	Airlines	To	Flight	Gate
06:50	Emirates	Dubai	EK 351	E2
07:10	Air Canada	Tokyo	AC 6230	D2
08:20	Qatar	Yangon	QR 4432	C1A
08:35	Etihad	Abu Dhabi	EY 403	G5
09:05	Tigerair	Singapore	TR 2103	A3

9. A B C D
☐ ☐ ☐ ☐

10. A B C D
☐ ☐ ☐ ☐

11. A B C D
☐ ☐ ☐ ☐

F Q12 and Q13

12. A B C D
☐ ☐ ☐ ☐

13. A B C D
☐ ☐ ☐ ☐

G Q14 and Q15

14. A B C D
    □ □ □ □

15. A B C D
    □ □ □ □

To err is human; to forgive, devine./ Alexander Pope

犯錯是人性，寬恕是神性。（亞歷山大·波普）

內容解析

Ⓐ Q1 and Q2

1. Where are they?

    (A) At the department store
    (B) In a restaurant
    (C) At the zoo
    (D) At the train station

2. Please look at picture again. Are they waiting for their train to arrive?

    (A) Yes, they are looking at the station departures board.
    (B) No, they are going to the beach.
    (C) No, they are discussing their course.
    (D) Yes, they are reading a sign in the street.

1. 他們在哪裡?

    (A) 百貨公司
    (B) 餐廳
    (C) 動物園
    (D) 火車站

2. 再看圖 A。他們正在等火車進站嗎?

    (A) 是的,他們在看火車進站時間表。
    (B) 不,他們正要去海邊。
    (C) 不,他們正在討論課程。
    (D) 是的,他們正看著街上的指示告牌。

3 Where is this scene taking place?

(A) A church

(B) A building

(C) A wedding

(D) A temple

4 Look at the picture again. What is the man wearing?

(A) He is wearing a wedding suit.

(B) He is wearing a school uniform.

(C) He is wearing a swimming suit.

(D) He is wearing a welding suit.

3. 這個場景在哪裡舉辦？

(A) 教會

(B) 大樓

(C) 婚禮

(D) 廟宇

4. 再看此圖。這個男士穿著什麼？

(A) 他穿著結婚禮服。

(B) 他穿著學校制服。

(C) 他穿著泳衣。

(D) 他穿著焊接工人制服。

Weather Warning Report			January 18, 2017
City	Temperature	Chance of Rain	Visibility
London	7°C	30%	6.4 km
Cambridge	5°C	50%	6.4 km
Oxford	8°C	60%	6.4 km
Southampton	8°C	50%	11.3 km
Exeter	7°C	20%	16.1 km
Bath	9°C	40%	12.9 km
Visibility:5-10 km/moderate 10-15 km/good 16 km +/very good			

氣象預報			2017 年 1 月 18 日
城市	溫度	降雨機率	能見度
倫敦	7°C	30%	6.4 公里
劍橋	5°C	50%	6.4 公里
牛津	8°C	60%	6.4 公里
南安普敦	8°C	50%	11.3 公里
希艾特	7°C	20%	16.1 公里
巴斯	9°C	40%	12.9 公里
能見度：5-10 公里 / 中等 10-15 公里 / 良好 16 公里 + / 佳			

5. Where is the best place to hold an outside activity?

(A) Cambridge
(B) Oxford
(C) Southampton
(D) Exeter

5. 哪一個地方最適合舉辦戶外活動？

(A) 劍橋
(B) 牛津
(C) 南安普敦
(D) 艾希特

6. Look at the table again. Where is this weather report from?

(A) The United States of America
(B) The United Kingdom
(C) France
(D) Germany

6. 再看此圖表。這份氣象預報是來自何處？

(A) 美國
(B) 英國
(C) 法國
(D) 德國

D Q7 and Q8

BBC One TV Programming

Time	Program	Type
1300-1400	Sherlock Series 4:3 The Final Problem	Detective
1400-1600	Let It Shine Episode 2	Musical
1600-1700	Not Going Out Series 8:1 Romance	Romance
1700-1800	Death in Paradise Series 6:Episode 2	Science

BBC 第一頻道節目表

時間	節目	型態
1300-1400	Sherlock 神探夏洛克 第四季第三集：最後一案	偵探型
1400-1600	音樂真人秀閃耀新星 第二集	音樂劇
1600-1700	別走 第八季第一集：愛情降臨	浪漫愛情劇
1700-1800	天堂島疑雲 第六季第二集	科學

7. Which program will be about music and performance?

   (A) Sherlock
   (B) Let It Shine
   (C) Not Going Out
   (D) Death in Paradise

7. 哪一個節目跟音樂表演有關？

   (A) 神探夏洛克
   (B) 音樂真人秀閃耀新星
   (C) 別走
   (D) 天堂島疑雲

8. Look at the table again. Hannah loves chemistry and likes to discover the mysteries of the earth. Which program will she be fond of?

   (A) Sherlock
   (B) Let It Shine
   (C) Not Going Out
   (D) Death in Paradise

8. 再看圖表。Hannah 熱愛化學而且喜歡探索地球的奧秘。她會喜歡哪一個節目？

   (A) 神探夏洛克
   (B) 音樂真人秀閃耀新星
   (C) 別走
   (D) 天堂島疑雲

E Q9 and Q11

 Departure

Time	Airlines	To	Flight	Gate
06:50	Emirates	Dubai	EK 351	E2
07:10	Air Canada	Tokyo	AC 6230	D2
08:20	Qatar	Yangon	QR 4432	C1A
08:35	Etihad	Abu Dhabi	EY 403	G5
09:05	Tigerair	Singapore	TR 2103	A3

「離境班機」

時間	航空公司	前往	班機	登機門
06:50	阿聯酋航空	杜拜	EK 351	E2
07:10	加拿大航空	東京	AC 6230	D2
08:20	卡達航空	仰光	QR 4432	C1A
08:30	阿提哈德航空	阿布達比	EY 403	G5
09:05	虎航	新加坡	TR 2103	A3

9. Michael is going to Singapore for a conference. Which airlines will he take?

   (A) Emirates (B) Air Canada
   (C) Qatar (D) Tigerair

10. Look at the table again. Natalie is looking for flight QR 4432 at 08: 20. Which gate should she go?

   (A) E2 (B) D2
   (C) C1A (D) G5

11. Please look at picture again. Josh is going to Tokyo. What time is his flight?

   (A) 05:50 (B) 07:10
   (C) 08:30 (D) 09:05

9. Michael 準備去新加坡參加會議。他會搭哪一家航空班機？

   (A) 阿聯酋航空。 (B) 加拿大航空。
   (C) 卡達航空。 (D) 老虎航空。

10. 同圖表。Natalie 查詢八點二十分的航班 QR 4432。她應該去哪個登機門？

   (A) E2 (B) D2
   (C) C1A (D) G5

11. 再看此圖表。Josh 正前往東京。他的班機時間是什麼時候？

   (A) Six fifty. /Ten to six.
   (B) Seven ten. /Ten past seven.
   (C) Eight thirty. /Half past eight.
   (D) Nine O five. /Nine O five.

一、時間的表達

1. 表達整點時，其句型為：It's ＋數字（ ＋ o'clock).
   E.g. It's twelve.（現在十二點。）＝ It's twelve o'clock.

2. 表達幾點幾分時，代名詞用 it，「時」與「分」皆以數字表示。
   「分」若為兩個英文字的數字時，中間要加上連字號「-」，如 thirty-five（35 分），但「時」與「分」之間不用連字號。若「分」為個位數，常會用英文字 O 代表「零」，如 11:07 唸作 eleven O seven。
   E.g. 1:08 → one O eight
   　　　2:10 → two ten
   　　　7:25 → seven twenty-five

3. 用時鐘形狀作換算

It's ＋ 幾分鐘 ＋ to ＋ 幾點鐘（再過幾分幾點）通常用於 30 分之後	to....past	It's ＋ 幾分鐘 +past/after+ 幾點鐘（幾點又幾分）通常用於 30 分之前
	It's 10:20	It's twenty past ten.
It's twenty to nine.	It's 8:40	
	It's 6:15	It's a quarter past six. 因為每小時有 4 個 15 分鐘，所以表達 15 分或 45 分時，用 quarter 代替 fifteen
It's a quarter to eight.	It's 7:45	
	It's 4:30	It's half past four. 表達剛好 30 分鐘，用 half 代替 thirty。

4. 英文不會用 24 小時制來表達時間，所以要更明確的表達時間在哪一個時段，可在時間後加 a.m. / p.m. 或加上時間副詞（in the morning/ in the afternoon/in the evening/at night）。

時刻	時間副詞
中午 12:00 以前	a.m.（上午，指凌晨到中午的時間）或 in the morning（早上）
中午 12:00 以後	p.m.（下午，指中午到晚上的時間） in the afternoon（下午）、in the evening（傍晚；晚上）、 at night（晚上）

E.g.

(1) It's three o'clock in the afternoon.（現在是下午三點鐘。）

(2) It's nine a.m.（現在是上午九點。）

二、詢問時間

1. 詢問「現在幾點」，要以疑問詞 what time 開頭，而主詞一律用代名詞 it 來表達，不可使用其他代名詞。

2. 詢問「現在幾點」的句型為「What time is it?」，也可用「What is the time?」，其中 time 加上定冠詞 the 表特定（此刻）的時間。

   E.g.

   (1) A: What time is it?（現在幾點了？）= What is the time?

   　　B: It's 11:10.（現在是十一點十分。）

   (2) Do you have the time?（請問現在幾點）/ Do you have time?（你有空嗎？）

三、補充

1. 表達「某事在幾點」發生時，需用介系詞 at，其句型為「S + be-V + at +時間 .」。

   E.g.

   (1) The party is at half past seven.（派對在七點半開始）

   (2) The class is at eight in the morning, not at eight in the evening.

   　　（課程時間是早上八點開始，不是晚上八點）

2. 詢問「某事在幾點」發生時，其句型為「What time + be-V + S ?」，其中主詞為「某事」。

   E.g.

   (1) What time is the film?（電影幾點開始？）

   　　The film is at five p.m.（電影五點開始。）

   (2) A: What time is the meeting?（會議幾點開始？）

   　　B: It's at ten.（十點。）

F Q12 and Q 13

12. What is wrong with the woman?

    (A) She has a pair of shoes.

    (B) She has a broken leg.

    (C) She wears a scarf.

    (D) She wears a hat.

13. Please look at the picture again. What is wrong with the man?

    (A) He has broken his arm.

    (B) He has beautiful hands.

    (C) He likes to read books.

    (D) He looks at the woman.

12. 這位女士發生什麼事？

    (A) 她有一雙鞋子。

    (B) 她腳骨折。

    (C) 她戴了圍巾。

    (D) 她戴一頂帽子。

13. 再看此圖。這位男士怎麼了？

    (A) 他的手臂受傷了。

    (B) 他有一雙漂亮的手。

    (C) 他喜歡閱讀書籍。

    (D) 他看著這位女士。

14. Nick would like to visit the tallest building in Taiwan. Which part of Taiwan should he go to?

    (A) the eastern part
    (B) the southern part
    (C) the northern part
    (D) the western part

15. Look at the picture again. In the eastern Taiwan, what will Nick see?

    (A) A lighthouse
    (B) A Ferris wheel
    (C) A dolphin
    (D) A zoo

14. Nick 想去參觀台灣最高的大樓。他應該去台灣哪個區域？

    (A) 東部
    (B) 南部
    (C) 北部
    (D) 西部

15. 再看此圖。在東台灣，Nick 可以看到什麼？

    (A) 燈塔
    (B) 摩天輪
    (C) 海豚
    (D) 動物園

Well begun is half done./ Horace
好的開始是成功的一半。(赫瑞斯)

▶▶ Part 2：Q & A 問與答

Ann 的小叮嚀

此部分共 15 題，每題光碟播放出一英文問句或是直述句之後，請從四個選項 A 、B 、C 、D 四個回答或是回應中，選出一個最合適的答案。

Example：

1. Where is your sister?

   (A) She is 20.
   (B) She is in the United Kingdom.
   (C) She is watching TV.
   (D) She is hungry.

Ann's notes

Where 的問句，答案必定跟地方或是地點有關。(A) 答案與 how 有關 (How old is your sister?)，(C) 答案與 what 有關 (What is your sister doing?)，(D) 答案跟 what 或是 how 有關 (what's wrong with your sister? 或是 How is your sister doing?) 因此，答案選 (B)She is in the United Kingdom 她在英國。

2. Danny is the last person that I would like to talk to!

   (A) I talked with him yesterday.
   (B) No, he was the first one that arrived.
   (C) What's wrong between you and Danny?
   (D) It's time to go home.

Ann's notes

S. + V. + the last person that S. + V. 意思為「最不想 ... 的人」，這句話意思是「我最不想跟 Danny 說話」，此題為直述句，依據題意，可以得知 speaker 跟 Danny 之間可能有誤會，所以答案選 C。

★ 補充 1：(A) 我昨天才跟他通話過。(B) 不，他是最早到達的人。(D) 該回家了。
★ 補充 2：it is time to + V. 該是做 ... 時候了。

這個部分的作答技巧，是留意 speaker 使用什麼疑問詞，用句子中的疑問詞來判斷合適的答案。

For example:

What is the weather like today?

    (A) It is 7 o'clock.
    (B) It is cloudy.
    (C) It is over there.
    (D) It is done.

Ann's notes

問題以 what 開始，回答則需要跟狀態有關，如果選項有 yes 跟 no 的話，首先就可以先刪去這樣的答案了。

翻譯： 今天天氣如何？

(A) 現在七點鐘。(B) 今天天氣多雲。(C) 在那邊。(D) 做完了。

依據題目 what，加上有 weather 這個字，很明顯就是問天氣狀態。有時候問天氣狀況可以說「what is today?」或是「How is it today?」所以答案選 (B)。

The future belongs to those who believe in the beauty of their dreams.

/ Eleanor Roosevelt

未來是屬於那些相信自己美夢的人。(埃莉諾‧羅斯福)

牛刀小試

1.
   (A) Nando's
   (B) Her Majesty's Theatre
   (C) Covent Garden
   (D) King's College London

2.
   (A) She is sleeping.
   (B) She is watching an astronomy show.
   (C) She is playing the piano.
   (D) She is reading poems.

3.
   (A) Sure. Let's have some tea.
   (B) I am going to take a coach.
   (C) We can eat outside.
   (D) They are arguing.

4.
   (A) I am doing my homework.
   (B) I am washing the dishes.
   (C) I am good.
   (D) I am good at creating medical devices.

5.
   (A) Yes, he is running.
   (B) Yes, he is cooking.
   (C) No, he is eating lunch at home.
   (D) No, he is going out for dinner.

6.
   (A) You can buy stamps at the post office.
   (B) You can eat your breakfast first.
   (C) You can take the train to that place.
   (D) You can visit Eton College.

7.
   (A) Yes, I am going out this morning.
   (B) No, I don't want to go out this evening.
   (C) I don't understand the question.
   (D) I am meeting friends this afternoon.

8.
   (A) It is fine.
   (B) It is good weather.
   (C) It costs 10 pounds.
   (D) It refers to luxury.

9.
   (A) He must be tired.
   (B) He was excited.
   (C) He was fond of the show.
   (D) He likes to sleep.

10.
   (A) Yes, he likes to sing songs.
   (B) No, he likes painting.
   (C) He doesn't know what to choose.
   (D) He likes to decorate his flat.

11.
- (A) Yes, she is cooking at home.
- (B) No, she is eating lunch outside.
- (C) Yes, she likes studying in the library.
- (D) No, she likes reading books at a cafe.

12.
- (A) It is scary.
- (B) It is fun.
- (C) It is not interesting.
- (D) It is about ecology.

13.
- (A) I don't like boring things.
- (B) Yes, I like boring books.
- (C) I am doing some research so I need to read this book.
- (D) I don't like this book.

14.
- (A) It is rubbish.
- (B) It is hungry.
- (C) It is in the forest.
- (D) It likes the city.

15.
- (A) Yes, I am looking for a book.
- (B) Yes, I like this restaurant.
- (C) No, I don't like watching films.
- (D) No, I am not particularly interested in old things.

16.
- (A) You are wrong.
- (B) I don't like it.
- (C) You can say that again.
- (D) It is a piece of cake.

17.
- (A) I am fine.
- (B) Nothing is wrong with me.
- (C) I am very right.
- (D) I am a giraffe.

18.
- (A) Oh, but that is not my favorite color.
- (B) This is my house.
- (C) No, it's not.
- (D) This is silly.

19.
- (A) I like hot chocolate milk.
- (B) I like pizza.
- (C) I play basketball.
- (D) I watch the film.

20.
- (A) I take the same journey every day.
- (B) Yes, I have never been there before.
- (C) Yes, I enjoy tennis.
- (D) This is very delicious.

Life is not all roses.

人生並不是康莊大道。

1. Which restaurant will we go to celebrate Mike's birthday?

   (A) Nando's
   (B) Her Majesty's Theatre
   (C) Covent Garden
   (D) King's College London

1. 我們要去哪一間餐廳慶祝 Mike 的生日？

   (A) Nando's 烤雞餐廳
   (B) 女王陛下劇院
   (C) 柯芬園
   (D) 倫敦大學國王學院

Ann's notes

Nando's 是英國非常常見的葡式烤雞連鎖餐廳，是相當普遍的食物。本店於 1987 年在南非創立，如今在世界上 30 幾個國家有超過 1,000 間分店。Nando's 被稱為葡式烤雞餐廳，是因為創辦人 Fernando Duarte 跟 Robert Brozin 是葡萄牙人，但烤雞的料理方式跟葡萄牙沒有什麼關係。Nando's 是 Ann 在英國求學時最愛的餐廳之一，因為價錢合理，烤雞則是現烤的。最愛的 one quarter chicken（四分之一雞）加上 two sides（兩個配菜 -- 有薯條、沙拉、奶油烤玉米…等）。在高消費的英國，一餐不到 10 英鎊的美味烤雞餐，實在是既滿足口腹之慾、價錢又親民的選擇。前些日子回到當初留學居住的南安普敦 (Southampton)，發現 Nando's 又開了新店面，而 Nando's 在大倫敦總共有約莫 150 間分店，而且大部分距離地鐵站都非常近，所以有機會到英國時，一定不要錯過 Nando's 烤雞喔！

這題的答案跟英國文化比較相關，沒有去過英國的讀者可能覺得較難選出正確答案，不過考試中也很有可能遇到題目超出我們原有的背景知識，這時候就可以選擇用刪去法來解題。首先 B 選項 (Her Majesty's Theatre) 跟 D 選項 (King's College London) 和題目問的餐廳明顯不合，所以我們可以先刪除。剩下 A 跟 C 選項，C 選項的 Covent Garden「柯芬園」是英國倫敦的一個自治市鎮 (city)，位於英國倫敦西區的聖馬丁巷與德魯里巷之間。區內的皇家歌劇院與小商店是柯芬園的一大特色，其中的 art market 是英國有名的手工藝市場之一，東側的河岸街，則保存著眾多 17 至 18 世紀建造的建築物。

因此，刪去了所有不可能的選項，答案就選 A。

2. What is Ann doing at the planetarium?

   (A) She is sleeping.
   (B) She is watching an astronomy show.
   (C) She is playing the piano.
   (D) She is reading poems.

2. Ann 在天文館做什麼？

   (A) 她在睡覺。
   (B) 她正在看一場天文電影。
   (C) 她在彈鋼琴。
   (D) 她正在閱讀詩集。

3. It is windy. Maybe we can stay in a restaurant.

   (A) Sure. Let's have some tea.

   (B) I am going to take a coach.

   (C) We can eat outside.

   (D) They are arguing.

3. 風真大。或許我們可以待在餐廳。

   (A) 好啊。喝點茶吧。

   (B) 我正要去搭客運。

   (C) 我們可以到外面吃飯。

   (D) 他們在正吵架。

4. How are you doing today?

   (A) I am doing my homework.

   (B) I am washing the dishes.

   (C) I am good.

   (D) I am good at creating medical devices.

4. 你今天如何呢？

   (A) 我正在寫作業。

   (B) 我正在洗完盤。

   (C) 我很好。

   (D) 我擅長創造醫療設備。

Ann's notes

除了「How are you?」之外，還有其他許多與問候有關的句型，例如「How are you doing?」、「What's everything?」、「How have you been up to?」等。所以，當聽到 doing 的時候，容易直覺想到跟做什麼事情有關。不過也有些例外的狀況，例如要問職業相關用的句型是「What do you do?」或「What are you doing?」，因此要特別注意把句子聽清楚喔。

5. Is Michael going out for lunch?

   (A) Yes, he is running.

   (B) Yes, he is cooking.

   (C) No, he is eating lunch at home.

   (D) No, he is going out for dinner.

5. Michael 準備出門吃午餐嗎？

   (A) 是的，他正在跑步。

   (B) 是的，他正在煮飯。

   (C) 不，他在家吃午餐。

   (D) 不，他正出門吃晚餐。

6. Where can we buy stamps for sending postcards?

   (A) You can buy stamps at the post office.

   (B) You can eat your breakfast first.

   (C) You can take the train to that place.

   (D) You can visit Eton College.

6. 我們可以去哪裡買寄明信片的郵票呢？

   (A) 你可以去郵局買郵票。

   (B) 你可以先吃早餐。

   (C) 你可以搭火車去那個地方。

   (D) 你可以參觀伊頓中學。

7. What are you going to do this afternoon?

   (A) Yes, I am going out this morning.
   (B) No, I don't want to go out this evening.
   (C) I don't understand the question.
   (D) I am meeting friends this afternoon.

7. 你今天下午要做什麼？

   (A) 是的，我今天早上會出門去。
   (B) 不，我今天晚上不想外出。
   (C) 我不清楚這個問題。
   (D) 我今天下午要跟朋友見面。

8. How much is it?

   (A) It is fine.
   (B) It is good weather.
   (C) It costs 10 pounds.
   (D) It refers to luxury.

8. 這個多少錢？

   (A) 沒事的。
   (B) 天氣很好。
   (C) 10 英鎊。
   (D) 它代表奢侈品。

Ann's notes

refer to + N./Ving 代表 / 意味

9. Polo's Dad was sleeping when the show began.

   (A) He must be tired.
   (B) He was excited.
   (C) He was fond of the show.
   (D) He likes to sleep.

9. Polo 的爸爸在表演一開始時就睡著了。

   (A) 他一定很累。
   (B) 他很興奮。
   (C) 他很喜歡這個表演。
   (D) 他喜歡睡覺。

Ann's notes

「喜歡」除了 like 之外，還可以用「be fond of + N./Ving.」
E.g. Laura is fond of watching the film on Friday evening.（Laura 喜歡週五晚上看電影）。

10. What does Michael like to do?

   (A) Yes, he likes to sing songs.
   (B) No, he likes painting.
   (C) He doesn't know what to choose.
   (D) He likes to decorate his flat.

10. Michael 喜歡做什麼？

   (A) 是的，他喜歡唱歌。
   (B) 不，他喜歡畫畫。
   (C) 他不知道要選擇什麼。
   (D) 他喜歡佈置他的公寓。

11. Is Hannah studying in the library?

    (A) Yes, she is cooking at home.

    (B) No, she is eating lunch outside.

    (C) Yes, she likes studying in the library.

    (D) No, she likes reading books at a cafe.

11. Hannah 在圖書館讀書嗎？

    (A) 是的，她在家做飯。

    (B) 不，她在外面吃午餐。

    (C) 是的，她喜歡在圖書館讀書。

    (D) 不，她喜歡在咖啡廳讀書。

Ann's notes

題目是問「Hannah 在圖書館讀書嗎？」而不是「Hannah 喜歡在圖書館讀書嗎？」所以，D 選項不符合問題。

12. What is the main idea behind this film?

    (A) It is scary.

    (B) It is fun.

    (C) It is not interesting.

    (D) It is about ecology.

12. 這部電影的主旨是什麼？

    (A) 驚悚的。

    (B) 好玩的。

    (C) 無聊的。

    (D) 與生態有關。

13. Why are you reading this book? It seems boring.

    (A) I don't like boring things.

    (B) Yes, I like boring books.

    (C) I am doing some research so I need to read this book.

    (D) I don't like this book.

13. 為什麼你要讀這本書？看起來很無聊。

    (A) 我不喜歡無聊的事情。

    (B) 是的，我喜歡無聊的書籍。

    (C) 我正在做一些研究所以必須看這本書。

    (D) 我不喜歡這本書。

14. Look! There is a fox searching for food on the street.

    (A) It is rubbish.

    (B) It is hungry.

    (C) It is in the forest.

    (D) It likes the city.

14. 看！街上有一隻狐狸在找食物。

    (A) 牠是垃圾。

    (B) 牠很餓。

    (C) 牠待在森林裡。

    (D) 牠喜歡城市。

15. Do you like this shop? It sells antiques.

    (A) Yes, I am looking for a book.

    (B) Yes, I like this restaurant.

    (C) No, I don't like watching films.

    (D) No, I am not particularly interested in old things.

15. 你喜歡這個商店嗎？它販賣古董。

    (A) 是的，我正在找一本書。

    (B) 是的，我喜歡這間餐廳。

    (C) 不，我不喜歡看電影。

    (D) 不，我對舊東西沒有特別興趣。

16. I think Simon is the most interesting person I have ever met.

    (A) You are wrong.

    (B) I don't like it.

    (C) You can say that again.

    (D) It is a piece of cake.

16. 我覺得 Simon 是我認識的人中最有趣的一個。

    (A) 你錯了。

    (B) 我不喜歡。

    (C) 我同意你說的！（再同意不過了！）

    (D) 小事一件。

Ann's notes

C 選項 You can say that again. 意思指的是「我同意你的看法。」也就是 I agree with you. 或是 I can't agree more.，所以請同學們別用「直譯法」，以為這句話的意思是「你可以再說一次」，意思相差甚遠喔！

D 選項 a piece of cake 意思指的是小事一件（不足掛齒），當然也可以翻譯為「一小塊蛋糕」但必須依前後文來定義，不過外國人不會因為有人問他要不要來塊蛋糕而說 I want a piece of cake.，通常比較會說 Oh, thanks. Please give me some/a bit.（謝謝，請給我一些）。

17. What's wrong with you?

    (A) I am fine.

    (B) Nothing is wrong with me.

    (C) I am very right.

    (D) I am a giraffe.

17. 怎麼了嗎？

    (A) 我很好。

    (B) 我沒事啊。

    (C) 我才是對的。

    (D) 我是一隻長頸鹿。

18. This is my favourite colour.

    (A) Oh, but that is not my favorite color.

    (B) This is my house.

    (C) No, it's not.

    (D) This is silly.

18. 這是我最喜歡的顏色。

    (A) 喔，但那不是我最喜歡的顏色。

    (B) 這是我的房子。

    (C) 不，才不是。

    (D) 這很蠢。

19. What kinds of drink do you like most?

    (A) I like hot chocolate milk.

    (B) I like pizza.

    (C) I play basketball.

    (D) I watch the film.

19. 你最喜歡什麼飲料？

    (A) 我喜歡巧克力牛奶。

    (B) 我喜歡披薩。

    (C) 我打籃球。

    (D) 我看電影。

Ann's notes

favourite (a.) =favorite (a.) 最喜歡的，favourite 是英式英文而 favorite 是美式英文；colour (n.) =color (a.) 顏色，前者是英式英文；後者是美式英文。不知道大家是否有發現，英式英文的某些單字會有『u』而美式則省略了『u』呢？其實發音沒有不同，只是使用的拼字方式不同。另外，當然每個地區會有腔調（accent）上的不同，即使是在一些非英語系國家，音調也會有所不同。英文是國際通行的語言，所以大家也要學著適應不同的腔調喔！

20. You must be excited with the journey.

    (A) I take the same journey every day.

    (B) Yes, I have never been there before.

    (C) Yes, I enjoy tennis.

    (D) This is very delicious.

20. 你一定對於這個旅程感到非常興奮。

    (A) 我每天都有同樣的行程。

    (B) 是的，我還沒去過那個地方。

    (C) 是的，我很喜歡網球。

    (D) 這東西非常美味。

The more we do, the more we can do./ William Hazlitt

當做的愈多，能做的也就愈多。（威廉‧哈茲里特）

▶▶ Part 3：Short talk 簡短對話

此部分共 15 題，每題光碟播放出一英文對話之後，請從四個選項 A 、B、C、D 四個回答或是回應中，選出一個最合適的答案。

Ann's notes

此部分的作答技巧就是：在聽的同時，一邊將關鍵字 taking notes「做筆記」，特別針對一些數字、日期、時間等，或是先後順序的細節內容。另外，了解對話中的內容地點或場合，有助於回答 where 的問題。注意 speaker 以哪種疑問詞發問，來選擇合適回覆的答案，或是以提醒的對話方式問與答。

Example：

1. (At the airport)

Passenger A: Do you need help?

Passenger B: Oh, thanks. I think I can try once.

Passenger A: Maybe this massage machine is not working. Would you like to try this one?

Passenger B: Ok, thank you. It's kind of you. By the way, what's your name?

Passenger A: I am Ann. Nice meeting you. What's your name?

Passenger B: My name is James. Nice to meet you too.

Q: What has happened to the man?

   (A) He is sleeping.

   (B) His name is James.

   (C) He tries to use the massage machine.

   (D) He is a passenger at the airport.

1.（機場）

旅客 A: 需要幫忙嗎？

旅客 B: 喔，謝謝。我想我可以再試一次。

旅客 A: 或許這台按摩機壞掉了。你要不要試試這一台？

旅客 B: 好的，謝謝你。你人真好。對了，請問你叫什麼名字？

旅客 A: 我叫 Ann。很高興認識你。請問你的名字？

旅客 B: 我叫 James。我也很高興認識你。

問題：那位男士怎麼了？

   (A) 他正在睡覺。

   (B) 他名字是 James。

   (C) 他試著使用按摩機。

   (D) 他是機場的旅客。

Ann's notes

使用 What 的問句，回答的答案需和事情有關。(A) 選項與 what 和 doing 相關 (What is the man doing?)，(B) 選項與姓名有關 (What is the man's name?)，(D) 選項跟 who 有關 (Who is this man at the airport?) 因此，答案選 (C) He ties to use the massage machine 他嘗試著使用按摩機。(hint:this massage machine is not working.)

2.　(on the flight)

F:　Are you ok? You fainted.

M:　Yes, I am fine, just a little bit uncomfortable.

F:　Please take a seat. I'll ask for help from the flight attendant.

M:　Thank you.

Q:　What will the woman do?

　　(A) She fainted.

　　(B) She will ask for assistance.

　　(C) She feels uncomfortable.

　　(D) She is looking at the man.

2.　（在飛機上）

女士：你還好嗎？你剛剛昏倒了。

男士：嗯，我沒事，只是有一點不舒服。

女士：請坐。我幫你跟空服員請求協助。

男士：謝謝。

問題：這位女士將做什麼？

　　(A) 她昏倒了。

　　(B) 她將尋求協助。

　　(C) 她感到不舒服。

　　(D) 她看著那個男士。

Ann's notes

使用 What 的問句，回答的答案需和事情有關。(A) 答案與 what 和 doing 無關，而且昏倒的人不是她。(C) 答案與 how 有關聯，題目如果是 How is the man? 答案就可以回應 He feels uncomfortable. 或是 He is sick.。(D) 答案跟對話內容無關。因此，答案選 (B) She will ask for assistance. 她將請求協助。(hint:I'll ask for help from the flight attendant.)

Never put off what you can do today until tomorrow.

今日事今日畢。

43

牛刀小試

1.

    (A) She wants to water the plants.

    (B) She wants to read a book.

    (C) She wants to watch a film.

    (D) She wants to take a bath.

2

    (A) He doesn't like Mr D.

    (B) He wants to contact Mr D.

    (C) He thinks the woman can be more active to contact Mr D.

    (D) He hopes to break up with Mr D.

3.

    (A) At the entrance of Sailor's Trail

    (B) At the destination of Sailor's Trail

    (C) At the tourist information center

    (D) At the bus station

4.

    (A) No, she doesn't like the man.

    (B) No, she has a meeting.

    (C) Yes, she loves the man.

    (D) Yes, she wants to attend the workshop.

5.

    (A) It is on Wednesday.

    (B) It is not available anymore.

    (C) It's an online workshop.

    (D) It is on the 21st of June.

6.

    (A) Apple juice

    (B) Hot chocolate

    (C) Coffee without sugar

    (D) Sugary milk

7.

    (A) She does not like apple juice.

    (B) Mark is mean to her.

    (C) She drank too much apple juice.

    (D) She does not sleep well.

8.

    (A) Buy her new shoe.

    (B) Cut her hair.

    (C) Take her to the hairdresser.

    (D) Let her cut his hair.

9.

    (A) Mable was late.

    (B) Angela was not hungry.

    (C) Mable does not eat meal.

    (D) Angela is fasting.

10.

    (A) The bus will be too hot.

    (B) The train is cheaper.

    (C) The bus will take too long.

    (D) The cinema is far away.

11.

(A) Her mum will be very happy.

(B) Her mum will be telling a truth.

(C) Her mum may scold her.

(D) Her mum should take the test herself.

12.

(A) They will have mushrooms

(B) Tom cannot decide.

(C) They will have a pizza.

(D) Tom and Jerry decide to wait for breakfast.

13.

(A) Go to US.

(B) Become a scientist.

(C) Study for his masters.

(D) Do working-holiday programme in the UK.

14.

(A) Ann did not like the colour pink.

(B) Ann preferred the blue handbag.

(C) Ann preferred the pink handbag.

(D) Ann thought the handbag was too expensive.

15.

(A) Toast

(B) Yogurt

(C) Both toast and yogurt

(D) Cereal

Genius only means hard-working all one"s life./ Mendeleyer

天才只意味著終身不懈的努力。（門捷列夫）

1.

Simon: What's your plan this afternoon? Doing some gardening?

Katy: Maybe yes. But I would rather watch a film first.

Simon: Perhaps you can be watering the plants in the garden later.

Katy: Well, watering the plants should be done before evening. I will do it. No worries.

Simon: Brilliant.

Q: What will the woman like to do first?

(A) She wants to water the plants.
(B) She wants to read a book.
(C) She wants to watch a film.
(D) She wants to take a bath.

1.

Simon: 你今天下午有什麼計畫？忙花園的東西嗎？

Katy: 可能吧！但是我比較想先看一部電影。

Simon: 或許你可以晚一點再幫花園的植物澆水。

Katy: 不過，幫植物澆水的工作應該在晚上之前完成。我會做完的。不用擔心。

Simon: 太好了。

問題：這位女士想先做什麼事？

(A) 她想要幫植物澆水。
(B) 她想讀一本書。
(C) 她想看電影。
(D) 她想泡澡。

2.

Laura: Do you think Mr D is nice?

Mike: Yes, he really is.

Laura: But he doesn't contact me when we are apart.

Mike: I think you can try to be more active.

Laura: I am not sure. Maybe I would want to break up with him.

Mike: Are you sure?

Q: What is the man's thought?

(A) He doesn't like Mr D.
(B) He wants to contact Mr D.
(C) He thinks the woman can be more active to contact Mr D.
(D) He hopes to break up with Mr D.

2.

Laura: 你覺得 D 人怎麼樣？

Mike: 他很好啊。

Laura: 但是我們分開的時間他都不跟我聯絡。

Mike: 我覺得你可以試著主動一點。

Laura: 我不知道耶。或許我會跟他分手吧。

Mike: 你確定？

問題：這位男士的想法是什麼？

(A) 他不喜歡 D 先生。
(B) 他想跟 D 先生聯絡。
(C) 他認為這位女士應該更積極跟 D 先生聯絡。
(D) 他希望跟 D 先生分手。

3.

Woman: Where are we?

Man:　　We are at the entrance of Sailor's Trail.

Woman: So it is about 1.5 miles to the destination, isn't it?

Man:　　Yes, I guess so. Let's start walking now?

Woman: Sure.

Q:　Where are the man and the woman?

(A) At the entrance of Sailor's Trail
(B) At the destination of Sailor's Trail
(C) At the tourist information center
(D) At the bus station

3.

女士： 這裡是哪裡？

男士： 我們在「水手道」的入口。

女士： 所以，到達目的地大約是 1.5 英里嗎？

男士： 我想是吧！那我們現在出發嗎？

女士： 是的。

問題：這位男士與女士在哪裡？

(A)「水手道」的入口車站
(B)「水手道」的終點
(C) 旅客服務中心
(D) 公車站

4.

Man:　　Would you like to go to Tate Modern?

Woman: Yes, I'd love to, but today I have a meeting. I am afraid I can't go with you.

Man:　　Oh, that's a shame. But it's ok. We can go together next time.

Q:　Does the woman go to Tate Modern with the man?

(A) No, she doesn't like the man.
(B) No, she has a meeting.
(C) Yes, she loves the man.
(D) Yes, she wants to attend the workshop.

4.

男士： 你想去泰德現代藝術博物館嗎？

女士： 嗯，我很想去，不過我今天有一個會議。我恐怕沒辦法跟你去。

男士： 噢，那太可惜了。沒關係，我們下次再一起去。

問題： 這位女士要跟這男士去泰德現代藝術博物館嗎？

(A) 不，她不喜歡這位男士。
(B) 不，她有會議。
(C) 是的，她很喜歡這個男士。
(D) 是的，她想去參加這個研習會。

5.

Man: Michael Rosen is a famous writer of children's books. Here is a workshop he will hold.

Woman: Really? When is it?

Man: It is on the 21st of June. Will you like to sign up for it online?

Woman: Definitely, I will.

Q: When is Michael Rosen's workshop?

(A) It is on Wednesday.

(B) It is not available anymore.

(C) It's an online workshop.

(D) It is on the 21st of June.

6.

Woman: Hi there. What would you like to drink?

Man: May I have a cup of latte?

Woman: Sure. With sugar or not?

Man: No sugar please.

Q: What does the man want to drink?

(A) Apple juice

(B) Hot chocolate

(C) Coffee without sugar

(D) Sugary milk

5.

男士： Michael Rosen 是一位有名的童書作家。他將舉辦一場研習。

女士： 真的嗎？什麼時候？

男士： 就在 6 月 21 日。你想上網報名嗎？

女士： 一定的。

問題：Michael Rosen 的研習在什麼時候？

(A) 星期三。

(B) 已經不再受理報名。

(C) 那是一個網路研習。

(D) 6 月 21 日。

6.

女士： 你好。想喝點什麼嗎？

男士： 請給我一杯拿鐵。

女士： 沒問題。加糖嗎？

男士： 不加糖。

問題：這位男士想喝什麼？

(A) 蘋果汁。

(B) 熱巧克力。

(C) 無糖咖啡。

(D) 加糖牛奶。

7.

Annie: I'm not feeling very well.

Mark: Oh dear. What is the problem?

Annie: I think I drank too much apple juice.

Mark: You should take a rest.

Q: Why is Annie not feeling well?

(A) She does not like apple juice.

(B) Mark is mean to her.

(C) She drank too much apple juice.

(D) She does not sleep well.

7.

Annie: 我人不大舒服。

Mark: 哎，發生什麼事嗎？

Annie: 我覺得我喝太多蘋果汁了。

Mark: 你休息一下吧。

問題：為什麼 Annie 覺得不大舒服？

(A) 她不喜歡蘋果汁。

(B) Mark 對她很不好。

(C) 她喝太多蘋果汁了。

(D) 她沒睡好。

Ann's notes

對話中的 oh dear 本來有「我的天啊」或是「又來了 ...」之意，常用來回應發生麻煩的事（台灣人比較常用的 oh my god 其實是一種比較不禮貌、不文雅的表達方式），在這裡的 oh dear 依據上下文可推測因為 Annie 不舒服，所以 Mark 替 Annie 感到遺憾。What is the problem? 等於 What happened to you? 或是 What's wrong with you? 的用法。另外，選項 B 中的 mean (a.) 形容詞指：卑鄙的、小人的，當動詞 mean (v.) 則是：意指、表示之意。

8.

Abbie: I'm going to have my hair cut.

Mark: Do you want me to cut your hair?

Abbie: No! You are not a hairdresser!

Mark: But I will cut your hair for free.

Q: What does Mark offer to do for Abbie?

(A) Buy her new shoe.

(B) Cut her hair.

(C) Take her to the hairdresser.

(D) Let her cut his hair.

8.

Abbie: 我想去剪頭髮。

Mark: 你想要我幫你剪嗎？

Abbie: 不要。你又不是髮型設計師。

Mark: 但是我可以免費幫你剪頭髮。

問題：Mark 可以提供 Abbie 什麼服務？

(A) 買新鞋送她。

(B) 幫她剪頭髮。

(C) 帶她去髮型設計師那邊。

(D) 讓她幫他剪頭髮。

9.

Mable: I am back. Let's have lunch now.

Angela: I have already eaten lunch.

Mable: But I have not eaten anything.

Angela: You are late. I became hungry.

Q: Why did Angela not have with lunch with Marble?

(A) Mable was late.

(B) Angela was not hungry.

(C) Mable does not eat meal.

(D) Angela is fasting.

9.

Marble: 我回來了。一起吃午餐吧。

Angela: 我已經吃過了。

Marble: 可是我還沒吃東西。

Angela: 你回來晚了。我很餓。

問題： 為什麼 Angela 沒跟 Marble 一起吃午餐？

(A) Marble 太晚回家了。

(B) Angela 已經不餓了。

(C) Mable 沒有吃飯。

(D) Angela 正在禁食。

Ann's notes

fast 當作形容詞跟副詞是「快速」的意思，當動詞時則是「禁食」或是「齋戒」的意思。例如回教徒每年到了齋戒月，他們都會 be fasting 來遵守他們的宗教與文化信仰。fasting (n.) 就是「禁食」。

10.

Bob: How will we get to the cinema?

Mike: We can take the bus.

Bob: The train is quicker.

Mike: Ok. If we take the bus, we may be late.

Q: Why will Mike and Bob take the train to the cinema?

(A) The bus will be too hot.

(B) The train is cheaper.

(C) The bus will take too long.

(D) The cinema is far away.

10.

Bob: 我們要怎麼去電影院呢？

Mike: 我們可以搭公車。

Bob: 火車比較快。

Mike: 好吧。如果我們搭公車的話，可能會遲到。

問題： 為什麼 Mike 跟 Bob 搭火車去看電影？

(A) 公車太熱了。

(B) 火車比較便宜。

(C) 公車花費比較長的時間。

(D) 電影院太遠了。

11.

May: I failed on my maths test. I think my mum will be crazy and tell me off.

Ray: Don't worry. I think telling the ruth is better than telling a lie. She will understand.

May: No, she will be mad. But I will still tell her the true result.

Q: What would May's mum do after she tells the true outcome of her test?

(A) Her mum will be very happy.
(B) Her mum will be telling a truth.
(C) Her mum may scold her.
(D) Her mum should take the test herself.

11.

May: 我數學沒過關。我想我媽會抓狂而且罵我。

Ray: 別擔心。我覺得告訴她事實比說謊來得好。她一定會理解的。

May: 不，她會生氣的。不過我還是會告訴她真實的成績。

問題： May 的媽媽在她說真實的結果之後會怎麼樣？

(A) 她媽媽會很開心。
(B) 她媽媽會說實話。
(C) 她媽媽可能會罵她。
(D) 她媽媽應該自己去考試。

12.

Jerry: What do you want to eat for dinner?

Tom: I don't mind.

Jerry: I will get a pizza.

Tom: Ok. Please get a pizza without mushrooms.

Q: What will Tom and Jerry eat for dinner?

(A) They will have mushrooms
(B) Tom cannot decide.
(C) They will have a pizza.
(D) Tom and Jerry decide to wait for breakfast.

12.

Jerry: 你晚餐想吃什麼？

Tom: 我都可以。(我不介意)。

Jerry: 我會買一個披薩。

Tom: 好啊。請買一個不加蘑菇的披薩。

問題： Tom 跟 Jerry 晚餐吃什麼？

(A) 他們將吃蘑菇。
(B) Tom 無法做決定。
(C) 他們要吃披薩。
(D) Tom 跟 Jerry 決定等吃早餐。

13.

Woman: Where are you going to work on your masters next year?

Man: The University of Edinburgh.

Woman: That's in Scotland, the UK, right?

Man: Yes. It's in the UK.

Q: What will the man do next year?

(A) Go to US.

(B) Become a scientist.

(C) Study for his masters.

(D) Do working-holiday programme in the UK.

13.

女士： 你明年要去哪裡攻讀碩士？

男士： 愛丁堡大學。

女士： 在英國的蘇格蘭，是嗎？

男士： 是的，就在英國。

問題： 這位男士明年將要做什麼？

(A) 去美國。

(B) 成為一位科學家。

(C) 攻讀碩士。

(D) 參加英國打工旅遊計畫。

Ann's notes

選項 D 的 programme (n.) 節目、計畫，為英式英文，美式英文是 program。

14.

Ann: These handbags are nice. I like the pink one best.

Hannah: Shall we buy one now?

Ann: I think I will buy it later.

Hannah: Ok, we will come back later.

Q: Did Ann like the pink handbag?

(A) Ann did not like the colour pink.

(B) Ann preferred the blue handbag.

(C) Ann preferred the pink handbag.

(D) Ann thought the handbag was too expensive.

14.

Ann: 這些手提包真漂亮。我最喜歡粉紅色的包。

Hannah: 我們要不要來買一個啊？

Ann: 我想我之後才會買。

Hannah: 好吧。我們之後再回來看看。

問題：Ann 喜歡那個粉紅色手提包嗎？

(A) Ann 不喜歡粉紅色。

(B) Ann 比較喜歡藍色的手提包。

(C) Ann 比較喜歡粉紅色的手提包。

(D) Ann 認為這個手提包太貴了。

Ann's notes

這個對話著重在兩位女生討論買包與否，Ann 覺得之後再回來買，「I think I will buy it later.」有考慮的意思，所以 Hannah 才會說「那麼我們之後再回來看看」。

15.

Mike: Do you want toast or a yogurt for breakfast?

Ann: I want both.

Mike: Do you think you can eat that much?

Ann: Yes, I'm very hungry.

Q: What does Ann want for breakfast?

(A) Toast

(B) Yogurt

(C) Both toast and yogurt

(D) Cereal

15.

Mike: 你早餐想吃吐司或是優格？

Ann: 都想要。

Mike: 你覺得你可以吃那麼多嗎？

Ann: 是的，我非常餓。

問題： Ann 早餐吃什麼？

(A) 吐司。

(B) 優格。

(C) 吐司跟優格。

(D) 穀片。

I have nothing to offer but blood, toil tears and sweat./ Winston Churchill
我所能奉獻的沒有其他，只有熱血、辛勞、眼淚與汗水。(邱吉爾)

Listening Module 1
聽力模擬測驗

▼

本測驗分三部分，全為四選一之選擇題，每部分各為 15 題，共 45 題，作答時間約 30 分鐘。

Part 1：看圖辨義

本部分共 15 題，試題冊上有數幅圖畫和照片，每一個圖畫有 1~3 個描述該圖的題目，每題請聽錄音播出題目以及 A、B、C、D 四個英語敘述之後，選出與所看到的圖畫最相符的答案，每題只播出一遍。

....

A Questions 1-2

1. A B C D
   □ □ □ □

2. A B C D
   □ □ □ □

A Questions 3-4

3. A B C D
   ☐ ☐ ☐ ☐

4. A B C D
   ☐ ☐ ☐ ☐

B Questions 5-6

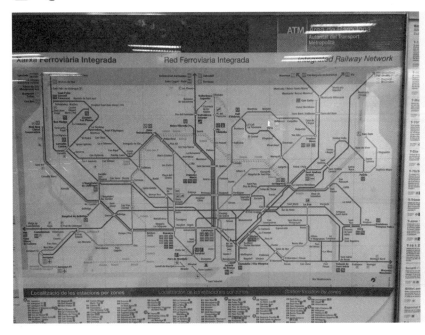

5. A B C D
   ☐ ☐ ☐ ☐

6. A B C D
   ☐ ☐ ☐ ☐

C Questions 7-9

7. A B C D
   ☐ ☐ ☐ ☐

8. A B C D
   ☐ ☐ ☐ ☐

9. A B C D
   ☐ ☐ ☐ ☐

D Questions 10-11

10. A B C D
    ☐ ☐ ☐ ☐

11. A B C D
    ☐ ☐ ☐ ☐

E **Questions 12-13**

12. A B C D
    □ □ □ □

13. A B C D
    □ □ □ □

F **Questions 14-15**

14. A B C D
    □ □ □ □

15. A B C D
    □ □ □ □

Part 2：Q & A 問與答

本部分共 15 題，每題請聽錄音播出英語問句或直述句之後，從試題冊上 A、B、C、D 四個回答或回應中，選出一個最適合作答。每題只播出一遍。

16.

    (A) That's great.

    (B) I'm ok. Thanks.

    (C) How exciting!

    (D) It's a piece of cake.

17.

    (A) Yes, I mean it.

    (B) Yes, I mention it.

    (C) Yes, I am not serious.

    (D) No, I don't intend to do it.

18.

    (A) Yes, I am like dogs.

    (B) Yes, dogs are not cats.

    (C) No, I prefer cats.

    (D) No, it rains cats and dogs.

19.

    (A) Thanks. It's very slow.

    (B) Thanks. It's very nice.

    (C) Thanks. I like my old phone.

    (D) You don't need a new phone.

20.

    (A) It's very long.

    (B) It's very short.

    (C) You look very nice.

    (D) I want to get my hair cut.

21.

    (A) It's boring.

    (B) It's expensive.

    (C) It's addictive.

    (D) It's luxurious.

22.

    (A) It's 10 to 10.

    (B) It's great old day.

    (C) Thank you.

    (D) It is yesterday.

23.

    (A) It smells lovely.

    (B) I want to make dinner.

    (C) You have eaten dinner, haven't you?

    (D) I am in the dinning room.

24.

    (A) It's very hot.

    (B) I like showers.

    (C) Take your time and relax.

    (D) You don't need to run so fast.

25.

    (A) It's very delicious.

    (B) I gave my presentation yesterday

    (C) I am doing a project.

    (D) I am going jogging today.

26.

    (A) I am studying engineering.

    (B) I am a college student.

    (C) I go to Oxford University.

    (D) I only study on weekends.

27.

    (A) It was very tasty. Thank you.

    (B) Yes, his name is Floppy.

    (C) No, his name is Floppy.

    (D) I like rabbits.

28.

    (A) I was quiet.

    (B) The weather was nice.

    (C) It was busy.

    (D) I was doing my work.

29.

    (A) I don't know how to use the facilities.

    (B) It's a good idea.

    (C) I know something about fixing.

    (D) It's nice weather for the ducks.

30.

    (A) Yes, I like films.

    (B) I always have popcorns.

    (C) I like the film About Time.

    (D) I don't the film About Time.

Part 3：簡短對話

本部分共 15 題，每題請聽錄音播出一段對話及一個相關的問題之後，從試題冊上 A、B、C、D 四個選項中選出一個最適合者作答。每段對話及問題只播出一遍。

31.

    (A) Yes, he plays often.

    (B) No, Dave hasn't played for a long time.

    (C) No, Dave has never played.

    (D) Yes, Dave has just started to play the piano.

32.

    (A) She gets handmade strawberry wine and vinegar.

    (B) She buys strawberries.

    (C) She gets one bottle of vinegar.

    (D) She buys one souvenir.

33.

    (A) It is a blue hat.

    (B) It is a white hat.

    (C) It is a red spot.

    (D) It's a white hat with red spots.

34.

    (A) She shows her ID.

    (B) She should have had her ID.

    (C) She can get in the library.

    (D) She goes back to her flat.

35.

    (A) She is going for a vacation.

    (B) She is visiting friend.

    (C) She will participate workshops and a conference.

    (D) She will work for her Masters.

36.

    (A) Yes, they do.

    (B) Yes, they will watch different films.

    (C) No, they don't like it.

    (D) No, they will watch a film tomorrow.

37.
- (A) She is going rock-climbing.
- (B) She is doing jogging.
- (C) She needs to mind the head.
- (D) She is going to St Michael's Mount.

38.
- (A) She is pregnant.
- (B) She is giving birth to a baby.
- (C) She will compliment the man.
- (D) She will wear a gorgeous dress.

39.
- (A) She wants marmalade.
- (B) She wants yogurt only.
- (C) She wants to have toast and yogurt.
- (D) She does not want anything.

40.
- (A) She will have a cup of coffee.
- (B) She will have a presentation.
- (C) She will be sleepy after a presentation.
- (D) She will focus on how to make coffee.

41.
- (A) Touch the hedgehog.
- (B) Be scared of the hedgehog.
- (C) Look at the hedgehog.
- (D) Go into the hedge.

42.
- (A) Maths is easy.
- (B) She is not good at maths.
- (C) Maths puzzles are difficult to solve.
- (D) She does not study maths.

43.
- (A) She likes salt and vinegar flavour crisps
- (B) She takes one crisp.
- (C) She eats the whole packet.
- (D) She does not like crisps.

44.
- (A) It doesn't work.
- (B) Michael breaks it.
- (C) Ann is silly and does not know how to use it.
- (D) Ann is an engineer but she breaks it.

45.
- (A) Talking about her oral defense.
- (B) Showing her a great project.
- (C) Telling her she gets an 'A' in her oral defense.
- (D) Hiding her grade from her oral defense.

Patience is bitter, but its fruit is sweet./ Jean Jacques Rousseau

忍耐是痛苦的，但它的果實是甜蜜的。（盧梭）

Part 1：看圖辨義

本部分共 15 題，試題冊上有數幅圖畫和照片，每一個圖畫有 1~3 個描述該圖的題目，每題請聽錄音播出題目以及 A、B、C、D 四個英語敘述之後，選出與所看到的圖畫最相符的答案，每題只播出一遍。

A Questions 1-2

1. What is the man on the left doing?

   (A) He is fishing.
   (B) He is sailing.
   (C) He is having his lunch.
   (D) He is writing his assignment.

2. Where are the men?

   (A) They are at the train station.
   (B) They are walking along the riverside.
   (C) They are on the water.
   (D) They are playing board games.

1. 左邊的男人正在做什麼？

   (A) 他在釣魚。
   (B) 他在划船。
   (C) 他在吃午餐。
   (D) 他在寫作業。

2. 這些人在哪裡？

   (A) 他們在火車站。
   (B) 他們在河邊走路。
   (C) 他們在水上。
   (D) 他們在玩桌遊。

3. What is Mike doing?

   (A) He is working on a project.
   (B) He is cleaning his flat.
   (C) He is playing the violin.
   (D) He is watching a film.

4. Which of the following items is not close to him?

   (A) A lamp.
   (B) A computer.
   (C) A bin.
   (D) A notice board.

3. Mike 正在做什麼？

   (A) 他正在做一個報告。
   (B) 他在打掃他的公寓。
   (C) 他在拉小提琴。
   (D) 他在看電影。

4. 下列哪一個東西沒有在他旁邊？

   (A) 檯燈。
   (B) 電腦。
   (C) 垃圾桶。
   (D) 公布欄。

ⓒ Questions 5-6

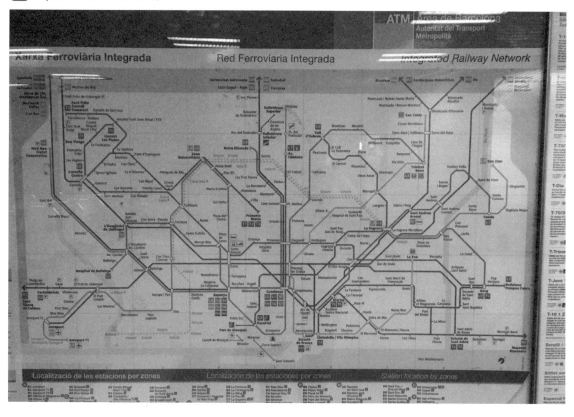

5. What is shown in the photo?

    (A) A car-parking map.
    (B) A radio show.
    (C) A website map.
    (D) A tube map.

6. Who will find it useful?

    (A) Passengers.
    (B) Farmers.
    (C) Animals.
    (D) Car mechanics.

5. 照片顯示的是什麼？

    (A) 停車場地圖。
    (B) 廣播表演。
    (C) 網站地圖。
    (D) 地鐵地圖。

6. 誰會覺得這個很有用？

    (A) 旅客。
    (B) 農夫。
    (C) 動物。
    (D) 修車廠。

7. What are they playing?

   (A) They are swimming.
   (B) They are driving a boat.
   (C) They are playing volleyball.
   (D) They are doing crosswords.

8. What is between the two teams?

   (A) A net.
   (B) A needle.
   (C) A pair of trousers
   (D) A bag.

9. Where is the venue according to the picture?

   (A) On the beach.
   (B) At the coach station.
   (C) At the department store.
   (D) At a gym.

7. 他們正在玩什麼？

   (A) 他們在游泳。
   (B) 他們駕駛船隻。
   (C) 他們在打排球。
   (D) 他們在玩拼字遊戲。

8. 這個隊伍之間有什麼？

   (A) 網子。
   (B) 針。
   (C) 褲子。
   (D) 袋子。

9. 根據圖片，這個地方在哪裡？

   (A) 沙灘上。
   (B) 客運站。
   (C) 百貨公司。
   (D) 健身房。

10. What are these people most likely doing?

    (A) They are doing physical exercise on the school field.
    (B) They are studying in the classroom.
    (C) They are infants in the hospital.
    (D) They are talking in the park.

11. Are they happy to answer the question?

    (A) No, they are not students.
    (B) No, they are not volunteers.
    (C) Yes, they are keen to answer the question.
    (D) Yes, they easily get to know each other.

10. 這些人最有可能在做什麼？

    (A) 他們學校運動場做身體運動。
    (B) 他們正在教室上課。
    (C) 他們是醫院的嬰兒。
    (D) 他們在公園聊天。

11. 他們開心回答問題嗎？

    (A) 不，他們不是學生。
    (B) 不，他們不是自願者。
    (C) 是的，他們熱烈地回答問題。
    (D) 是的，他們很容易認識彼此。

F Questions 12-13

12. What does the sign mean?

    (A) Keep going straight.
    (B) Be quiet when passing by this area.
    (C) No smoking.
    (D) Stop to smoke.

13. Where would you see this sign?

    (A) Under trees.
    (B) Inside a box.
    (C) At the shopping centre.
    (D) On the top of a mountain.

12. 這個標誌説明什麼？

    (A) 向前直走。
    (B) 經過這個地區請肅靜。
    (C) 禁菸。
    (D) 他們在潛水。停下來去抽菸。

13. 你可以在哪裡看到這個標誌？

    (A) 樹下。
    (B) 盒子裡面。
    (C) 購物商場。
    (D) 山頂上。

14. What activity are they taking part in?

    (A) They are running.

    (B) They are playing hockey.

    (C) They are doing yoga.

    (D) They are scuba diving.

15. What would this event be?

    (A) It would be a singing competition.

    (B) It would be a clearance sale.

    (C) It would be a marathon.

    (D) It would be a wedding.

14. 他們正參加什麼運動？

    (A) 他們在跑步。

    (B) 他們在打曲棍球。

    (C) 他們在做瑜伽。

    (D) 他們在潛水。

15. 這個活動可能是什麼？

    (A) 可能是一個唱歌比賽。

    (B) 可能是清倉大拍賣。

    (C) 可能是一場馬拉松。

    (D) 可能是一場婚禮。

All things in their being are good for something.

天生我才必有用。

Part 2：Q & A 問與答

本部分共 15 題，每題請聽錄音播出英語問句或直述句之後，從試題冊上 A、B、C、D 四個回答或回應中，選出一個最適合作答。每題只播出一遍。

16. Would you like to have some dessert?

    (A) That's great.
    (B) I'm ok. Thanks.
    (C) How exciting!
    (D) It's a piece of cake.

16. 你想要來些甜點嗎？

    (A) 太好了。
    (B) 不用了，謝謝。
    (C) 好刺激阿！
    (D) 小事一件。

> **Ann's notes**
>
> 通常我們說「I am ok.」指的是客氣的拒絕，直接說「No, thank you.」也是可以，在外國人們一般不會那麼直接用「No」來拒絕，除非是很嚴重的事情才會用這麼重的語氣，因此「I'm ok. Thanks.」是客氣的對人說「不用了」的方式。另外，「a piece of cake」是指小事一件，當然如果真的想說「只要一片蛋糕」之類的話，可以說「Please give me some cake.」會比較恰當。

17. Are you serious?

    (A) Yes, I mean it.
    (B) Yes, I mention it.
    (C) Yes, I am not serious.
    (D) No, I don't intend to do it.

17. 你是認真的嗎？

    (A) 是的，我是說真的。
    (B) 是的，我有提這個
    (C) 是的，我不是認真的。
    (D) 不，我不是故意的。

18. Do you like dogs?

    (A) Yes, I am like dogs.
    (B) Yes, dogs are not cats.
    (C) No, I prefer cats.
    (D) No, it rains cats and dogs.

18. 你喜歡狗嗎？

    (A) 是的，我很像狗。
    (B) 是的，狗不是貓。
    (C) 不，我比較喜歡貓。
    (D) 不，現在下超大的雨。

19. I got you a new phone.

    (A) Thanks. It's very slow.
    (B) Thanks. It's very nice.
    (C) Thanks. I like my old phone.
    (D) You don't need a new phone.

19. 我買了新的電話給你。

    (A) 謝謝。它真的很慢。
    (B) 謝謝。這真的很棒。
    (C) 謝謝。我喜歡我的舊電話。
    (D) 你不需要一支新的電話。

20. I got my hair cut today.

    (A) It's very long.

    (B) It's very short.

    (C) You look very nice.

    (D) I want to get my hair cut.

21. Why do you keep playing that game?

    (A) It's boring.

    (B) It's expensive.

    (C) It's addictive.

    (D) It's luxurious.

22. What is the time?

    (A) It's 10 to 10.

    (B) It's great old day.

    (C) Thank you.

    (D) It is yesterday.

23. I made you dinner.

    (A) It smells lovely.

    (B) I want to make you dinner.

    (C) You have eaten dinner, haven't you?

    (D) I am in the dinning room.

24. I'm going to run a bath.

    (A) It's very hot.

    (B) I like showers.

    (C) Take your time and relax.

    (D) You don't need to run so fast.

25. Are you giving a presentation today?

    (A) It's very delicious.

    (B) I gave my presentation yesterday

    (C) I am doing a project.

    (D) I am going jogging today.

20. 我今天去剪了頭髮。

    (A) 真的很長。

    (B) 真的很短。

    (C) 你看起來很不錯呢。

    (D) 我想要去剪頭髮。

21. 為什麼你一直玩那個遊戲？

    (A) 很無聊。

    (B) 很貴。

    (C) 真讓人著迷。

    (D) 很豪華。

22. 現在幾點？

    (A) 十點十分。

    (B) 美好的舊時光。

    (C) 謝謝。

    (D) 是昨天

23. 我幫你弄了晚餐。

    (A) 聞起來很香呢。

    (B) 我想要煮晚餐。

    (C) 你已經吃晚餐了，不是嗎？

    (D) 我在飯廳。

24. 我正要來泡個澡。

    (A) 天氣好熱。

    (B) 我喜歡洗澡。

    (C) 享受美好時光放鬆一下。

    (D) 你不需要跑那麼快。

25. 你今天要上台報告嗎？

    (A) 真是美味。

    (B) 我昨天做完報告了。

    (C) 我正在做一個報告。

    (D) 我今天要去跑步。

26. What are you studying?

    (A) I am studying engineering.

    (B) I am a college student.

    (C) I go to Oxford University.

    (D) I only study on weekends.

26. 你目前唸什麼？

    (A) 我目前唸工程學。

    (B) 我是一個大學生。

    (C) 我要去牛津大學。

    (D) 我只在週末唸書。

27. Do you own a rabbit?

    (A) It was very tasty. Thank you.

    (B) Yes, his name is Floppy.

    (C) No, his name is Floppy.

    (D) I like rabbits.

27. 你養兔子嗎？

    (A) 非常好吃。謝謝你。

    (B) 是的，他的名字叫做小毛。

    (C) 不，他的名字叫做小毛。

    (D) 我喜歡兔子。

28. What have you done today?

    (A) I was quiet.

    (B) The weather was nice.

    (C) It was busy.

    (D) I was doing my work.

28. 你今天做了什麼？

    (A) 我很安靜。

    (B) 天氣很好。

    (C) 交通繁忙。

    (D) 我做完我的工作了。

Ann's notes

「busy」的用法有很多種意思，需要用上下文判斷句中的意思。如果問的是交通狀況，那麼可以用「It is busy.」，當然也可以說「The traffic is busy.」，去到某個城市旅行發現人很多也可以用「It is quite busy.」來表示。簡單扼要是生活英文的表達方式，「Less is more.」就是他們的溝通態度，跟我們中文直譯成英文的說話模式很不同喔！

29. You should use the facilities after a long journey.

    (A) I don't know how to use the facilities.

    (B) It's a good idea.

    (C) I know something about fixing.

    (D) It's nice weather for the ducks.

29. 長途旅行後你應該去盥洗一下。

    (A) 我不知道怎麼使用設備。

    (B) 好主意。

    (C) 我知道怎麼修理這東西。

    (D) 今天天氣真不錯。

30. What's your favourite film?

    (A) Yes, I like films.

    (B) I always have popcorns.

    (C) I like the film *About Time*.

    (D) I don't the film *About Time*.

30. 你最喜歡的電影是什麼？

    (A) 是的，我喜歡電影。

    (B) 我很喜歡吃爆米花。

    (C) 我喜歡「珍愛每一天」。

    (D) 我不喜歡「珍愛每一天」。

Part 3：簡短對話

本部分共 15 題，每題請聽錄音播出一段對話及一個相關的問題之後，從試題冊上 A、B、C、D 四個選項中選出一個最適合者作答。每段對話及問題只播出一遍。

31.

Fred:　Can you play the piano?

Dave:　I used to play, but it was a long time ago.

Fred:　Do you want to play me a song?

Dave:　I will need to practice first.

Q:　Does Dave play the piano?

(A) Yes, he plays often.

(B) No, Dave hasn't played for a long time.

(C) No, Dave has never played.

(D) Yes, Dave has just started to play the piano.

31.

Fred:　你會彈鋼琴嗎？

Dave:　我以前會彈，不過那是很久以前的事了。

Fred:　你想彈一首歌給我聽嗎？

Dave:　那我需要先練習一下。

問題：Dave 會彈鋼琴嗎？

(A) 是的，他常常彈鋼琴。

(B) 不，Dave 已經好久一段時間沒彈了。

(C) 不，Dave 從沒彈過鋼琴。

(D) 是的，Dave 才剛開始彈鋼琴而已。

32.

Salesman:　Hi there. Can I help you?

Ann:　Yes. I'd like to find some souvenirs. What is the most special thing here?

Salesman:　We have special handmade strawberry wine and black vinegar.

Ann:　Oh, that's brilliant. Can I have both?

Salesman:　Sure. Here you are.

32.

銷售人員：你好。需要為您服務的嗎？

Ann:　是的，我想要找一些紀念品。這裡有什麼最特別的東西嗎？

銷售人員：我們有特別的手工釀造草莓酒和黑醋。

Ann:　嗯，那太棒了。可以給我兩個各一嗎？

銷售人員：沒問題。這兩個給您。

Q: What does Ann get for souvenirs?

   (A) She gets handmade strawberry wine and vinegar.

   (B) She buys strawberries.

   (C) She gets one bottle of vinegar.

   (D) She buys one souvenir.

問題：Ann 買了什麼紀念品。

   (A) 她買了手工釀造草莓酒跟醋。

   (B) 她買了草莓。

   (C) 她買了一瓶醋。

   (D) 她買了一個紀念品。

33.

M: Hello, have you seen my hat?

W: What does it look like?

M: It's white with red spots.

W: No, sorry. The one I saw is blue.

Q: What colour is the man's hat?

   (A) It is a blue hat.

   (B) It is a white hat.

   (C) It is a red spot.

   (D) It's a white hat with red spots.

33.

男士：你好，你有看到我的帽子嗎？

女士：它長什麼樣子？

男士：白色有紅點。

女士：很抱歉。我只看到一個藍色的。

問題：這位男士的帽子是什麼顏色？

   (A) 藍色的帽子。

   (B) 白色的帽子。

   (C) 紅色的帽子。

   (D) 白色帽子上面有紅點。

34.

M: Can I see your ID please?

W: Oh, just a second. Let me check. I think I left it at my flat.

M: I am sorry. I can't let you in.

Q: What should the woman have in this moment?

   (A) She shows her ID.

   (B) She should have had her ID.

   (C) She can get in the library.

   (D) She goes back to her flat.

34.

男士：麻煩您的身分證？

女士：噢，請等一下，我找一下。我想我把它放在我的公寓了。

男士：很抱歉，那無法讓您進入。

問題：這位女士這時候應該要有什麼？

   (A) 她拿出她的身分證。

   (B) 她應該要帶她的身分證。

   (C) 她可以進入圖書館。

   (D) 她現在要回她的公寓去。

35.

Customs officer: Your passport, please.

Ann: Here you are.

Customs officer: How long do you plan to stay in the UK?

Ann: One month.

Customs officer: What are you planning to do?

Ann: I will attend two workshops and one conference.

Customs officer: Welcome to the UK.

Q: What is Ann going to do in the UK?

(A) She is going for a vacation.

(B) She is visiting friend.

(C) She will participate workshops and a conference.

(D) She will work for her Masters.

36.

M: I want to watch a film this evening.

A: Which one do you want to watch?

M: I think 'Despicable Me III' is nice. I like Minions.

A: It's a lovely film. Can I go with you?

M: Sure. Let's watch it together.

Q: Do Michael and Ann go to watch a film together?

(A) Yes, they do.

(B) Yes, they will watch different films.

(C) No, they don't like it.

(D) No, they will watch a film tomorrow.

35.

海關人員：麻煩護照。

Ann: 這裡。

海關人員：你計畫在英國停留多久？

Ann: 一個月。

海關人員：你計畫在這裡做什麼？

Ann: 我將參加兩場研討會跟一個會議。

海關人員：歡迎來到英國。

問題：Ann 來英國做什麼？

(A) 她來度假的。

(B) 她來找朋友。

(C) 她將參加研討會跟會議。

(D) 她來這裡唸碩士。

36.

男士： 今天晚上我想看電影。

女士： 你想看哪一部電影？

男士： 我覺得「神偷奶爸 3」很不錯。我喜歡小小兵。

女士： 很可愛的一部電影。我可以跟你一起去嗎？

男士： 當然可以。我們一起去吧！

問題：Michael 跟 Ann 一起去看電影嗎？

(A) 是的，他們一起去。

(B) 是的，他們看不同的電影。

(C) 不，他們不喜歡這部電影。

(D) 不，他們明天去看電影。

37.

M: Where are you going?

A: I am going to St Michael's Mount.

M: Mind the steps. They are very slippery.

A: Thanks for reminding me. I will be careful.

Q: What is Ann going to do?

  (A) She is going rock-climbing.

  (B) She is doing jogging.

  (C) She needs to mind the head.

  (D) She is going to St Michael's Mount.

38.

M: You look gorgeous in this dress.

W: Thank you. I think I don't look very good because of my big body.

M: You are pregnant and it is natural to be big.

W: I just hope that I could only look a bit heavier than I used to be.

M: I am sure you will be back to normal soon.

Q: What will happen to the woman in the future?

  (A) She is pregnant.

  (B) She is giving birth to a baby.

  (C) She will compliment the man.

  (D) She will wear a gorgeous dress.

37.

男士：你要去哪裡？

Ann：我要去聖麥克山。

男士：小心階梯。那裡很滑。

Ann：謝謝你的提醒。我會注意小心的。

問題：Ann 要去做什麼？

  (A) 她要去攀岩。

  (B) 她要去跑步。

  (C) 她需要小心頭撞到。

  (D) 她要去聖麥克山。

38.

男士：妳穿這件洋裝真美。

女士：謝謝。我覺得因為我的大身軀所以看起來不怎麼好看。

男士：妳懷孕所以身體變胖是很自然的事情。

女士：我希望我能比我平常樣子看起來重一些些就好了。

男士：我相信你很快就會恢復原來的樣子了。

問題：這位女士未來會怎麼樣。

  (A) 她現在懷孕。

  (B) 她準備生小孩。

  (C) 她會讚美這個男士。

  (D) 她會穿這件超美的洋裝。

39.

M: What do you want to have for breakfast?

W: Toasts with marmalade.

M: Anything else?

W: I want some yogurt please.

M: No problem.

Q: What does the woman have for breakfast?

(A) She wants marmalade.

(B) She wants yogurt only.

(C) She wants to have toast and yogurt.

(D) She does not want anything.

40.

M: Are you awake?

W: Yes, but I am so sleepy. I will have a presentation tomorrow.

M: If you want to prepare for it, you can have some coffee to help you focus.

W: Thanks. I think I will have a cup of coffee soon.

Q: What will the woman have tomorrow?

(A) She will have a cup of coffee.

(B) She will have a presentation.

(C) She will be sleepy after a presentation.

(D) She will focus on how to make coffee.

39.

男士： 你想吃什麼早餐？

女士： 柑橘醬吐司。

男士： 還有嗎？

女士： 麻煩再一些優格。

男士： 沒問題。

問題：這位女士想吃什麼早餐。

(A) 她想要柑橘醬。

(B) 她只想要優格。

(C) 她想吃吐司跟優格。

(D) 她不想吃任何東西。

40.

男士： 妳還醒著的嗎？

女士： 是的，不過我很睏。我明天還有一個報告。

男士： 如果你想要準備報告，你可以喝一些咖啡讓你可以專注。

女士： 謝謝。我想我待會就會喝一杯咖啡。

問題：這位女士明天要做什麼？

(A) 她要喝一杯咖啡。

(B) 她有一個報告。

(C) 她在做完報告後會想睡覺。

(D) 她會專注如何沖泡咖啡

41.

M: Oh look, it's a hedgehog.

A: I don't want to look at it. I'm scared.

M: Don't worry. It won't hurt you

A: Are you sure? I still don't want to look.

Q: What does Ann not want to do?

　(A) Touch the hedgehog.

　(B) Be scared of the hedgehog.

　(C) Look at the hedgehog.

　(D) Go into the hedge.

42.

M: Can you solve this puzzle?

A: I'm not good at puzzles. My maths is bad.

M: Don't worry. This one's easy.

A: Ok, I'll try to solve it.

Q: What does Ann think about maths?

　(A) Maths is easy.

　(B) She is not good at maths.

　(C) Maths puzzles are difficult to solve.

　(D) She does not study maths.

41.

男士： 快看！有一隻刺蝟！

Ann ： 我不想看。我很怕。

男士： 別怕。它不會傷害妳的。

Ann ： 確定？我還是不想看。

問題：Ann 不想做什麼？

　(A) 觸摸這隻刺蝟。

　(B) 害怕這隻刺蝟。

　(C) 看那隻刺蝟。

　(D) 進到樹籬裡。

42.

男士： 你可以解決這個謎題嗎？

Ann ： 我不擅長解謎題。我的數學很差。

男士： 別擔心。這個很簡單。

Ann ： 好吧！那我試試看。

問題：Ann 覺得數學怎麼樣？

　(A) 數學很簡單。

　(B) 她不擅長數學這科目。

　(C) 數學謎題很困難解決。

　(D) 她不喜歡唸數學。

Ann's notes

「maths」英式英文的數學縮寫，而「math」則是美式英文的數學縮寫，兩者都可用，而數學這個單字是「mathematics」。

43.

M: Would you like a crisp?

A: No thanks, I'm full.

M: Are you sure? They are salt and vinegar flavour.

A: Oh ok then, I'll just have one.

Q: What does Ann do when offered a crisp?

(A) She likes salt and vinegar flavour crisps

(B) She takes one crisp.

(C) She eats the whole packet.

(D) She does not like crisps.

43.

男士： 你想來一包洋芋片嗎？

Ann： 不用了謝謝。我很飽。

男士： 你確定？鹽跟醋醬口味的洋芋片喔。

Ann： 喔好吧！來一包好了。

問題： 人家要給 Ann 一包洋芋片時，Ann 怎麼做？

(A) 她想吃鹽跟醋醬口味的洋芋片。

(B) 她拿了一包。

(C) 她吃了整包。

(D) 她不想吃洋芋片。

Ann's notes

在英國，crisp (n.) 是指洋芋片，美國則是用 potato chips 或是 chips。而在英國，chips 指的是薯條，所以「fish and chips」是英國名菜「炸魚薯條」。在美國，薯條是「French flies」或是「flies」。因應文化風情不同，在兩國點菜的時候，別搞混了喔。

44.

A: Something is wrong with my vacuum. It doesn't work.

M: Let me check it.

A: Are you sure you know how to fix the problem?

M: Of course. I am an engineer. See, it's working now.

A: Wow, amazing.

Q: What's wrong with Ann's vacuum?

   (A) It doesn't work.

   (B) Michael breaks it.

   (C) Ann is silly and does not know how to use it.

   (D) Ann is an engineer but she breaks it.

45.

A: I got an 'A' in my oral defense.

M: Fantastic. You did a great job.

A: I want to tell my mum on her birthday. So, I am not going to tell her now.

M: I think it will surprise her.

Q: What does Ann want to give as a birthday gift for her mum?

   (A) Talking about her oral defense.

   (B) Showing her a great project.

   (C) Telling her she gets an 'A' in her oral defense.

   (D) Hiding her grade from her oral defense.

44.

Ann： 我的吸塵機壞掉了。它不動了。

男士： 我看一下。

Ann： 你確定你知道怎麼修理它的問題嗎？

男士： 當然。我是工程師。看吧！現在不就動了！

Ann： 哇！真厲害！

問題：Ann 的吸塵機怎麼了？

   (A) 它不動了。

   (B) Michael 弄壞了。

   (C) Ann 很傻而且不知道怎麼使用它。

   (D) Ann 是一個工程師，但她把它弄壞了。

45.

Ann： 我的論文答辯拿到「A」。

男士： 厲害！你真強！

Ann： 我想在我媽生日時候告訴她。所以我現在不打算告訴她。

男士： 我想這一定會讓她很驚訝。

問題： Ann 想要給她媽媽什麼作為生日禮物？

   (A) 談論有關她的論文答辯。

   (B) 做一個很棒的報告給她看。

   (C) 告訴她母親她論文答辯成績拿到「A」。

   (D) 把她的論文答辯成績藏起來。

Man proposes, God disposes.

謀事在人，成事在天。

Listening Module 2
聽力模擬測驗

▼

本測驗分三部分，全為四選一之選擇題，每部分各為 15 題，共 45 題，作答時間約 30 分鐘。

Part 1：看圖辨義

本部分共 15 題，試題冊上有數幅圖畫和照片，每一個圖畫有 1~3 個描述該圖的題目，每題請聽錄音播出題目以及 A、B、C、D 四個英語敘述之後，選出與所看到的圖畫最相符的答案，每題只播出一遍。

⋯⋯⋯⋯⋯⋯⋯⋯⋯⋯⋯⋯⋯⋯⋯⋯⋯⋯⋯⋯⋯⋯⋯⋯⋯⋯⋯⋯⋯⋯⋯⋯⋯

A Questions 1-2

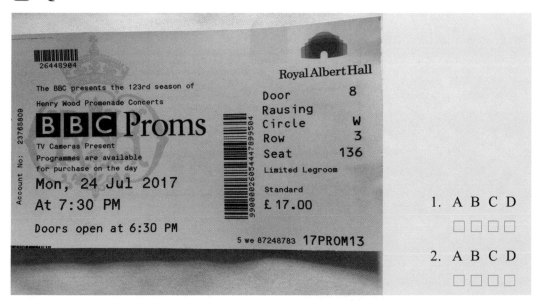

1. A B C D
   ☐ ☐ ☐ ☐

2. A B C D
   ☐ ☐ ☐ ☐

B **Questions 3-5**

3. A B C D
   ☐ ☐ ☐ ☐
4. A B C D
   ☐ ☐ ☐ ☐
5. A B C D
   ☐ ☐ ☐ ☐

C **Questions 6-7**

6. A B C D
   ☐ ☐ ☐ ☐
7. A B C D
   ☐ ☐ ☐ ☐

D **Questions 8-9**

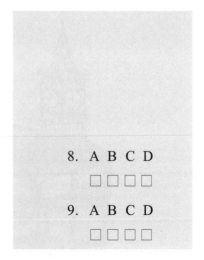

8. A B C D
☐ ☐ ☐ ☐

9. A B C D
☐ ☐ ☐ ☐

E **Questions 10-11**

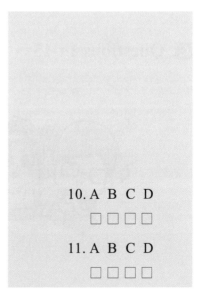

10. A B C D
☐ ☐ ☐ ☐

11. A B C D
☐ ☐ ☐ ☐

F **Questions 12-13**

12. A B C D
    ☐ ☐ ☐ ☐
13. A B C D
    ☐ ☐ ☐ ☐

G **Questions 14-15**

14. A B C D
    ☐ ☐ ☐ ☐
15. A B C D
    ☐ ☐ ☐ ☐

Part 2：Q & A 問與答

本部分共 15 題，每題請聽錄音播出英語問句或直述句之後，從試題冊上 A、B、C、D 四個回答或回應中，選出一個最適合作答。每題只播出一遍。

16.

  (A) Stop running.
  (B) In 2018.
  (C) In the evening.
  (D) Probably at half past 8.

17.

  (A) Yes, I don't speak English.
  (B) Yes, I enjoy it a lot.
  (C) No, I speak Chinese.
  (D) No, I like it.

18.

  (A) He hurt his nose because he walked into the glass door.
  (B) He is in the class.
  (C) He is ok with the dessert.
  (D) He is a sweets lover.

19.

  (A) Her family and relatives.
  (B) Wide animals.
  (C) Strangers and passengers in the train station.
  (D) A man who lives on the streets.

20.

  (A) It must be amazing.
  (B) I am sorry to hear that.
  (C) It was a funny story.
  (D) I am not going to Europe.

21.

  (A) She will dance to the music.
  (B) She will do art painting.
  (C) She will be with friends.
  (D) She will work until next year.

22.

  (A) He has finished his meal.
  (B) He sometimes runs a concert.
  (C) He must enjoy reading a lot.
  (D) He doesn't read anymore.

23.

  (A) Are they studying in the primary schools?
  (B) Are they all working now?
  (C) Does she live in Bournemouth?
  (D) Has she grown up?

24.

  (A) Me neither.
  (B) Me too.
  (C) How amazing!
  (D) What a coincidence.

25.

  (A) Would you like to have some coffee?
  (B) Would you like to go home?
  (C) Could you give me a hand?
  (D) May I have some coke?

26.

 (A) Thanks. I like it too.

 (B) I like my hairstyle too.

 (C) I have no idea.

 (D) The top of the mountain is amazing.

27.

 (A) No, I don't like a desert.

 (B) Yes, I like Egypt.

 (C) Thanks. I am ok.

 (D) Don't give me the menu.

28.

 (A) What are you going to sue?

 (B) Can I join you?

 (C) Why don't you sleep on Saturday?

 (D) Where are you going?

29.

 (A) I am ok. Thanks.

 (B) No, I am not feeling ill.

 (C) Yes, I am feeling good.

 (D) I don't know why you are dizzy.

30.

 (A) He always asks me to do lots of work I don't like.

 (B) He tries to solve problems by fighting.

 (C) He seems to worry about argument.

 (D) He likes to do volunteering jobs in his free time.

Part 3：簡短對話

本部分共 15 題，每題請聽錄音播出一段對話及一個相關的問題之後，從試題冊上 A、B、C、D 四個選項中選出一個最適合者作答。每段對話及問題只播出一遍。

31.

(A) She will arrive at 9.

(B) She will take the tube and the bus.

(C) She has a hospital appointment tomorrow.

(D) She will have a long journey tomorrow.

32.

(A) She likes her old house.

(B) She has a fabulous house with a big garden.

(C) She doesn't want to do gardening.

(D) She needs to rent a house.

33.

(A) A normal man.

(B) An adorable man.

(C) A muscle man.

(D) A crazy man.

34.

(A) She will have an interview of a dram performance.

(B) She will choose the correct dress code.

(C) She will interview people.

(D) She will put on a formal suit.

35.

(A) They sympathize him a lot.

(B) They think he should not have been like that.

(C) They think he is awesome.

(D) They think he needs to work harder.

36.

(A) Training the boat drivers.

(B) Opening Tower Bridge to let boats under.

(C) Controlling London city.

(D) Driving a boat.

37.

(A) She became trapped.

(B) She is going to ask for help.

(C) Her luggage was stolen.

(D) Her friends' luggage was stuck in the gate.

38.

(A) They are too easy.

(B) They are too interesting.

(C) Sometimes they are not challenging.

(D) There are many old words that Ann doesn't understand.

39.

    (A) He listens to his parents.

    (B) He gets punishment because he watches too much TV.

    (C) He is too naughty.

    (D) He gets an idea.

40.

    (A) It was Black Friday.

    (B) It was Thanksgiving Day.

    (C) It was Mother's Day.

    (D) It was Christmas' Eve.

41.

    (A) Her passport has expired.

    (B) Her driving license has expired.

    (C) She doesn't have passport and driving license with her.

    (D) None of the above.

42.

    (A) The woman will have a business meeting.

    (B) The woman is on holidays.

    (C) The woman doesn't have a reference number.

    (D) The woman wants to stay in the hotel for three nights.

43.

    (A) Roses

    (B) Lilies

    (C) Sunflowers

    (D) Bugs

44.

    (A) He has a room for a rent.

    (B) He has a telephone.

    (C) He has a contact book.

    (D) He gets a new flatmate.

45.

    (A) She had an accident.

    (B) She went to accident and emergency in the hospital at midnight.

    (C) She supported the man.

    (D) She bothered the man.

Haste makes waste.

欲速則不達。

Part 1：看圖辨義

本部分共 15 題，試題冊上有數幅圖畫和照片，每一個圖畫有 1~3 個描述該圖的題目，每題請聽錄音播出題目以及 A、B、C、D 四個英語敘述之後，選出與所看到的圖畫最相符的答案，每題只播出一遍。

A Questions 1-2

1. What day of the week does Ann go to the event?

   (A) At 7.30pm.
   (B) On the 24th of July.
   (C) In 2017.
   (D) On Monday.

2. What can you infer from the ticket?

   (A) It is a concert.
   (B) It is a tennis match.
   (C) It is an open-air museum.
   (D) It is a writing workshop.

1. Ann 這週的哪一天會去這個活動？

   (A) 晚上 7 點 30 分。
   (B) 7 月 24 日。
   (C) 2017 年。
   (D) 星期一。

2. 從這張票券你可以推測出什麼？

   (A) 這是一場音樂會。
   (B) 這是一場網球比賽。
   (C) 這是一個露天博物館。
   (D) 這是一個寫作研討會。

B **Questions 3-5**

3. What is this place?

   (A) A swimming pool.
   (B) A palace garden.
   (C) A road.
   (D) A beach.

4. What is it in the middle?

   (A) It is a fountain.
   (B) It is a function.
   (C) It is a candle.
   (D) It is a light.

5. What can William do in this place?

   (A) He can go mountain climbing.
   (B) He can attend a test.
   (C) He can go for a walk.
   (D) He can't jump into the river.

3. 這個地方在哪裡？

   (A) 游泳池。
   (B) 皇宮花園。
   (C) 一條路。
   (D) 海灘。

4. 中間是什麼東西？

   (A) 噴泉。
   (B) 功能。
   (C) 蠟燭。
   (D) 燈光。

5. William 可以在這個地方做什麼？

   (A) 他可以爬山。
   (B) 他可以參加考試。
   (C) 他可以散步。
   (D) 他不能跳進河裡面去。

6. What is it in the photo?

    (A) Big trees.
    (B) Purple bricks.
    (C) House facilities.
    (D) Beautiful flowers.

7. What are the animals in the photo?

    (A) They are hedgehogs.
    (B) They are bumblebees.
    (C) They are cats.
    (D) They are mice.

6. 圖片裡面是什麼？

    (A) 大樹。
    (B) 紫色磚塊。
    (C) 房子設施。
    (D) 漂亮的花。

7. 照片裡面的動物是什麼？

    (A) 刺蝟。
    (B) 大黃蜂。
    (C) 貓。
    (D) 老鼠。

8. Why David is falling asleep?

   (A) He may have stayed up late last night.
   (B) He should sleep on time.
   (C) He must be late for work.
   (D) He may be presenting now.

8. 為什麼 David 快睡著了？

   (A) 他昨天晚上可能熬夜了。
   (B) 他應該準時睡覺了。
   (C) 他一定是工作時遲到了。
   (D) 他現在可能在做報告。

9. David is tired now. What can he do to stay awake?

   (A) He can read some books.
   (B) He can freshen up.
   (C) He can sleep on the bed.
   (D) He can go to hospital.

9. David 現在很累。他可以做什麼讓他保持清醒？

   (A) 他可以讀幾本書。
   (B) 他可以去盥洗一下。
   (C) 他可以去床上睡覺。
   (D) 他可以去醫院。

E **Questions 10-11**

10. Is it a school prom?

   (A) Yes, they are high school students.
   (B) Yes, it is a school sport contest.
   (C) No, it is a dancing competition.
   (D) No, it is a university entrance test.

11. What are they doing?

   (A) They are having a dancing audition.
   (B) They are playing the instruments.
   (C) They are playing football.
   (D) They are having a mine tour.

10. 這是學校舞會嗎？

   (A) 是的，他們是高中生。
   (B) 是的，這是學校運動會。
   (C) 不，這是舞蹈比賽。
   (D) 不，這是大學入學考。

11. 他們在做什麼？

   (A) 他們參加舞蹈試鏡會。
   (B) 他們在演奏樂器。
   (C) 他們在踢足球。
   (D) 他們體驗礦藏之旅。

12. What is it in the photo?

    (A) It is a cab.

    (B) It is a double decker.

    (C) It is a skyscraper.

    (D) It is an airplane.

13. What is shown in the background?

    (A) They are city landmarks.

    (B) They are city dwellers.

    (C) They are country maps.

    (D) They are sweets.

12. 圖片中的東西是什麼？

    (A) 計程車。

    (B) 雙層巴士。

    (C) 魔天倫。

    (D) 飛機。

13. 背景裡面是什麼？

    (A) 城市地標。

    (B) 城市居民。

    (C) 國家地圖。

    (D) 糖果。

14. What is the man in the middle doing?

    (A) He is delivering a speech.
    (B) He is playing the piano.
    (C) He is shouting at the police.
    (D) He is running in the park run.

14. 中間的男士正在做什麼？

    (A) 他正在演講。
    (B) 他正在彈鋼琴。
    (C) 他對著警察大喊呼嘯。
    (D) 他正在公園路跑活動跑步。

15. Are there many people happily listening to him?

    (A) No, it doesn't matter.
    (B) No, many people have gone.
    (C) Yes, people like the event.
    (D) Yes, there is only one person there.

15. 大家很開心聽他說話嗎？

    (A) 不，沒關係。
    (B) 不，很多人都離開了。
    (C) 是的，大家很喜歡這個活動。
    (D) 是的，只有一個人在那裡。

A fall into the pit, a gain in your wit.

吃一塹，長一智。

Part 2：Q & A 問與答

本部分共 15 題，每題請聽錄音播出英語問句或直述句之後，從試題冊上 A、B、C、D 四個回答或回應中，選出一個最適合作答。每題只播出一遍。

16. When are we leaving for the morning run?
    (A) Stop running.
    (B) In 2018.
    (C) In the evening.
    (D) Probably at half past 8.

16. 我們什麼時候要去晨跑？
    (A) 嚴禁跑步。
    (B) 2018 年。
    (C) 晚上。
    (D) 大該是八點半。

17. Do you like English?
    (A) Yes, I don't speak English.
    (B) Yes, I enjoy it a lot.
    (C) No, I speak Chinese.
    (D) No, I like it.

17. 你喜歡英文嗎？
    (A) 是的，我不會講英文。
    (B) 是的，我非常喜歡。
    (C) 不，我講中文。
    (D) 不，我很喜歡。

18. What's wrong with Simon?
    (A) He hurt his nose because he walked into the glass door.
    (B) He is in the class.
    (C) He is ok with the dessert.
    (D) He is a sweets lover.

18. Simon 怎麼了？
    (A) 他鼻子受傷了，因為他撞到玻璃門。
    (B) 他在上課。
    (C) 他很喜歡甜點。
    (D) 他是個甜食愛好者。

19. Who will go to Jessie's birthday party?
    (A) Her family and friends.
    (B) Wide animals.
    (C) Strangers and passengers in the train station.
    (D) A man who lives on the streets.

19. 誰會去 Jessie 的生日會？
    (A) 她家人跟朋友們。
    (B) 野生動物。
    (C) 火車站的陌生人跟旅客。
    (D) 住在街上的那個男士。

20. An incident regarded as a terrorist attack happened in London.

  (A) It must be amazing.
  (B) I am sorry to hear that.
  (C) It was a funny story.
  (D) I am not going to Europe.

21. When will Katy retire from her job?

  (A) She will dance to the music.
  (B) She will do art painting.
  (C) She will be with friends.
  (D) She will work until next year.

22. Bill is good at writing fantasy stories.

  (A) He has finished his meal.
  (B) He sometimes runs a concert.
  (C) He must enjoy reading a lot.
  (D) He doesn't read anymore.

23. Sally has four children and they are all grown-ups.

  (A) Are they studying at the primary schools?
  (B) Are they all working now?
  (C) Does she live in Bournemouth?
  (D) Has she grown up?

24. I don't know why he doesn't like meals with mushroom.

  (A) Me neither.
  (B) Me too.
  (C) How amazing!
  (D) What a coincidence.

20. 倫敦發生了一個事件被視為是恐怖攻擊。

  (A) 那一定很棒。
  (B) 很遺憾聽到這件事情。
  (C) 那是一件有趣的故事。
  (D) 我沒準備去歐洲。

21. Katy 什麼時候退休？

  (A) 她會隨著音樂跳舞。
  (B) 她會去上藝術繪畫課。
  (C) 她會跟朋友一起。
  (D) 她會一直工作到明年。

22. Bill 擅長寫奇幻故事。

  (A) 他已經吃完飯。
  (B) 他有時會辦演唱會。
  (C) 他一定很喜歡閱讀。
  (D) 他完全不看書。

23. Sally 有四個小孩，而且他們都是大人了。

  (A) 他們正在唸小學嗎？
  (B) 他們全部都在工作了嗎？
  (C) 她住在伯恩茅斯。
  (D) 她長大了嗎？

24. 我不知道他為什麼不喜歡吃有蘑菇的餐點。

  (A) 我也不知道。
  (B) 我也是。
  (C) 太棒了！
  (D) 真是巧啊！

neither (adv.) 也不，用於否定句的回應。/ too (adv.) 也，用於肯定句的回應。例如：

肯定用法

Ann: I like to watch musicals. 我喜歡看音樂劇。

Emma: Me too. 我也是。（表示我也想歡看音樂劇）

否定用法

Michael: I don't like mushroom. 我不喜歡蘑菇。

Laura: Me neither. 我也是。（表示我也不喜歡蘑菇）

感嘆句 (how/what 的用法)

1. how + Adj. + (S. + V.)!

    E.g. How lovely the photo is! = How lovely! 這照片真是太美了！

2. what + (冠詞 + adj.) N. + (S. + V.)!

    E.g. What an amazing book it is! = What an amazing book! 真棒的一本書！

25. It is cold. I hope to have a hot drink.

    (A) Would you like to have some coffee?

    (B) Would you like to go home?

    (C) Could you give me a hand?

    (D) May I have some coke?

25. 天氣冷了。我希望喝個熱飲。

    (A) 要不要來點咖啡呢？

    (B) 你想回家嗎？

    (C) 你可以幫我一下嗎？

    (D) 麻煩給我可樂？

26. I like your top. It's nice.

    (A) Thanks. I like it too.

    (B) I like my hairstyle too.

    (C) I have no idea.

    (D) The top of the mountain is amazing.

26. 我喜歡你的上衣。看起來很不錯。

    (A) 謝謝。我也很喜歡。

    (B) 我也很喜歡我的髮型。

    (C) 我不知道。

    (D) 山的頂端很漂亮。

27. Do you want some dessert?

    (A) No, I don't like a desert.

    (B) Yes, I like Egypt.

    (C) Thanks. I am ok.

    (D) Don't give me the menu.

27. 你想來點甜點嗎？

    (A) 不，我不喜歡沙漠。

    (B) 是的，我喜歡埃及。

    (C) 謝謝，我很飽了。

    (D) 不要給我菜單。

28. We will go to Hampton Court Palace this Saturday.

    (A) What are you going to sue?

    (B) Can I join you?

    (C) Why don't you sleep on Saturday?

    (D) Where are you going?

28. 我們這禮拜六要去漢普頓皇宮。

    (A) 你要去哪裡控訴什麼？

    (B) 我可以跟你們一起去嗎？

    (C) 為什麼你星期六不睡覺？

    (D) 你要去哪裡？

29. You look sick. Are you ok?

    (A) I am ok. Thanks.

    (B) No, I am not feeling ill.

    (C) Yes, I am feeling good.

    (D) I don't know why you are dizzy.

29. 你看起來生病的樣子。還好嗎？

    (A) 我沒事，謝謝。

    (B) 不，我沒覺得不舒服。

    (C) 是的，我覺得很好。

    (D) 我不知道你為什麼昏昏的。

30. What are you arguing about?

    (A) He always asks me to do lots of work I don't like.

    (B) He tries to solve problems by fighting.

    (C) He seems to worry about argument.

    (D) He likes to do volunteering jobs in his free time.

30. 你們在吵什麼？

    (A) 他一直要求我做我不想做的事情。

    (B) 他試著用吵架來解決問題。

    (C) 他似乎很擔心吵架。

    (D) 他喜歡在空閒時間做義工。

Life is not an exact science, it is an art./ Samuel Butler
生活不是嚴謹科學，而是一種藝術。（塞繆爾‧巴特勒）

Part 3：簡短對話

本部分共 15 題，每題請聽錄音播出一段對話及一個相關的問題之後，從試題冊上 A、B、C、D 四個選項中選出一個最適合者作答。每段對話及問題只播出一遍。

31.

M: When is your hospital appointment?

W: I will go to hospital tomorrow morning at 9.

M: How do you plan to get there?

W: Well, I will take the underground first and then the bus.

M: Have a safe journey.

Q: How does the woman go to the hospital?

(A) She will arrive at 9.

(B) She will take the tube and the bus.

(C) She has a hospital appointment tomorrow.

(D) She will have a long journey tomorrow.

31.

男士：妳什麼時候要去醫院看診？

女士：我明天九點到醫院。

男士：妳打算怎麼去？

女士：嗯，我先搭地鐵再轉公車。

男士：一路平安。

問題：這位女士怎麼去醫院？

(A) 她會在九點到達。

(B) 她將搭地鐵然後轉公車。

(C) 她明天有醫院門診。

(D) 她明天有長途旅行。

32.

M: Do you like your new house?

W: Yes, it's fabulous. My new house has a big garden.

M: Amazing. I know you like gardening. You must be excited to have the garden.

W: Definitely.

32.

男士： 妳喜歡妳的新家嗎？

女士： 很喜歡，簡直是太棒了！我新家有一個大花園。

男士： 好棒啊！我知道妳喜歡園藝。妳一定很高興有一個花園。

女士： 當然。

Q: What does the woman have?

   (A) She likes her old house.

   (B) She has a fabulous house with a big garden.

   (C) She doesn't want to do gardening.

   (D) She needs to rent a house.

問題：這位女士有什麼？

   (A) 她喜歡她的舊房子。

   (B) 她喜歡有大花園的漂亮房子。

   (C) 她不喜歡園藝。

   (D) 她需要租一個房子。

33.

M: I don't know why Laura likes David so much; he is such a normal man.

W: He has big muscles and I think he is Laura's type.

M: She even adores him and puts his photos on her wall.

W: She must have a crush on him. A man with muscles is charming to her.

Q: What does Laura like?

   (A) A normal man.

   (B) An adorable man.

   (C) A muscle man.

   (D) A crazy man.

33.

男士：我不知道 Laura 為什麼那麼喜歡 David。他只是一個普通的男生。

女士：他有大肌肉而且我覺得他是 Laura 的菜。

男士：她迷戀他不已而且還在她的牆上貼他的照片。

女士：她一定是愛上他了。有肌肉的男生對她來說真的很迷人。

問題：Laura 喜歡什麼？

   (A) 普通男人。

   (B) 可愛的男生。

   (C) 肌肉男。

   (D) 瘋狂男子。

34.

W: I will have an interview next week. I don't know what I should wear.

M: I suggest you follow a normal and safe dress code, like a formal suit.

W: But, I am going for a special interview, which is a drama performance.

M: Ok then, you can check what role or character you will have and pick up suitable clothes.

W: Maybe I am too excited and a bit nervous.

M: Just try your best and good luck.

34.

女士：我下週有一個面試。我不知道我應該穿什麼。

男士：我建議妳著正式且安全的服飾，例如正式西裝。

女士：但是，我要去一個特別的面試，是一個戲劇表演。

男士：喔好，那妳可以查一下妳會接什麼角色然後挑合適的衣服。

女士：或許我太興奮也有點緊張。

男士：盡力就好，祝妳順利。

Q: What will the woman have next week?

    (A) She will have an interview of a dram performance.

    (B) She will choose the correct dress code.

    (C) She will interview people.

    (D) She will put on a formal suit.

問題：這位女士下週有什麼事情？

    (A) 她下週有一個戲劇表演試鏡。

    (B) 她將選擇合適的衣服。

    (C) 她要面試別人。

    (D) 她會穿正式服裝。

35.

M: What's wrong with Robert? He seems not happy.

W: He kicked over a chair when he lost the game.

M: Oh dear.

W: What a sore loser!

Q: What do the man and the woman think of Robert?

    (A) They sympathize him a lot.

    (B) They think he should not have been like that.

    (C) They think he is awesome.

    (D) They think he needs to work harder.

35.

男士： Robert 怎麼了？他看起來不太開心。

女士： 比賽輸的時候他把椅子踢飛了。

男士： 天啊！

女士： 真是輸不起！

問題： 這位男士與女士覺得 Robert 怎麼樣？

    (A) 他們很同情他。

    (B) 他們覺得他不該這樣。

    (C) 他們覺得他很厲害。

    (D) 他們認為他需要更認真。

Ann's notes

sore 是「疼痛的」意思，常用來表示肌肉或是身體上其他部位疼痛。另外一個常見搭配為 sore throat，指的是「喉嚨痛」。sore 在口語上也有「生氣的；不高興的」意思，因此 sore loser 就是指「輸不起的人」。

36.

W: Look! Tower Bridge is opening! Amazing!

M: I've lived in London for 7 years, but I have never seen this.

W: I am so lucky. I am wondering how the bridge can be opened.

M: There are six bridge drivers who work for Tower Bridge. They will manage to open the bridge to let boats pass underneath.

W: It sounds a wonderful job—being a bridge driver.

Q: What does a bridge driver do?

(A) Training the boat drivers.
(B) Opening Tower Bridge to let boats under.
(C) Controlling London city.
(D) Driving a boat.

36.

女士：快看！塔橋打開了！真是驚訝！

男士：我住在倫敦七年了，但我從來沒看過這個景象。

女士：我真幸運。我想知道這個橋怎麼打開的。

男士：有六個人在塔橋工作。他們執行開橋的工作讓船隻通過。

女士：聽起來是一個很棒的工作，開橋人員。

問題：開橋人員要做什麼事情？

(A) 訓練船隻駕駛人員。
(B) 打開塔橋讓船隻從底下通過。
(C) 控制整個倫敦城市。
(D) 駕駛船隻。

> Ann's notes

倫敦塔橋 London's Tower Bridge，除了航船需要而開啟之外，也會因為一些重要且特定的時刻打開。例如 2012 年倫敦奧運，英國足球金童貝克漢在泰晤士河行駛著船帶著奧運火炬前往會場，當他行駛經過 Tower Bridge 時，倫敦塔橋就於萬眾注目下緩緩開啟。在倫敦，水上交通的優先權高於公路交通，只要擁有船隻的駕駛，在 24 小時前告知塔橋工作人員，塔橋工作人員便會打開塔橋讓船隻行駛通過。當塔橋打開時，所有行經塔橋的車輛和行人，都必須停下來讓船隻先行，而且這個服務是全年無休喔！在塔橋工作的人稱為 Tower Bridge controllers，也被稱為 bridge drivers，他們必須先經過一年的訓練，目前於塔橋擔任打開塔橋門的 bridge drivers 有 6 個人，這個工作感覺滿 cool 的吧！

37.

M: Mind the door. Oh, are you ok?

A: My luggage is stuck in the gate.

M: I'll go to the staff office and ask for help.

A: Thanks. I am waiting here.

Q: What happened to Ann?

    (A) She became trapped.

    (B) She is going to ask for help.

    (C) Her luggage was stolen.

    (D) Her friends' luggage was stuck in the gate.

38.

A: What do British people like to do so they don't get bored?

M: Well, most British people like to do crosswords.

A: Crosswords sometimes confuse me a lot because there are many old words.

M: That's right. So is it challenging?

A: Yes, it is.

Q: Why do crosswords confuse Ann sometimes?

    (A) They are too easy.

    (B) They are too interesting.

    (C) Sometimes they are not challenging.

    (D) There are many old words that Ann doesn't understand.

37.

男士：小心門。喔喔，你還好吧？

Ann：　我的行李卡在閘門了。

男士：我去找服務人員請求協助。

Ann：　謝謝。那我在這裡等。

問題：Ann 怎麼了？

    (A) 她被困住了。

    (B) 她去找人幫忙。

    (C) 她的行李被偷了。

    (D) 她朋友的行李卡在閘門。

38.

Ann：　英國人喜歡做什麼，那麼他們才不會覺得無聊？

男士：嗯，大部分的英國人喜歡玩拼字遊戲。

Ann：　有時候拼字遊戲讓我覺得困擾因為有太多古老單字了。

男士：沒錯。所以很有挑戰性吧？

Ann：　確實是。

問題：為什麼拼字遊戲有時候很困擾 Ann？

    (A) 太簡單了。

    (B) 太有趣了。

    (C) 有時候沒那麼有挑戰性。

    (D) 有太多 Ann 不懂的古老單字。

39.

M: Why does Mark become so quiet?

A: He is too naughty to listen to his parents and he gets punishment.

M: What is his punishment?

A: His parents don't allow him to watch TV for the whole day.

M: I understand.

Q: What does Mark do?

    (A) He listens to his parents.

    (B) He gets punishment because he watches too much TV.

    (C) He is too naughty.

    (D) He gets an idea.

40.

A: What is happening in the store? Many people are gathering there.

M: You don't know what day it is?

A: I have no idea.

M: Today is Black Friday. You forget what we have had yesterday.

A: Oh, yesterday was Thanksgiving Day.

Q: What was yesterday?

    (A) It was Black Friday.

    (B) It was Thanksgiving Day.

    (C) It was Mother's Day.

    (D) It was Christmas' Eve.

39.

男士： 為什麼 Mark 變得那麼安靜？

女士： 他太頑皮不聽他爸媽的話，所以他被處罰了。

男士： 他的處罰是什麼？

女士： 他爸媽不准他這一整天看電視。

男士： 了解。

問題：Mark 做了什麼事情？

    (A) 他聽他爸媽的話。

    (B) 他被處罰，因為他看太多電視了。

    (C) 他太頑皮了。

    (D) 他想到一個方法。

40.

Ann: 那間商店發生什麼事情？好多人聚集在那裡。

Michael: 你不知道今天是什麼日子？

Ann: 我不知道。

Michael: 今天是「黑色星期五」。你忘了我們昨天過什麼日子了。

Ann: 噢，昨天是「感恩節」。

問題：昨天是什麼？

    (A) 黑色星期五。

    (B) 感恩節。

    (C) 母親節。

    (D) 聖誕夜。

41.

A: Hi, I would like to rent a car.

M: Sure. Can you show me your passport and driving license?

A: Here you are.

M: Ms. Wang, I am sorry but your international driving license has expired.

A: Can I provide a permanent one which is from my country?

M: Sorry I am afraid not.

Q: Why does the woman fail to rent a car?

(A) Her passport has expired.

(B) Her driving license has expired.

(C) She doesn't have passport and driving license with her.

(D) None of the above.

42.

W: Hi, I would like to cancel my booking.

M: Yes. Can you give me your reference number?

W: Wait a second.

M: Sure, no problem.

W: My reference is F542509.

M: Three nights for Logger Inn?

W: Yes. I have a business meeting. Therefore, I can't make the trip.

M: No problem. I will cancel the booking for you.

41.

Ann: 您好，我想要租車。

男士： 好的。麻煩您的護照跟駕照？

Ann: 這裡給您。

男士： 很抱歉王小姐，您的國際駕照已經過期了。

Ann: 我可以提供我國家的永久駕照嗎？

男士： 很抱歉恐怕不行。

問題：為什麼這位女士無法租車？

(A) 她的護照過期了。

(B) 她的駕照過期了。

(C) 她身上沒有護照跟駕照。

(D) 以上皆非。

42.

女士： 你好，我想要取消我的訂房。

男士： 沒問題。麻煩您的訂房代碼？

女士： 等一下。

男士： 沒問題。

女士： 我的訂房代碼是 F542509。

男士： 洛格小棧三晚嗎？

女士： 是的。我有一個工作會議。所以我無法成行。

男士： 沒問題。我幫您取消您的訂房。

Q: Why is the booking canceled?

   (A) The woman will have a business meeting.

   (B) The woman is on holidays.

   (C) The woman doesn't have a reference number.

   (D) The woman wants to stay in the hotel for three nights.

問題：訂房為什麼取消了？

   (A) 這位女士有一個工作會議。

   (B) 這位女士去度假。

   (C) 這位女士沒有訂房代碼。

   (D) 這位女士想在這個旅館住三個晚上。

43.

M: Which flower do you like most?

A: I like roses. Also, I like lilies. They smell so good.

M: I like sunflowers.

A: I am so scared of sunflowers because some bugs are attracted to them.

M: Don't worry about the bugs. They won't hurt you.

Q: What is the woman scared of?

   (A) Roses

   (B) Lilies

   (C) Sunflowers

   (D) Bugs

43.

男士：你最喜歡什麼花？

Ann：我喜歡玫瑰花。我也喜歡百合花。它們聞起來真香。

男士：我喜歡向日葵。

Ann：我很怕向日葵，因為有蟲吸附在裡面。

男士：不用怕那些蟲。牠們不會咬妳。

問題：這位女士怕什麼東西？

   (A) 玫瑰花。

   (B) 百合花。

   (C) 向日葵。

   (D) 蟲。

44.

M: I am looking for a flatmate. I have one room which is available now.

W: My friend William is looking for a place to live.

M: That's brilliant. Can you tell him my contact details or can you give me his number?

W: Sure. I will ring him and give him your contact details.

M: Perfect. Thanks.

44.

男士：我正在找一個室友。我現在有一個空房。

女士：我朋友 William 正在找一個地方住。

男士：太好了。妳可以告訴他我的聯絡方式或者妳可以給我他的電話嗎？

女士：沒問題。我打電話給他，給他你的聯絡方式。

男士：太好了，謝謝妳。

Q: What does the man have?

    (A) He has a room for a rent.

    (B) He has a telephone.

    (C) He has a contact book.

    (D) He gets a new flatmate.

問題： 這位男士有什麼？

    (A) 他有一個房間要出租。

    (B) 他有一支電話。

    (C) 他有一本聯絡簿。

    (D) 他有一個新室友。

45.

M: Why don't you try to ask me for help?

A: I just don't want to bother you.

M: You never bother me. You shouldn't have gone to accident and emergency at midnight by yourself. I can go with you if you need any help.

A: Thank you for your support.

Q: What happened to Ann?

    (A) She had an accident.

    (B) She went to accident and emergency in the hospital at midnight.

    (C) She supported the man.

    (D) She bothered the man.

45.

男士： 妳為什麼不找我幫忙啊？

Ann: 我就不想打擾你啊。

男士： 妳不會打擾我啊。妳不應該半夜自己去急診室的。如果妳需要幫忙，我可以跟妳去的。

Ann: 謝謝你的幫忙。

問題：Ann 發生什麼事情？

    (A) 她出了意外。

    (B) 她半夜自己去醫院的急診室。

    (C) 她直持這位男士。

    (D) 她打擾了這位男士。

Well begun is half done./ Horace
好的開始是成功的一半。(赫瑞斯)

Section Two：Reading
閱讀練習與講解

全民英檢第二部分為閱讀能力測驗，該測驗涵蓋三種題型：詞彙和結構、段落填空、閱讀理解，滿分為 120 分。通過此項測驗即表示能閱讀短文、私人信件、廣告、簡介與使用說明等，也能閱讀工作須知、操作手冊、傳真、電報等。聽力與閱讀兩項測驗成績總和須達 160 分，且其中任一項成績不低於 72 分。

Ann 的小叮嚀

閱讀測驗中的題型大致為學生在國、高中時期會遇到的題型，例如第一部分的詞彙與結構，著重在詞彙量、基本文法結構與時態變化；第二部分的段落填空除了單字用法與時態變化外，介系詞、轉折語氣詞、副詞語氣詞的用法也是考題重點；第三部分的閱讀理解主要為短文閱讀或資訊擷取，建議閱讀時邊畫重點，以免在作答時忘記細節。留意詢問文章單字含義的題目，通常會在文章中有補充資訊以利解題。在閱讀測驗中，最容易讓學生打瞌睡的就是第三部分。因為看不懂文意而挫折只好猜題作答，或是以自己認知的知識作答。切記！文章提供的是「答題的資訊」，所以，正確答案當然是從文章中有提到的「資訊」取得。簡言之 Ann 常說「寫閱讀測驗時，不要在人家的文章中自己加入自己的意思，你又不是在寫作文需要闡述自己的想法…」。那麼就開始以下的練習吧！

全民英檢中級的閱讀內容配置如下：

	Content	Questions
Part 1	Vocabulary & Structure	15
Part 2	Passage	10
Part 3	Reading Comprehension	15

▶▶ Part 1：Vocabulary and Structure 詞彙與結構

說明

閱讀能力測驗第一部分為詞彙與結構共 15 題，全為四選一之選擇題，主要測試考生詞彙記憶與句子文法結構，選出符合句意的單字或是詞彙用法亦為文法。

I. 詞彙 Vocabulary

For example:

The ISIS is a terrifying _____ that has launched several attacks to claim the lives of lots of people.

    (A) relation   (B) organization

    (C) committee   (D) employment

ISIS 是一個令人驚恐的組織，到目前為止已經發動許多攻擊奪走很多生命。

因此，答案選 (B)，符合句子題意。

★ 補充：(A) 關係 (C) 委員會 (D) 工作

Ann's reminder

熟記中級程度的單字，注意一些外型相像詞彙；除此之外，注意一些時事內容，即使遇到不是很懂的句子時，能夠大略知道題目要表達的意思。例如 ISIS 是目前國際之間棘手的一個恐怖組織，相關恐怖攻擊的單字可以一並背誦，以便應付同議題不同詞彙的考題。

例如 terrorism (n.) 恐怖主義，terrify (v.) 使恐懼，launch (v.) 發動，attack (v. n.) 攻擊，claim (v.) 宣稱 / 奪走，organization (n.) 組織等。

1. attack (v. n.) 攻擊
   E.g. A woman was attacked and robbed by a gang of youths.
   一位婦女遭到一夥年輕人的襲擊與搶劫。

2. attach (v.) 附著 附件（檔案）
   E.g. I attach a copy of my notes for your information.
   我附上筆記一份供你參考。

Genius is one percent inspiration and ninety-nine percent perspiration./ Edison
天才是一分靈感加上九十九分的努力。（愛迪生）

Let's have a go at Vocabulary!

1. We _____ our friends, but we don't often joke around with strangers.

   (A) tease   (B) praise   (C) protect   (D) mind

2. A music-lover of the nineteenth century might have had to make a _____ sacrifice of time and money to follow his hobby.

   (A) considerate   (B) considerable   (C) complimentary   (D) complementary

3. I _____ an old friend of mine on my way home.

   (A) broke out   (B) broke up with   (C) came across   (D) came up with

4. Do not _____ time and money doing such meaningless things.

   (A) expand   (B) expend   (C) retain   (D) tolerate

5. _____ the dictionary if you don't know the word.

   (A) Maintain   (B) Insist   (C) Conceal   (D) Consult

6. The eternal triangle is always a problem hard to _____.

   (A) cooperate with   (B) keep in touch with

   (C) cope with   (D) wait on

7. People around the world are _____ against terrorism.

   (A) finding   (B) fighting   (C) planning   (D) handling

8. It was devastating that the plane _____ immediately after it took off.

   (A) crushed   (B) crashed   (C) landed   (D) lent

9. Hard work is the only secret _____ success.

   (A) to   (B) for   (C) of   (D) with

10. Though they are twin brothers, they have nothing _____.

   (A) the same   (B) in all   (C) in common   (D) a few

Answers: 1. A   2. B   3. C   4. B   5. D   6. C   7. B   8. B   9. A   10. C

內容解析

1. 我們會揶揄我們的朋友，但是不會常常對身旁的陌生人開玩笑。

   (A) 揶揄　　　　　(B) 讚美　　　　　(C) 保護　　　　　(D) 介意

2. 一位十九世紀音樂愛好者或許會犧牲相當的時間與金錢來投注他的喜好。

   (A) 考慮周到的　(B) 相當的　　　　(C) 讚美的　　　　(D) 補充的

> ### Ann's notes
>
> 特別注意 considerate 跟 considerable 這個形容詞。這兩個形容詞是由 consider (v.)「思考、考慮」延伸出的兩個形容詞。
>
> E.g. Charles is so considerate that he always cares for others' feelings.
>   Charles 非常體貼，所以他總會顧及別人的感受。(considerate = thoughtful)
>
> E.g. The project wasted a considerable amount of time and money.
>   這項工程耗費了相當多的時間與資金。
>
> ★「許多」除了 many（可數）跟 much（不可數）用法之外，還有其他的表達方式：
> 用於可數名詞：a(+ adj.) number of + 可數名詞　E.g. a great number of books
> 用於不可數名詞：a(n)（+ adj.) amount of + 不可數名詞　E.g. a huge amount of money

3. 我在回家的路上巧遇一位老朋友。

   (A) 爆發　　　　　　　　　　(B) 分手
   (C) 巧遇 = run across　　　　(D) 想到

4. 不要耗費時間跟金錢做一些沒有意義的事情。

   (A) 擴張　　　　　(B) 耗費　　　　　(C) 保留　　　　　(D) 忍受

5. 如果你不懂這個字就查字典。

   (A) 維持　　　　　(B) 堅持　　　　　(C) 隱蔽　　　　　(D) 查閱

6. 三角戀情一直是很難處理的問題。

   (A) 合作　　　　　(B) 保持聯繫　　　(C) 處理 =deal with　(D) 指望

1. wait on 等待／指望（別人來做決定）的含義
   E.g. We are waiting on the manager's answer. Once we get that, we will be able to manage the project.
   我們在等候經理的答覆。一旦得到消息，我們就可以進行這個計畫。
2. wait for 等待（人、物），期望（事情發生）
   E.g. The boy is waiting for his parents to pick him up.
   這男孩等待著父母來接他。

7. 全世界的人們都在對抗恐怖主義。

   (A) 發現   (B) 對抗   (C) 計畫   (D) 操控

fight(v.) 打仗／搏鬥／反對
fight for+ N./Ving. 為 ... 努力／奮鬥
fight against+ N./Ving. 反對／對抗

8. 這架飛機起飛後立即墜落的事情令人心碎難過。

   (A) 壓碎   (B) 墜落   (C) 降落   (D) 借出

9. 努力是成功的唯一訣竅。

   此題的用法是 the secret to N.「... 的秘密或是訣竅」，類似用法例如 the answer to N.「... 的答案」。

10. 雖然他們是雙胞胎兄弟，但他們沒有什麼交集。

   此題的用法是 have N. in common（有 ... 的共識或是交集），所以 have nothing in common 意為「沒有交集」或是「沒有共識」或者「沒有共同點」。

You can't judge a book by its cover.
人不可貌相；海水不可斗量。

II. 結構 Structure

For example:

Over the past seven years of teaching career, Ann has instructed many students,

_____ have successfully entered into ideal universities.

    (A) some of them

    (B) some of whom

    (C) some of which

    (D) some of that

在過去的七年教學生涯中，Ann 指導了許多學生，當中的一些學生成功進入理想大學就讀。

此題是測驗關係代名詞的用法，不過此句屬於複雜的關係代名詞用法。因為學生是人，所以選擇的關係代名詞必須是 who、whom 或是 that，而 that 前面不得有介系詞，因此答案選 (B)。

> **Ann's reminder**
>
> 關係代名詞是形容詞子句的一種，用來補充、強調，或說明句子當中特定的名詞。關係代名詞的用法主要分為 1. 人與非人 2. 主格受格與所有格用法，that 則可以代替人與非人的主格與受格用法，但不得代替所有格 whose。很多人學習英文時害怕關係代名詞是因為關係代名詞子句讓句子變得複雜，建議多複習關係代名詞的用法，多做題目了解句意，可以減少考試時的作答時間，並特別留意句型必須用 that 或是不得使用 that（例如本題因為前方有介系詞的關係，故不得使用 that），關係代名詞是為考試中比較棘手的題型，需多費心研讀。

Let's have a go at Structure!

1. _____ from space, the earth is almost perfectly round.

   (A) Seeing   (B) Seem   (C) To see   (D) See

2. One is _____ by the company he keeps.

   (A) decided   (B) looked   (C) considered   (D) known

3. It was teamwork that _____ our success.

   (A) contributes to   (B) contributed to   (C) is contributed to   (D) was contributed to

4. The Olympics games are _____ contests of sports, music, and literature.

   (A) made up of   (B) made of   (C) made from   (D) made in

5. _____ farmers attend the rally.

   (A) A huge number of   (B) A huge amount of
   (C) The huge number of   (D) The huge amount of

6. It was then _____ I began to understand the necessity of learning English.

   (A) which   (B) when   (C) that   (D) at which

7. Despite being an ordinary star, our sun is more important to man than _____.

   (A) any other star   (B) any star   (C) all the stars   (D) any star else

8. He doesn't like the city life because he _____ in the country.

   (A) used to live   (B) is used to living   (C) is used to live   (D) is used as living

9. It sometimes happens that an artist will acquire traditional skills then, _____ to break away from the past.

   (A) wished   (B) wishes   (C) wish   (D) wishing

10. Charles M. Schulz's comic strip _____ psychology, social commentary and humor was worth discussing from a child's viewpoint.

    (A) dealing with   (B) is dealt with   (C) was dealt with   (D) dealt with

Answers: 1. B   2. D   3. B   4. A   5. A   6. C   7. A   8. B   9. D   10. A

1. 從外太空看來，地球幾近完美圓潤。

   句子原本是 When the earth is seen from space, it is almost perfectly round.

   此句為「分詞構句」，逗點前的子句中，省略連接詞 when 及主詞 the earth，將動詞 (is seen) 降為分詞 (Vpp.) seen。

2. 觀其友而知其人。= A man is known by the company he keeps.

   這是一個英文諺語。One 在這裡指的是 a man 或者 one person，這句話以被動語態呈現「一個人能被瞭解多少可以從他身旁認識的朋友中得知」的意思。company 除了有「公司」的意思，還有「同伴、朋友」的含義。

3. 團隊工作促成我們的成功。

   此題型重點於 contribute to 的運用。contribute to + N/Ving 為有助於或是促進 / 促成的意思。這句話前面的 It was teamwork 可知道使用的是「過去式」，所以 that 子句後面也必須使用同一時態。另外一個重點「 It be-V + 強調的人事物、時間、地點 that S + V」是所謂的「分裂句」，也就是強調句的用法。將強調的人事物或是時間地點放置到 it be-V 後面，之後再接一個關係代名詞子句來修飾所要強調的名詞。

   例如：

   It is in the park that Danny walks his dog.（Danny 就是在這個公園遛狗）

   → 強調地點 in the park

   It is this Sunday that we will have a BBQ.（我們會在這個星期日烤肉）

   → 強調時間 this Sunday

4. 奧運是由運動、音樂跟文學這些比賽所組成的。

   (A) be made up of 由 ... 組成

   　　E.g. The Taipei Universiade is made of many countries' representative teams.

   　　台北世大運是由多國家代表隊所組成的世界運動會。

   (B) be made of 由 ... 材料製成

   　　（當原材料製成成品後，原材料仍保持原有性質。）

   　　E.g. This chair is made of metal. 這把椅子是用金屬製成的。

   (C) be made from 由（原料）... 製成（尤其指食物製成）

   　　E.g. Brandy is made from grapes. 白蘭地酒是用葡萄釀造的。

   (D) be made in 於（某地）製造

   　　E.g. This leather coat was made in Italy. 這件皮外套是義大利製造的。

5. 很多農民參與這場集會。

Ⅰ.「許多」除了 a lot of（＋可數／不可數名詞）之外，常見的有 many ＋ 可數名詞跟 much ＋ 不可數名詞的用法。除外，還有其他的片語方式呈現：

可數／不可數	a lot of, lots of, a quantity of, a wealth of, plenty of
可數	a (great/large/huge) number of
不可數	a (great/large/huge) amount of, a (great/large/huge) deal of

E.g.

There is a wealth of books in our library. 我們圖書館裡有很多書。（可數）

I have plenty of working experience. 我有很豐富的工作經驗。（不可數）

He has a great number of songs in my iPod. 他的 iPod 裡有很多首歌。（可數）

Emma spends a great deal of time studying English every day.

Emma 每天都花很多時間學英文。（不可數）

Ⅱ. The number of（＋可數名詞）與 The amount of（＋不可數名詞）的語意雖然跟 a number of（＋可數名詞）還有 an amount of（＋不可數名詞）相同，都是「許多」的意思，不過 the number of 跟 the amount of 著重在「一大群」意思，所以兩者為主詞的時候，動詞皆以單數連接。

E.g.

The number of students gather in the basketball court.

一群學生聚集在籃球場。(the number of students)

The great amount of scholarship is the result of this book.

這些學術成集結而成這本書。（the great amount of scholarship 學術成就）

6. 不久之後我開始了解到學習英文的必要性。

這個題型同第三題「分裂句」（強調句型）的用法，所以選擇連接詞 that。

7. 雖然太陽是一個普通的恆星，它比起其他的恆星對人類還來得重要。

首先，star 是指太空中的物體、恆星、星星；表演者、明星、符號。這題答案選擇 A，any other star 是指除了太陽以外的恆星。選項 B 的 any star 指的是全部恆星，包含太陽在內，必須加上 other 才正確。選項 C 的意思也是指所有的恆星，跟 B 選項不同是以複數呈現。選項 D 在 else 的用法不正確。

1. else 是個副詞，可用在以 any-、every-、no- 和 some- 開頭的一群字後面來表示「其他；別的；另外」的意思。這群字包括 anybody、everybody、nobody、somebody、anyone、everyone、no one、someone、anything、everything、nothing、something 等不定代名詞以及 anywhere、everywhere、nowhere、somewhere（或美國口語的 anyplace、everyplace、no place、someplace）等副詞。例如：

   ★ Anybody else would have condemned her foolish behavior.
   （換了誰都會譴責她的愚蠢行為。）

   ★ Joseph stayed at work when everybody else had gone home.
   （別人都回家了，約瑟還在工作。）

   ★ No one else can do it.（沒有其他人能做這件事了。）

2. else 亦可用在 how、what、where、who、why、whatever 和 whoever 等疑問和關係代名詞詞後面來表示「其他；別的；另外」的意思。例如：

   What else did Rachel tell you?（Rachel 還告訴了你什麼？）

   Who else is coming over?（還有誰要來？）

8. 他不喜歡城市的生活，因為他習慣鄉村的生活。

   ★ S + used to + V. 某人過去習慣做 ...（現在沒有這個習慣）

   E.g. Jenny used to walk to school when she was in senior high.
   　　 Jenny 以前高中的時候習慣走路去上學。

   ★ S + be-V + used to + N./ Ving. 習慣於 ...、逐漸 ...

   E.g. I am used to the life in the university. 我很習慣大學生活。

   此外，選項 C 是「被動語態」(be used to V.)，所以不符合題意。選項 D 也是「被動語態」，連接 as 的意思有「以 ...（狀態）作為 ...（身份）」。

9. 有時候藝術家可能授傳統技巧的訓練，然而會希望擺脫過去的學習。

   原本句子是 It sometimes happens that an artist will acquire traditional skills then and wish to break away from the past.。省略連接詞 and 後，將用 wishing 接下 acquire (v.)「獲得」之後的動作。

10. 由於查爾斯·舒茲的連環漫畫跟心理學相關，從小孩的觀點來看，社會評論跟幽默在他的漫畫中很值得討論。

此句話原本是 As Charles M. Schulz's comic strip was dealt with psychology, social commentary and humor was worth discussing from a child's viewpoint. 在省略連接詞 as 的情況之下形成分詞構句，另外 A +be dealt with + B「A 與 B 相關」的用法在省略 as 連接詞後，be-V. 也省略留下分詞 dealt with。分詞構句的用意在於文字修辭美化，所以會有些複雜。以一個大原則方向思考，分詞構句主要省略連接詞，因為連接詞連接兩個句子，少了連接詞，附屬子句（也就是連接詞帶出來的子句）必須變化成分詞構句，以語氣來劃分，主動的狀態用 Ving，被動用 Vpp.。

分詞構句

★ Ving..., S + V....（主動）

When I found that my parents were not home, I got something outside.

= Finding that my parents were not home, I got something outside.

知道我爸媽不在家時，我就在外面吃飯了。（主動）

★ Vpp..., S + V...（被動）

Since Ann was noticed to fall asleep in the planetarium, she was waken up by the staff.

= Noticed to fall asleep in the planetarium, Ann was waken up by the staff.

因為 Ann 在天文館裡面睡著了，她被工作人員叫醒了。（被動）

Ann's notes

查爾斯·舒茲（Charles M. Schulz）。漫畫以小狗史努比（Snoopy）和查理·布朗（Charlie Brown）、莎莉（Sally Brown）、萊 斯（Linus Van Pelt）、露西（Lucy Van Pelt）、謝勒德（Schroeder）等幾位小學生為主要角色，以小孩生活為題材，觀察這個簡單又複雜的世界。《花生》(Peanut) 漫畫是漫畫發展史上首部多角色系列漫畫，從 1950 年 10 月 2 日開始發行，到 2000 年 2 月 13 日作者病逝之時停止。

Love makes the world go round.

愛的力量是無限的。

牛刀小試

1. Lily was _____ by the pop-up ads that kept interrupting her while she was surfing the Internet.

   (A) amused

   (B) irritated

   (C) satisfied

   (D) interested

2. Many consumers are _____ by the store's constant price increases, and they are asking or assistance from the Consumer's Foundation.

   (A) ranged

   (B) rated

   (C) outraged

   (D) ranked

3. When Banny asked my advice on what to do, I _____ all the possible solutions for a while before answering.

   (A) recreated

   (B) arranged

   (C) managed

   (D) pondered

4. Pickiness about food may not directly cause health problems; however, it can cause _____ problems for children, such as slow development and poor growth.

   (A) underlying

   (B) essential

   (C) proper

   (D) appropriate

5. Career counselors often advise their _____ on how to look for employment or how to make a career change.

   (A) patients

   (B) clients

   (C) dentists

   (D) artists

6. In the face of many questions about her private life, the actress _____ that it was none of their business.

   (A) repaired

   (B) recovered

   (C) restored

   (D) retorted

7. Lily compared the advantages of package tours _____ independent travel, and then chose the former because it was much more economical.

   (A) versus

   (B) against

   (C) under

   (D) behind

8. Questioned by the police for hours, Nick finally _____ that he had been involved in the kidnapping.

   (A) realized

   (B) understood

   (C) attained

   (D) confessed

9. James _____ at the waitress after he had waited for his order for forty minutes.

   (A) took into heart

   (B) lashed out

   (C) took over

   (D) put off

10. Monica _____ take the earliest bus to school when she was in junior high. However, it just takes her less than five minutes to walk to school.

    (A) is used to

    (B) was used to

    (C) used to

    (D) had been used to

11. Your application didn't _____ the company's requirements, so I am afraid that you should come up with another one.

(A) reach   (B) meet

(C) arrive   (D) accomplish

12. Steven spends lots of time _____ the Internet before he begins his assignments every day.

(A) surfing

(B) sailing

(C) sealing

(D) serving

13. Chinese New Year is a short term vacation _____ families get together, give red envelops for blessing and send friends gifts.

(A) when

(B) where

(C) which

(D) that

14. This speech contest is the only one _____ students can have a chance to deliver a speech on stage by this semester.

(A) which

(B) whom

(C) that

(D) where

15. After crying for a while, Johnson felt _____ better than the moment when he had known the test result.

(A) very

(B) even

(C) more

(D) extremely

解答	1. B	2. C	3. D	4. A	5. B
	6. D	7. A	8. D	9. B	10. C
	11. B	12. A	13. A	14. C	15. B

★第一部分為單字文意為主，詞彙量是答題拿分最大主力。

1. Lily 在瀏覽網頁的時候被那些不斷出現的廣告頁面打擾而感到惱怒。答案選 (B)。
   (A) 感到愉快 (C) 感到滿足 (D) 感到有趣

Ann's notes

此題為重點文法「情緒動詞用法」。

S (人) + be-V/ 連綴動詞 + Vpp (+ 介系詞 + N.) 某人 (對某事某物) 感到 ...

S (物) + be-V/ 連綴動詞 + Ving 某物令人 ...

E.g. Daniel is satisfied with his performance.
      Daniel 對他的表演感到滿意。

E.g. This astronomy course in the Royal Observatory Greenwich is exciting.
      Royal Observatory Greenwich 的天文學課程真刺激。

2. 許多顧客因這間商店的不斷漲價而感到憤怒,因而轉向消基會尋求協助。答案選 (C)。(A) 範圍 (B) 評比 (D) 排名

3. 當 Banny 向我詢問怎麼做的時候,在答覆他之前,我思索了所有可能解決的方法。答案選 (D)。(A) 娛樂 (B) 安排 (C) 管理

4. 挑食可能不會直接影響健康問題;然而,它會對孩童造成潛在性的問題,例如發展遲緩與營養不良。答案選 (A)。(B) 重要的 (C) 適當的 (D) 適合的

5. 職涯顧問通常會針對如何求職或者轉職給委託人建議。答案選 (B)。(A) 病人 (C) 牙醫 (D) 藝術家

6. 面對一連串有關於他私生活的問題,那女演員反駁說這不關別人的事情。答案選 (D)。(A) 修理 (B) 復原 (C) 恢復 / 修復

7. Lily 比較了跟團旅行跟自由行的優點,她選擇了前者因為跟團更加經濟實惠。答案選擇 (A) 與 ... 相比。(B) 反對 / 對抗 (C) 在 ... 之下 (D) 在 ... 後面。

8. 被警方訊問了好幾個小時之後,Nick 最後承認參與綁架事件。答案選擇 (D)。(A) 領悟 / 了解 (B) 理解 (C) 達到 / 獲得

9. James 等了他的餐點 40 分鐘之後,把服務生痛罵了一頓。答案選擇 (B)。(A) 非常介意 (C) 接管 (D) 推遲

10. Monica 念國中時習慣搭最早的公車上學。但現在只需不到五分鐘的時間的路程即可到達學校。答案選擇 (C) used to + V.

★ used to + V. 表示過去曾經，用於動作或事情

E.g. He used to live in the USA but now he lives in Taiwan.

　　他曾經住過美國，但現在他住在台灣。

★ be used to + Ving. 表示目前或是逐漸形成的習慣

E.g. Connie is used to drinking warm water when she gets up in the morning.

　　Connie 習慣每天早上起床喝溫開水。

11. 你的申請沒有符合這間公司的要求，所以我想你應該再申請其他試試看。答案為 (B) meet one's requirements（符合 ... 要求）。(A) 到達 (C) 抵達 (D) 完成

12. Steven 每天開始寫作業之前，花很多時間上網。答案選 (A)。(B) 航行 (C) 密封 / 保證 (D) 提供 / 服務

13. 春節是家人聚集在一起、給紅包作為祝福還有送禮物給朋友的假期時光（時間）。空格前的名詞為 a short term vacation（一段時間），因此選擇 (A) when 來補充說明這段時間可以從事什麼事情。(B) where 補充說明地點用法 (C) which 可作為一般關係代名詞用法 (D) that 可當作一般關係代名詞或其他用法。

14. 這個演講比賽是唯一一次學生可以在這個學期前參加上台演講的機會。答案選擇 (C)，因為先行詞 one 前面有 the only 的關係，所以只能選擇 that。

關係代名詞的用法：

關係代名詞	主格	受格
代替人	who	whom
代替事物	which	which
代替整個句子	which	which

★ (2 Don'ts) that 最常用來取代 who/whom/which，因為可以同時取代人或物，所以常常被拿來當作選擇答案的捷徑，不過，that 當關係代名詞時有兩個限制：

a. 只能用在限定用法，換句話說，that 前面不可加逗點

b. that 之前不能有介系詞

★ **(8 Musts)** 如果在下列情況之下，關係代名詞只能用 that，不用 who/whom/which

(1) 序數之後（the fir/ second...）

　　E.g. She was the first girl that came up in my mind.

(2) 最高級之後（the best/ the most + adj....）

　　E.g. He is the best coach that I have even seen.

(3) the very + N.（此為加強語氣的慣用法）

　　E.g. He is the very guy that I saw last week.

(4) All 之後（all/every... 表全部語詞後）

　　E.g. All that I said is true.

(5) the only + N.（慣用法，只接 that）

　　E.g. He is the only man that I want to marry.

(6) 句中有兩個相同的關係代名詞（避免重複）

　　E.g. He is clever, which is a fact that I is known to us.

　　　 = He is clever, which is a fact which is known to us.（原句）

(7) 關係代名詞在 be-V. 後面當補語（表示身份）

　　E.g. She is not the girl that she used to be.

(8) 兩個先行詞性質不同（人與非人）卻需要用一個關係代名詞時

　　E.g. Look at the lady and the dog that are walking on the beach.

15. 哭完一會兒，比起在知道考試結果那一刻，Johnson 感覺好更多。答案選 (B)。修飾比較級的副詞 much/even/far/a bit/a lot/rather/somewhat。一般形容詞用 very/too/quite 來修飾。

If at first you don't succeed, try, try again.

再接再勵；不輕言放棄。

· 閱 · 讀 · 練 · 習 ·

▶▶ Part 2：Passage 段落填空

說明

「段落填空」就是高中學測與指考的「克漏字測驗」。此項考題作答時，應慢慢細看文章，遇到空格題目時，從上下文 (context) 中找到合適文意與文法的答案。

Ann's reminder

> 此類型範圍廣，凡單字、慣用語、介系詞、時態、文法句型結構等，皆可能成為考題。建議平時大量閱讀文章，熟悉結構用字，同時增進閱讀數度與一些資訊的知識。

For example：（Tips: 此篇短文出現重要文法為假設語氣用法）

Last week, my dad and I went to the Science Museum. A crazy-looking professor was testing a new device for reading people's minds. My dad and I decided to give it a go. We put some helmets on and everything went dark. When I opened my eyes, I found that my mind was in my dad's body! I could see myself standing opposite me. The professor said he'd try to fix things, but it would take a week.

For the next few days, I had to go to work at my dad's job. I had no idea he had so many tasks! Luckily, one of his coworkers helped me a lot. Meanwhile, Dad went to my school. He couldn't believe how much homework I had to do. (與現在事實相反假設法)

Fortunately, the professor was able to put our minds back where they belong. Dad and I respect each other more now, because we know how hard we both have to work. I won't complain if he gets home late（條件式）, and he said he wouldn't put so much pressure on me about my studies（與現在事實相反假設法）. Had it not been for this crazy experience, we might never have understood each other so well（與過去事實相反假設法）.

翻譯

上週我跟我爸爸去科學博物館。一個看起來怪怪的教授當時候正在測試一個能讀人類心智的新器材。我跟我爸決定試試這個儀器。我們戴上安全帽，視野全部變暗。當我打開我的雙眼時，我發現我的意識居然在我爸的體內！我可以看見我自己（的身體）站在我的對面。這位教授說他還在嘗試修改一些東西，不過這得花上一週的時間。

接下來的幾天，我必須去做我爸爸的工作。我不知道他怎麼會有那麼多的任務！很幸運地，他一位同事幫了我許多忙。同時，爸爸去我的學校上課。他難以相信我竟然有那麼多的功課要寫。

好在這位教授能夠換回屬於我們的意識。爸爸跟我因此更尊重彼此,因為我們知道彼此都很努力。如果他回家晚了點,我不會再抱怨了;他也說他不會再對於我的課業加諸更多壓力。如果沒有這個瘋狂的經驗,我們可能永遠都無法那麼了解彼此。

Ann's notes

此文章的重點文法是「假設語氣」。假設就是和事實相反,如果可能發生或是真實事件就不必用假設語氣(應使用「條件式」也就是 If + S + 現在式動詞 S + will + V.)

舉例: If the strong typhoon comes tomorrow, the authorities will announce to have one day off. (如果這個強颱明天到來,那麼當局會宣布明天放假一天)。

請記住 Ann 的提醒,所謂「假設語氣法」就是「不會發生的事情」,而假設法有好幾種類型,廣義分為三種:

與過去事實相反的假設法 :(If + S + had + Vpp..., S + would/could/should/might + have + Vpp...)

E.g. If I had read more information online, I would have had some understanding about that country I was travelling. (如果之前我有上網做功課,那對於當時旅行的國家就能有更多的認識。)

與現在事實相反的假設法 :(If + S + were/ 過去式動詞 /could ...., S + would/could/should/ might + V...)

E.g. If I were a bird, I could fly over the sky. 如果我是一隻鳥,我就可以翱翔天際。

未來事實相反的假設法: (If + S + were to + V...., S + would/could/should/might + V...)。

E.g. If it were to have ghosts in the real life, I would like to see them in person without fear. (如果真實世界真的有鬼的話,那麼我一點也不害怕想親自看看。)

以上是三種常見的用法。我們常常可以在電視新聞上看到被訪問的政治人物或是明星名人回應媒體「我不回答假設性問題」,代表他 / 她認為這是不會發生的問題,所以他 / 她不想回應,當然,也取決於當事者自己的認知。因此在考試或是閱讀文章時,可以從上下文來理解是否使用假設語氣。

Better late than never.
亡羊補牢,猶未晚也。

Let's have a go at the exercises!

First published in 1943, *The Little Prince* is a children's book written by Antoine de Saint-Exupéry. *The Little Prince* is a fantasy story about a pilot stranded in the desert, who meets a boy from another planet—the Little Prince. The boy is searching for knowledge, and asks the pilot many questions. Its **(1)** is based on its charming way of addressing simple but important truths, especially those that adults often forget **(2)** they age. A famous quote from the story is that "It is only with the heart that one can see rightly; what is essential is **(3)** to the eye." Its straight, imaginative fantasy setting makes this story entertaining for children, and its universal concepts attract adults as well. This **(4)** makes the novel very popular. **(5)** , the story has been translated into more than 250 languages and is one of the top 50 best-selling books in the world.

___1. (A) peculiarity　(B) appeal　(C) criticism　(D) contribution

___2. (A) unless　(B) until　(C) as　(D) if

___3. (A) fundamental　(B) precious　(C) invisible　(D) impractical

___4. (A) combination　(B) contradiction　(C) distribution　(D) recognition

___5. (A) Nevertheless　(B) Otherwise　(C) Likewise　(D) In fact

---

Keywords:

children's book 童書　fantasy (n.) 幻想　strand (v.) 滯留擱淺　desert (n.) 沙漠

age (v.) 年紀增長　quote (n.) 引言　setting (n.) 情節背景　concept (n.) 概念

best-selling (adj.) 暢銷的

翻譯

《小王子》在 1943 年首度出版，是一本由安東尼・德・聖修伯里所撰寫的童書。它是一個幻想故事，描寫一名迫降在沙漠的飛行員遇見來自外星的小男孩 -- 小王子。這名男孩渴求知識，問了飛行員許多問題。這本書吸引人的地方，在於它以迷人的方式處理一些簡單卻重要的真相，特別是一些大人會隨著年齡增長而遺忘的事。出自這個故事的名言之一就是：「只有用心才能看清一切；真正重要的東西用眼睛是看不見的。」這本書直率而有想像力的幻想場景，使這個故事不只對兒童很有娛樂性，其中一些普世皆然的觀念也吸引了大人。這種結合使這本書非常暢銷。事實上，它已經被翻譯成超過 250 種語言，是全世界賣得最好的 50 本書籍之一。

Background knowledge:

Antoine de Saint-Exupéry 安東尼‧德‧聖修伯里 (1900-1944) 是 20 世紀出法國作家、飛行員，著有代表作《小王子》(Le Little Prince, 1943)、《夜間飛行》(Night Flight, 1931)、《風沙星辰》(Wind, Sand and Stars, 1939)。在二次世界大戰前是一位擔任運送郵件的飛行員，大戰開始後加入法國空軍，於 1944 年執行一次任務中不幸罹難。法國政府曾將旗肖像放置 50 法朗紙鈔上，另外家鄉里昂的機場，也以其名改為里昂聖修伯里機場紀念這位出色的作家。

解析

1. Its appeal is based on its charming way of addressing simple but important truths.

   (A) 奇異 (B) 吸引力 (C) 批評 (D) 貢獻。此句說明「這本書吸引人的地方在於用迷人的方式說明簡單的道理」，故最適合的答案為 (B)

2. especially those that adults often forget as they age.

   隨著人們年紀增長，會逐漸忘記這些道理。故最適合的連接詞為 (C) as。

3. "It is only with the heart that one can see rightly; what is essential is invisible to the eye."

   (A) 基礎的 (B) 珍貴的 (C) 看不見的 (D) 不實際的。此句前一句說明只有用心靈才能看得清楚，因此可推論出事物的基本道理時常是肉眼所看不見的，故答案選 (C)。

4. This combination makes the novel very popular.

   (A) 結合 (B) 矛盾 (C) 分配 (D) 認可。此上文可知本書的幻想情節吸引孩童，而講述的想法吸引成人，這兩點的結合使他受全世界讀者的歡迎。

5. In fact, the story has been translated into more than 250 languages and is one of the top 50 best-selling books in the world.

   此句更進一步說明本書受歡迎的程度，故最適合的選項為 (D)。(A) 然而 (B) 否則 (C) 同樣地 (D) 事實上。

A penny saved is a penny earned.

積少成多；積沙成塔。

牛刀小試

Unit 1

Below is one part of speech "I Have a Dream", which is delivered by Martin Luther King Jr. who is an important person for striving for African Americans' human rights in the early 20th century in the USA.

Five score years ago, a great American, in whose symbolic shadow we assemble, signed the Emancipation Proclamation. This historic decree came as a great light of hope to millions of Negro slaves, who had been seared in the flames of withering injustice. It came as joyous daybreak to end the long night of **(1)** .

But one hundred years later, the Negro is still not free. One hundred years later, the life of the Negro is still **(2)** by the manacles of segregation and the chains of discrimination. One hundred years later, the Negro lives on a lonesome island of poverty in the midst of a vast ocean of material prosperity. One hundred years later, the Negro is still left in the corners of American society and finds himself an **(3)** in his own land. It is time that we **(4)** the shameful condition. So, we've come to this holy spot to remind America of the fierce urgency of now. In a sense, we've come to our nation's capital to **(5)** a check, a check that will give us upon demand the riches of freedom and security of justice.

____1. (A) ability   (B) capacity   (C) captivity   (D) compassion
____2. (A) crippled   (B) delighted   (C) ranked   (D) isolated
____3. (A) exit   (B) exile   (C) existence   (D) examination
____4. (A) highlighting   (B) highlight   (C) highlighted   (D) were highlighted
____5. (A) recruit   (B) create   (C) toll   (D) cash

Answers: 1. C   2. A   3. B   4. C   5. D

翻譯

以下是馬丁路德金恩博士的演講 - 「我有一個夢」的部分擷取，他是美國二十世紀初期，爭取非裔美國人人權的重要人物。

一百年前，一位偉大的美國人簽署了「解放奴隸宣言」，我們現在就聚集在他的雕像前。這個歷史詔令，對於幾百萬名飽受不義之火煎熬的黑奴來說，猶如一道偉大的希望光芒。它的到來猶如歡樂的黎明，終結了被囚禁的漫漫長夜。

然而一百年後的今天，黑人仍未獲得自由。一百年後，黑人的生活仍然因種族隔離和歧視的束縛而癱瘓。一百年後的今天，黑人還是生活在被物質繁榮的汪洋大海所包圍的貧窮孤島上。一百年後的今天，黑人依然被遺留在美國社會的角落，並意識到自己在屬於他的土地上流亡。該是我們凸顯這可恥現狀的時候了。所以，我們來到這個聖地以提醒美國，現在是極度迫切的時刻。從某種意義上來說，我們來到我國首都兌現支票；一張給予我們充分的自由和公平保障的支票。

> Background knowledge:
>
> Martin Luther King Jr. 馬丁‧路德‧金恩二世 (1929-1968) 出生於 1929 年 1 月 15 日，卒於 1968 年 4 月 4 日。金恩博士出生於美國喬治亞周的馬特蘭大市，一生致力於美國黑人平權運動，並在 1964 年榮獲諾貝爾和平獎。

Ann's notes

馬丁路德金恩博士的「我有一個夢」演講是全球著名演講之一，對於美國的種族歧視和黑人人權有重要的歷史意義。

1. It came as joyous daybreak to end the long night of captivity.

   此題重點在於詞彙的了解。

   (A) 能力 (B) 容量 / 能力 (C) 捕抓 / 囚禁 (D) 同情心

2. One hundred years later, the life of the Negro is still crippled by the manacles of segregation and the chains of discrimination.

   此題重點在於詞彙的了解。

   (A) 壓榨 (B) 開心 / 愉悅 (C) 排名 (D) 隔離

3. One hundred years later, the Negro is still left in the corners of American society and finds himself an exile in his own land.

   此題重點在於前後詞彙意思的連貫性。

   (A) 出口 (B) 流亡 / 流亡者 (C) 存在 (D) 測驗

4. It is time that we highlighted the shameful condition.

   此題重點為「it is time to + for somebody + V...」的用法，表示「該是 ... 的時候到了」。

   It is time to + V... 用法之外，也可以用另外一種寫作呈現「It is time (that) S + were/V-ed...」，此句型屬於「與現在事實相反」的假設語氣，其中有幾點需要注意的：

A. 此句型中的 that 子句，其動詞時態應使用過去式以代表「現在該做而尚未做」的行為，且可以省略 that。

E.g. It is time (that) you faced the music. 該是你勇於承擔後果的時候了。

　→ It is time for you to face the music.

　→ You are supposed to face the music now, but you are not doing so.

E.g. It is time (that) we left the restaurant. 我們該離開餐廳了。

　→ It is time for us to leave the restaurant.

　→ We should leave the restaurant now, but we are not doing so.

B. 在 time 之前可使用 right、high 或 about 加以修飾：

E.g. It is about time that you were in bed. 你該上床睡覺了。

　→ It is about time for you to be in bed.

　→ You should be in bed now, but you are not doing so.

所以，基於以上的句型解釋，此題答案應該選擇 (C) highlighted (v.) 凸顯（過去式動詞）。

5. In a sense, we've come to our nation's capital to cash a check, a check that will give us upon demand the riches of freedom and security of justice.

從某種意義上來說，我們來到我國首都兌現支票；一張給予我們充分的自由和公平保障的支票。

此題重點在於詞彙（特別是動詞）的搭配詞用法。答案選擇 (D) 兌現。

(A) 招募　　(B) 創造　　(C) toll (v.) 徵收 / (n.) 通行費

(D) cash (v.) 把 ... 兌現 / (n.) 現金

The words you need to know:

1. assemble (v.) 聚集 召集
2. seared (sear v. 使烙印) 煎熬的
3. withering (adj.) 乾枯的
4. manacle (n.) 手銬 腳鐐

5. segregation (n.) 隔離
6. discrimination (n.) 歧視
7. prosperity (n.) 繁榮

Where there's smoke there's fire.

無風不起浪；事出必有因。

Unit 2

One of the top issues in 2016 is Brexit, which citizens in the UK voted to leave or remain in EU (European Union). This definitely became one of __(1)__ in British history. The controversial but democratic referendum campaign ended with the "LEAVE" voters winning 52% to 48%. This result __(2)__ the citizens in the UK to learn more about knowledge of Brexit.

There were two important factors, immigration and the economy, to influence the vote. "Remain" voters were afraid of losing out on the free trade agreements that come with EU membership, __(3)__ "Leave" voters hoped stopping the free movement of Europeans to the UK so that they could keep more job vacancies.

The result came out of "Leave", leading to many consequences. David Cameron, who __(4)__ the "Remain" campaign, resigned as prime minister. The process of exiting the EU remains unclear and so does the overall impacts of Brexit, __(5)__ will be seen in the future.

____1. (A) setbacks   (B) milestones   (C) blocks   (D) drawbacks

____2. (A) aroused   (B) attacked   (C) raised   (D) tamed

____3. (A) while   (B) when   (C) although   (D) as

____4. (A) rejected   (B) led   (C) put   (D) acted

____5. (A) where   (B) who   (C) that   (D) which

Answers: 1. B   2. A   3. A   4.B   5.D

翻譯

2016 年其中一個大事件就是英國脫歐公投，英國公民投票決定要離開或是續留歐盟。這必定是英國歷史上一個重大里程碑。這個極具爭議但民主的公投活動最後由 52% 決定離開歐盟的投票者勝過於 48% 的留歐。這個結果喚起英國國民更深入了解英國脫歐的知識。

有兩個重要因素影響這個投票，就是移民和經濟。留歐支持者害怕失去歐盟會員自由交易的協議，而脫歐支持者則希望禁止歐洲人享有移居到英國的自由，以便他們可以保有更多工作職缺。

這個公投結果最後是離開歐盟，同時導致許多後果。主導留歐運動的大衛麥卡隆因此辭去總理一職。離開歐盟的程序仍不明確，英國脫歐的整體衝擊也是，這將是未來可預見的。

Ann's notes

1. This definitely became one of milestones in British history.

   此題選擇符合前後文詞彙。答案選 B

   (A) 挫折　(B) 里程碑　(C) 阻塞　(D) 弱點 / 缺點

2. This result aroused the citizens in the UK to learn more about knowledge of Brexit. 此題選擇適合的動詞文意。答案選 A

   (A) 喚起　(B) 攻擊　(C) 升起　(D) 馴服

3. "Remain" voters were afraid of losing out on the free trade agreements that come with EU membership, while "Leave" voters hoped stopping the free movement of Europeans to the UK so that they could keep more job vacancies. 此題重點是連接詞選擇。答案選擇 A

   (A) 而　(B) 當　(C) 雖然　(D) 當 / 因為

連接詞用法「S1 + V ... + conj. + S2 + V...」或是「conj. + S1 + V..., S2 + V...」

顧名思義,「連接詞」可用來「連接」單字、片語或是子句的字詞。主要分為兩大類:

對等	I know you have a girlfriend, but I don't mind at all. 我知道你有女友,但我一點都不介意。 1. 對等連接詞放句中。 2. 對等連接詞連接兩個「地位同等重要」的子句,意指兩個子句都能單獨存在。「I know you have a girlfriend. I don't mind at all.」
附屬 / 從屬	My tutor will talk to you when he comes later. 我的老師待會過來時會跟你聊一下。 1. 附屬連接詞通常放句首或是兩句中間皆可。 2. 附屬連接詞放在「地位較次要的子句」前。 3. 附屬連接詞引導副詞子句若描述的是未來,常用現在簡單式代替未來式。 4. 附屬連接詞引導出的子句不能單獨存在。例外「When he comes later.」或是「Because he is studying now.」是錯誤的句子,但口語化說話方式不在此限。

1. while 除了有「當 ...」之外，也就是等於「when」的意思，另外還有一個重要的用法是相對的連接詞「而 ...」的意思。

   E.g. While I was taking a bath, the phone rang. 我在洗澡的時候，電話響了。

   E.g. I prefer watching the movies to learn English while he likes listening to the English radio programme. 我喜歡看電影學英文，而他喜歡聽英文廣播。

2. when 當 ...（附屬連接詞）

   E.g. When you realise that learning is never too late, you always have a chance to improve yourself.

   當你理解到學習永遠不嫌晚，你總有機會可以讓自己進步。

   E.g. When he looked up, he saw something like a UFO flying in the sky.

   當他抬頭看的時候，他看見某個像幽浮的東西在天空飛。

3. although 雖然（附屬連接詞，不可與其他連接詞連用，例如 but）

   E.g. Although Chinese literature is hard to understand, you can appreciate the living attitude of some philosophers' wisdom.

   雖然中國文學不好懂，但你可以從一些哲學家的智慧學到生活態度。

   E.g. Although I am not good-looking, I have a soft heart.

   雖然我其貌不揚，但我有一顆良善的心。

4. as 因為 =because/ 當 =when/ 既然 =since（附屬連接詞）

   E.g. As you know how to make up for your mistakes, you need to face them with courage.

   既然你知道怎麼去彌補你的錯誤，那你需要有勇氣去面對。

   E.g. As Alex came over, Lilly suddenly felt too shy to talk to him.

   當 Alex 走過來時，Lilly 突然間感到害羞而無法跟他說話。

   E.g. As Anny had a headache, she stayed home to rest.

   因為 Anny 頭痛，所以她待在家裡稍作休息。

4. David Cameron, who led the "Remain" campaign, resigned as prime minister. 此題選擇符合文意的動詞 (B) lead (過去式 led)

   (A) 拒絕 (B) 主導 / 領導 (C) 放置 (D) 表現 / 引起作用

5. The process of exiting the EU remains unclear and so does the overall impacts of Brexit, which will be seen in the future.

    此題為關係代名詞的「非限定」用法，這裡的「which」表示強調的「補述」說明。所以答案選擇 (D)。

    E.g. James is hard-working, which is the key to his success.

    　　James 的努力，是他成功的秘訣。

    （先行詞為 James is hard-working 整個子句，所以使用非限定關係代名詞 which，前面加上逗號做補充強調說明。

Background knowledge:

英國去留歐盟公投（英語：The United Kingdom European Union membership referendum）是英國國 就其歐盟成員資格去留問題於 2016 年 6 月 23 日舉行的公投。通稱「英脫歐公投」（Brexit vote），又簡稱「歐盟公投」（EU referendum）。2016 年 6 月 23 日這天，英國脫歐（Brexit）公投，英國人民將決定是否和歐盟「分手」，重回「單身」，掌握自己國家的命運；亦或者繼續和歐盟「在一起」，同舟共濟，想辦法克服許多複雜的「感情問題」。然而，無論分或合，決定公投的這個舉動猶如在感情中提出分手，不僅帶給英國本身一大震撼，也重重打擊了歐盟。自 2010 年以來，民意調查顯示英國人對於是否退出歐盟意見分歧，支持退出一方在 2012 年 11 月達到高位，有 56% 支持退出，只有 30% 希望留在歐盟，到 2015 年 6 月則有 43% 希望留在歐盟，支持退出的有 36%。至當時為止的最大型的民意調查（2 萬人，2014 年 3 月）顯示支持與反對退出歐盟的人數接近，41% 支持退出，41% 希望留在歐盟，18% 未有決定。不過，當被問到如果英國與歐盟重新議定英國作為歐盟成員國的條件，而英國的利益得到保障時，超過 50% 的人表示他們會支持英國留在歐盟。

對於歐盟公投此事，Ann 詢問過幾個英國友人，在歐盟公投之前，Ann 的英國友人們認為「歐盟公投」這件事情是一件「stupid thing」（屬於個人意見），當然這是大部分支持留歐人士們的想法，因為他們覺得留歐對於英國跟整個歐洲，在貿易與各項事務往來對彼此來說都是一件好事，因此，當時的 Prime Minister (PM) 為了讓那些一直嚷嚷著要脫歐的人們信服，索性就舉辦了公投這件事情，而 PM 沒想到公投結果竟然脫歐勝出，只好請辭下台。很多英國人其實不知道為什麼要留在歐盟，或者說留歐或是脫歐這件事情意義是什麼，導致公投這件事情爭議性之大。

Sources from:https://zh.wikipedia.org/wiki/英國去留歐盟公投 &Ann 英國友人意見

Look before you leap.

三思而後行。

Unit 3

Bullying takes many forms, verbal abuse being one of them. Verbal abuse occurs when someone uses foul language or hurls bitter accusation at others. The mental scars resulting from it can run very deep. The victims, constantly **(1)** to hurtful words, are likely to develop low self-esteem and may even be plagued by emotional problems. **(2)** upset and hopeless, some may even run an increased risk of committing suicide. What's worse, a few victims wind up imposing this pain on other people mainly because this is the only means of expression that they experience. **(3)** mental effects, recent studies have uncovered the long-term physical damage that verbal abuse can cause.

By examining the brain scans of these subjects, researchers discovered that the victims' brains looked much like those of disabled people. In some cases, the trauma can halt the left side of the brain from developing, which leads to a decline in memory as well as the loss of language ability and senses. Perhaps it is time to **(4)** our understanding of the power of words. As the proverb goes, "The words of the reckless pierce like swords, but the tongue of the wise brings healing." We should always bear in mind that our words can hurt and thereby we ought to choose our words wisely and cautiously before **(5)** them. May we all speak the words that build others up and not tear them down.

___1. (A) exposing　(B) exposed　(C) was exposed　(D) has exposed
___2. (A) Leaving　(B) To leave　(C) Leave　(D) Left
___3. (A) Regardless of　(B) With an eye to　(C) Except for　(D) In addition to
___4. (A) reassess　(B) supervise　(C) diminish　(D) discount
___5. (A) uttering　(B) utter　(C) having uttered　(D) uttered

Answers:　1. B　2. D　3. D　4. A　5. A

翻譯

霸凌有很多形式，語言霸凌是其中之一。語言暴力發生於有人口出惡言或是對別人嚴苛控訴的痛罵。語言暴力會在心裡留下深刻的傷痕。這些受害者不斷遭受傷害人話語的環境中，很有可能發展出低自尊心，深受情緒問題的困擾。在沮喪、無望的心態下，自殺的風險也較高。更糟的是，一些受害者會轉嫁這種痛苦到別人身上，主要因為這是一種他們抒發自己經歷過痛苦的方式。除了心理副作用之外，近期的研究揭露了語言霸凌可能造成長期的生理傷害。藉由腦部掃描，研究人員發現這些受害者的腦部看起來與身心障礙人士的大腦極為相似。有些案例中，創傷甚至使得左腦停止發

Reading

137

展，而這往往也導致記憶力的永久性衰退，語言能力降低，感官則可能鈍化。或許，該是我們重新評估我們話語力量的解讀。就如一句諺語說的：「說話浮躁的，如刀刺人；智慧人的舌頭卻為醫人的良藥。」我們應該常常銘記在心的是，我們的話語會傷害人，所以，在說出話語之前，我們應該明智與謹慎選擇我們的用語。但願我們都能說造就人的話語而不是讓人流淚不止的話。

Ann's notes

1. The victims, constantly exposed to hurtful words, are likely to develop low self-esteem and may even be plagued by emotional problems.
   be exposed to sth. 接觸到暴露於 ...。所以答案選擇 (B)。

2. Left upset and hopeless, some may even run an increased risk of committing suicide.
   此句話是省略了連接詞與相同主詞 victims of verbal abuse 的分詞構句。原本的句子是：As some victims are left upset and hopeless, they may even run an increased risk of committing suicide.

3. In addition to mental effects, recent studies have uncovered the long-term physical damage that verbal abuse can cause.
   此題重點為介系詞片語。為符合文意，答案選擇 (D) in addition to。
   (A) 不管 / 不顧　　(B) 考慮到 / 注意到
   (C) 除了 ... 之外　(D) 除了 ... 尚有

   (C) 與 (D) 都是「除了 ... 之外」的意思，但兩者用法意思都不一樣。
   1. except for 除了 ... 之外
      E.g. The composition is quite good except for the spelling.
      這篇文章除了拼寫以外，其他都不錯。(spelling 拼字被排除在外)
   2. in addition to 除了 ... 尚有
      E.g. In addition to those subjects, they also taught history and geography.
      除了教這些課程外，他們還教歷史和地理。(全部包含在內)

4. Perhaps it is time to reassess our understanding of the power of words.

此題選擇符合前後文題意的動詞，正確答案選擇 (A) reassess 重新評估。[assess (v.) 評估]

(A) 重新評估 (B) 監督管理 (C) 削弱減少 (D) 折扣低估貶值

5. We should always bear in mind that our words can hurt and thereby we ought to choose our words wisely and cautiously before uttering them.

此題空格前面 before 為介系詞，utter (v.) 意指「說出」。介系詞後面遇到動詞須將動詞改為現在分詞 Ving，因此答案選擇 (A)uttering。

Game：Puzzle for the search of bulling-related words

請在下列格子中圈出以下所列的 10 個霸凌相關單字：

1. bully　2. control　3. cyber　4. isolated　5. physical
6. power　7.self-esteem　8. verbal　9. victim　10. violence

B	W	N	C	U	C	Y	B	E	R	A	G	M	S	P
A	U	R	V	I	O	L	E	N	C	E	Y	W	H	O
Z	S	L	Y	J	N	X	S	F	D	X	D	Y	K	W
I	S	O	L	A	T	E	D	A	Q	V	S	G	R	E
F	G	Y	C	Y	R	M	T	C	G	I	V	N	F	R
J	Z	X	T	V	O	H	V	I	C	T	I	M	Z	M
V	E	R	B	A	L	C	Z	A	K	W	J	S	A	T
Q	V	A	H	F	S	E	L	F	E	S	T	E	E	M

Background knowledge:

此文說明語言暴力並不如一般認為的只會傷害情感，事實上，各種形式的語言暴力，舉凡侮辱性文字的適用、霸凌、孤立、冷漠、忽視等等，更是在這個網路科技發達的社會中，更會造成受害者嚴重的身心受創，例如出現憂鬱乃至企圖自殺種種情緒問題，更會造成腦部損傷，導致受害者記憶及語言能力退化。甚至有些受害者，會複製負面經驗而成為加害者，使得言語霸凌的情況變成惡性循環。因此，開口前謹記惡言的負面力量，以免造成不可逆的傷害。

Answers:

B	W	N	C	U	C	Y	B	E	R	A	G	M	S	P
A	U	R	V	I	O	L	E	N	C	E	Y	W	H	O
Z	S	L	Y	J	N	X	S	F	D	X	D	Y	K	W
I	S	O	L	A	T	E	D	A	Q	V	S	G	R	E
F	G	Y	C	Y	R	M	T	C	G	I	V	N	F	R
J	Z	X	T	V	O	H	V	I	C	T	I	M	Z	M
V	E	R	B	A	L	C	Z	A	K	W	J	S	A	T
Q	V	A	H	F	S	E	L	F	E	S	T	E	E	M

Good fences make good neighbours.

好牆睦鄰。

Unit 4

The Mary Rose sank to the bottom of the sea more than four hundred years ago, __(1)__ Sunday 19th July, 1545. It was calm and sunny at Portsmouth that day. King Henry VIII was nearby at Southsea Castle, __(2)__ his ships as they sailed slowly out of the harbour. First came the Great Harry, and then the beautiful ship __(3)__ the Mary Rose. Across the water near the Isle of Wight lay the French ships, waiting to attack. Some small ships with oars, called galleys, rowed towards the Great Harry. Just then, a gentle wind started to blow. The Mary Rose began to hoist her sails, ready for action.

__(4)__ King Henry saw that something was wrong. His fine ship was leaning far over to one side! When this happened soldiers and sailors slid and tumbled down the sloping decks. Great guns broke loose and rumbled across the ship. Men ran about in terror. A few fell or bumped into the sea and were sucked down around the ship. Most were trapped inside the hull or caught in ropes and netting on the upper deck. King Henry watched helplessly as the Mary Rose went down. Small boats rushed to the rescue but they could not do much to help. __(5)__ 600 and 700 men went out from Portsmouth on the Mary Rose that day but only about 35 came back. It was a big disaster.

___1. (A) in   (B) at   (C) on   (D) during

___2. (A) watched   (B) watch   (C) was watching   (D) watching

___3. (A) call   (B) called   (C) which calls (D) calling

___4. (A) Suddenly   (B) However   (C) Surprisingly (D) Fortunately

___5. (A) Between   (B) Among   (C) Over   (D) Of

Answers: 1. C   2. D   3. B   4. A   5. A

翻譯

瑪莉露絲號於 1545 年 7 月 19 日星期天，沉入海底距今已超過四百年。那日朴茨茅斯 (Porthmouth) 是一個風平浪靜晴朗的天氣。亨利八世在附近的南海城堡中，看著他的船隻慢慢行駛航向港口。首先到達的是哈利一號，接下來是名為瑪莉羅斯號的美麗船隻。法國艦隊在海另一端的懷特島附近，正等待攻擊。一些被稱為槳帆船的有槳的小船，划向哈利一號。然後，一陣溫暖的風開始吹起。瑪莉露絲號開始揚起帆板，準備發動攻擊。

突然間亨利國王發覺情況不對。他那艘精美的船隻竟向著另一邊傾斜！事件發生的當下，士兵跟水手們從傾斜的甲板滑入跌進海裡。巨大的槍枝鬆動且轟隆隆地掉出船外。人們恐慌地逃跑。一些人跌落或是被撞擊落海且被吸入捲進船底。多數人都被困

在船身，或被上層甲板的繩索困住。亨利國王絕望地看著這船沈入海裡。小船趕來救援，但是他們沒辦法拯救那麼多人。那一天約有 600 至 700 人乘坐瑪莉羅斯號從朴茨茅斯出港，但大概只有 35 人被救回。那真是一場災難。

Ann's notes

1. The Mary Rose sank to the bottom of the sea more than four hundred years ago, on Sunday 19th July, 1545.

   表示確切的時間介系詞 on。

2. King Henry VIII was nearby at Southsea Castle, watching his ships as they sailed slowly out of the harbour.

   此句話已有 Be-V（主要動詞）的情形下，以「Be-V + Ving」做強調語氣。或可解釋為：因為前面有一動詞，以省略連接詞連接下一個動詞時，第二個動詞使用分詞構句，所以句子也可以是：Henry VIII was nearby at Southsea Castle and watched his ships as they sailed slowly out of the harbour. = Henry VIII was nearby at Southsea Castle, watching his ships as they sailed slowly out of the harbour. [省略連接詞 and，將 watched 改成 watching]。

   PS. harbour (n.) 海港 / 港口 (英式拼音)；harbor (美式拼音)

4. Suddenly King Henry saw that something was wrong.

   依據上下文意，副詞修飾語選擇 (A) suddenly。
   (A) 突然間 (B) 然而 (C) 令人驚訝的是 (D) 幸運地

5. Between 600 and 700 men went out from Portsmouth on the Mary Rose that day but only about 35 came back.

   四個選項都有「在 ... 之間」的意思，但用法不同。此題須選擇 (A) between 兩者之間，因為 between 的用法為「between A and B」(介於 A 與 B 之間)，而 (B) among 跟 (D) of 意指三者以上的「當中」，(C) over 有超過的意思，依照文章句子結構跟文意，between 是最合適的答案。

The Words you should know...
1. harbour (n.) 港口 / 海港
2. oar (n.) 槳
3. galley (n.) 划槳小船
4. sail (n.) 風帆 / (v.) 航向
5. tumble (v.) 跌入 掉進
6. bump into (v.) 撞擊
7. disaster (n.) 災難

It is better to give than to receive.
施比受更有福。

Unit 5

Nell Gwynn is one of those fascinating characters from history __(1)__ name has entered folklore but about whom many know little except that she was an orange seller who became the mistress of King Charles II. The full story, __(2)__ , is complex and fascinating. It was in a milestone of change that Nell Gwynn found herself to be in the right place at the right time. Little is actually known about her early life __(3)__ that she was probably born in Coal Yard Alley in Covent Garden that her alcoholic mother was a former prostitute and brothel madam, and that her sister Rose and maybe Nell too worked for their mother.

Charles II had many mistresses. However, Nell Gwynn was different __(4)__ most of Charles' mistresses in that she did not seek a title for herself but only for her children. She was also smart enough to have the King give her the freehold to her residence rather than __(5)__ her with a 'grace and favour' apartment. She became an expert at negotiating the plots of the court but was helped in this by being, without doubt, Charles' favourite mistresses. It should also be said that she knew the timings to speak out in the court and had wits to deal with people who wanted to keep her away from the King.

___1. (A) who   (B) whose   (C) that   (D) which

___2. (A) as usual   (B) yet   (C) now and then   (D) alike

___3. (A) according to   (B) including   (C) in addition to   (D) except

___4. (A) with   (B) on   (C) from   (D) between

___5. (A) apply   (B) reply   (C) supply   (D) imply

Answers: 1. B   2. A   3. D   4. C   5. C

翻譯

Nell Gwynn 是歷史上迷人的人物之一，她的名字已進入民間傳說，但除了她由賣橘的小販成為查爾斯二世國王的情婦之外，許多人對她了解甚少。如同常理，整個故事複雜又有趣。改變的里程碑，是 Nell Gwynn 在對的時間點找到自己的定位。除了知道她大概出生在柯芬園的煤場巷弄，她的媽媽之前是一個妓女，之後成為妓院老鴇，還有她的姊姊 Rose 跟 Nell 也都曾經為了她們的母親工作之外，很少人真正地了解她早年的生活。

查理二世曾擁有許多情婦。然而，Nell Gwynn 跟查理二世的其他情婦很不一樣，因為她不曾要求自己的而是爭取給她兒子頭銜。她非常聰明，擁有國王給她的永久產權的

住所，而不僅是提供她 "恩寵和庇護" 的公寓。她是皇宮中事件協商的專家，也受惠於這個角色關係，無疑地，是查爾斯最喜歡的情婦。應該可以這麼說，她知道在皇宮裡在什麼時機發言，而且她非常機智，知道怎麼處理那些想盡辦法要把她驅離國王身邊的人。

Ann's notes

1. Nell Gwynn is one of those fascinating characters from history whose name has entered folklore.

   關係代名詞用法，句子呈現為 [___ N. + V.]，所以關係代名詞選擇所有格 whose。正確答案為 (B)。

2. The full story, as usual, is complex and fascinating.

   句子主詞與動詞中間插入一個轉折語氣副詞來加強句子語氣，合適答案選 (A) as usual。

   (A) 如同往常般　(B) 尚未　(C) 有時候　(D) 想似的

3. Little is actually known about her early life except that she was probably born in Coal Yard Alley in Covent Garden.

   此題型為選填介系詞，符合文意答案為 (D)。

   (A) 根據　(B) 包含　(C) 除了 ... 還有　(D) 除了 ... 之外

4. However, Nell Gwynn was different from most of Charles' mistresses in that she did not seek a title for herself but only for her children.

   此題重點為 be different from 的用法。除了 be different from 之外，表示不同於 ..... 的片語還有「differ from」的動詞片語，或是「have/has/had differences from」的用法。

5. She was also smart enough to have the King give her the freehold to her residence rather than supply her with a 'grace and favour' apartment.

   此題選合適的動詞文意，正確答案選擇 (C) supply。

   (A) apply (to) 應用 / apply (for) 申請　　(B) reply (to) 回覆
   (C) 提供　　　　　　　　　　　　　　　　(D) 暗示

The Words you need to know...

1. fascinating (adj.) 美好的 / 迷人的

2. folklore (n.) 民俗傳説故事

3. mistress (n.) 情婦

4. milestone (n.) 里程碑

5. alcoholic (a.) 含酒精的 / 酗酒的；(n.) 酒鬼 嗜酒者

6. residence (n.) 住所 / 官邸

7. favour (n.) 幫忙 / 善意行為 [英式拼法] / favor [美式拼法]

8. deal with (v.) 處理 / 解決

Live and let live.
待人如己；得饒人處且饒人。

Unit 6

23 April every year is World Book and Copyright Day, promoting reading, publishing and the protection of intellectual property through copyright. The ways and dates that many countries celebrate in and on are somehow diverse. The idea for celebrating this day **(1)** in Catalonia where on the 23rd of April, a rose is traditionally given as a gift for each book sold. The date of 23 April is also symbolic for world literature **(2)** on this date and in the same year 1616, Cervantes and Shakespeare died. In fact, the celebration of World Book and Copyright Day started from 1929 to honor and remember great authors. This is the inspiration that UNESCO made it.

In the UK and Ireland, **(3)** , World Book Day is celebrated earlier in the year, usually on the first Thursday in March, to **(4)** it falls outside of school holidays. Why not celebrate World Book and Copyright Day at school by using books with a global theme? Have a browse through the resources **(5)** on the Global Dimension database under the subject 'English:literature/story'. You can find many interesting things that are written a feature on literature and global issue, which includes lots of suggestions for books to read with a global theme. The aim of the World Book Day is to encourage young people to take books and read them because reading brings lots of fun.

___1. (A) originated   (B) originate   (C) is originated   (D) originating

___2. (A) due   (B) that   (C) for   (D) of

___3. (A) besides   (B) meanwhile   (C) recently   (D) for example

___4. (A) ensure   (B) correct   (C) arrange   (D) create

___5. (A) listing   (B) listed   (C) which lists   (D) are listed

Answers: 1. A   2. B   3. D   4. A   5. B

翻譯

每年的四月二十三日是世界圖書與版權日，推廣閱讀、出版與保護知識產權。世界各地慶祝世界圖書日的時間有些不同。慶祝這一天的想法是源自於加泰隆尼亞，每當四月十三日這一天，傳統上會將玫瑰當作禮物隨每本書售出。四月二十三日這一天對於世界文學也是一個象徵性的日子，1616 年的這日，塞萬提斯和莎士比亞逝世了。事實上，世界圖書和版權日的慶祝活動始於 1929 年，是為了紀念偉大的作家們。聯合國教科文組織的靈感也來自於此。

在英國，為了避免圖書日和中小學校的復活節假期衝突，所以，英國將三月的第一個周四定為世界讀書日。何不使用具有全球性主題的書籍在學校慶祝世界圖書與出版日呢？你可以翻閱列在全球維度資料庫英文文學與故事的資源。你可以找到許多有趣的文學跟全球議題事物，包含全球性題材的書籍建議。世界圖書日的主旨是倡導年輕人多多拿起書本讀書，因為讀書充滿了樂趣。

Ann's notes

1. The idea for celebrating this day originated in Catalonia where on the 23rd of April.
   originate from 起源自 ...。慶祝這一天的想法是源自於過去的加泰隆尼亞文化，所以使用過去式呈現。

2. The date of 23 April is also symbolic for world literature that on this date and in the same year 1616, Cervantes and Shakespeare died.
   答案選擇 (B) that，作為名詞子句的連接詞，補充說明具有象徵性的這一天，同時也是大文豪塞萬提斯和莎士比亞過世的日子。

3. In the UK and Ireland, for example, World Book Day is celebrated earlier in the year.

第二段以舉例開頭，說明在英國為了避免圖書日與中小學的復活節假期強碰，所以和西班牙訂定的日期 4 月 23 日不同天。

(A) 除此之外 (B) 同時 (C) 最近 (D) 舉例來說

4. In the UK and Ireland, for example, World Book Day is celebrated earlier in the year, usually on the first Thursday in March, to ensure it falls outside of school holidays.

依據題意選擇合適的動詞 (A) ensure (v.) 確認

(A) 確認 (B) 更正 (C) 安排 (D) 創造

5. Have a browse through the resources listed on the Global Dimension database under the subject 'English: literature/story'.

原本句子為：

「Have a browse through the resources which are listed on the Global Dimension database under the subject 'English: literature/story'.」這裡可以省略關係代名詞 which 跟 be-V，留下 listed（被列出來的）這個分詞修飾先行詞 resources 資源，意思是「列在全球維度資料庫英文文學與故事的資源」。

所以答案選擇 (B) listed。

Nothing great was ever achieved without enthusiasm. / Emerson

一切豐功偉業都要靠熱忱。（愛默生）

Unit 7

For many people, life gets busy and it's the best way to relax with sweet spiced chai. This strong mix of the tea, herbs, and spices is popular and enjoyed around the world. Yet, in India, it is **(1)** a drink, instead of a part of life there.

Most Indians drink chai at least twice a day. This habit was **(2)** by the British, who had begun producing large quantities of tea in India in the 1820s. English tea often called for milk and sugar, **(3)** Indians added spices as well to create masala chai.

In India, greeting a guest with a cup of chai is a social custom. As a matter of fact, if a person **(4)** an offer of tea, they will likely offend their host. That's because chai has become a sign of hospitality. It is used to build **(5)** . Without any surprise so many people enjoy taking a break from what they are doing to drink chai and chat.

____1. (A) nothing more than (B) more than just (C) much more like (D) no more than

____2. (A) improved (B) impressed (C) increased (D) influenced

____3. (A) so (B) since (C) though (D) unless

____4. (A) refuses (B) repairs (C) reveals (D) receives

____5. (A) confidence (B) convenience (C) connections (D) considerations

Answers:	1. B	2. D	3. C	4. A	5. C

翻譯

對很多人來說，生活忙碌而甜甜的印度香料奶茶是放鬆身心的最佳選擇。這種味道濃烈、混合著茶葉、藥草以及各種香料的印度奶茶在世界各地都受到喜愛。然而，在印度，它不僅是一種飲料，反倒是當地生活的一部分。

大部分的印度人一天至少得喝上兩次奶茶。這種習慣受到英國人影響，英國人在 1820 年代開始在印度大量製茶。英國茶經常會需要搭配牛奶跟糖，不過，印度人還會加上香料來製作印度奶茶。

在印度，用一杯印度奶茶招待客人是一種社會習俗。事實上，如果有人拒絕主人所提供的奶茶，很有可能就此得罪東道主。這是因為印度奶茶已經成為一種好客的象徵。它被用來建立人與人之間的聯繫。難怪有那麼多人喜歡停下手邊工作休息片刻，喝杯印度奶茶，然後彼此談天。

Ann's notes

1. Yet it's more than just a drink in India; instead it's a part of life there.

   文章第一段說明印度奶茶在各地受到歡迎，但這句話開頭以 yet 來做一個轉折語氣，表示奶茶「不只是」一種飲料，甚至融入到社會中的一部分。所以答案選擇 (B)。

   (A) 僅僅 / 只不過

   (B) 不只是

   (C) 比較像是

   (D) 僅僅 / 不超過

2. This habit was influenced by the British, who had begun producing large quantities of tea in India in the 1820s.

   本段開頭說明印度人一天至少喝兩杯以上的奶茶，這個習慣的養成是由於英國人在 1820 年代在印度大量種植茶葉，所以此習慣是受到英國人的「影響」。所以答案選擇 (D)。

   (A) 改進 / 改善

   (B) 使留下深刻印象

   (C) 增加 / 增長

   (D) 影響

3. English tea often called for milk and sugar, though Indians added spices as well to create masala chai.

   本句進一步說明英國奶茶跟印度奶茶的不同。英國奶茶通常需要加上牛奶跟糖，「但是」印度人會加上一些香料來製作印度奶茶。所以答案選擇 (C)。

   (A) 所以 / 因此

   (B) 自從 / 因此

   (C) 但是 / 不過

   (D) 除非

4. As a matter of fact, if a person refuses an offer of tea, they will likely offend their host.

   本段開頭提到用一杯奶茶招待客人已成印度社會習俗，本句話再進一步說明這個習俗的禁忌。由後面提到「他們可能會冒犯到主人」來推測，if 領導的條件式子句表示的「拒絕接受」主人提供的奶茶。所以答案選擇 (A)。

   (A) 拒絕接受

   (B) 修理 / 補救

   (C) 揭露 / 露出

   (D) 接受 / 收到

5. It is used to build connections.

   延續上一句話，拒絕奶茶會冒犯主人的招待，所以說明印度奶茶已經成為好客的象徵 (hospitality)。本句話再進一步說明，奶茶可以建立人之間的「聯繫」，所以答案選擇 (C)。

   (A) 自信心 / 信賴

   (B) 方便 / 便利

   (C) 聯繫 / 連結

   (D) 考慮

The business of life is to go forward. / Samuel Johnson

生命的本質就是勇往直前。（塞繆爾·詹森）

Unit 8

There's a new kind of star that is famous around the world but might be your next-door neighbour. They are the YouTubers, people who are known **(1)** their won YouTube videos. In some ways, they're now becoming more popular **(2)** many TV and movie stars. There is another new term to call them, Vloggers.

Anyone can become a YouTuber or Vlogger with the right **(3)** , message, and style. That's because it's easier to **(4)** YouTube than on TV or in movies. Anyone with a video camera and a YouTube account can **(5)** and build their online presence. Most YouTubers start by filming themselves in their bedroom, for example.

___1. (A) to   (B) for   (C) as   (D) in

___2. (A) than   (B) as   (C) instead of   (D) despite

___3. (A) person   (B) personality   (C) author   (D) frame

___4. (A) get on   (B) get out   (C) pick up   (D) run into

___5. (A) enter in   (B) log out   (C) sign up   (D) turn on

Answers: 1. B   2. A   3. B   4. A   5. C

翻譯

現在有種新一代的明星在全世界出名，但也有可能只是你隔壁的鄰居。他們就是所謂的 YouTubers，因自製的 YouTube 影片爆紅而成名的人。就某方面來講，他們現在甚至比許多電視或電影明星還要受歡迎。現在有另一個專有名詞來稱呼他們，Vloggers--影像網誌者。

任何人都能成為一名 YouTuber 或是 Vlogger，只要有適當的個性、訊息以及風格。這是因為要出現在 YouTube 上比電視或是電影簡單多了。任何擁有攝影機與 YouTube 帳號的人都能登入並創造自己的網路形象。舉例來説，大部分 YouTubers 都從自己房間拍影片開始。

Ann's notes

1. They are the YouTubers, people who are known for their won YouTube videos.

依據文意，「他們就是所謂的 YouTubers，因自製的 YouTube 影片爆紅而成名的人。」

be known/famous as + 身份 職位（以 ... 身份或是職位聞名）

E.g. Jay Chou is famous as a songwriter and composer in Asia .

周杰倫以歌詞作詞作曲人在亞洲聞名。

be known/famous for + N/Ving（以 ... 某事物聞名）

E.g. Taiwan is well known for delicious cuisine.

台灣以知名的美食小吃聞名。

2. In some ways, they're now becoming more popular than many TV and movie stars.

「就某方面來說，他們現在甚至比許多電視或電影明星還要受歡迎。」此句話有形容詞比較級，所以有由此得知 they 跟後面的 TV and movie stars 做比較，答案選擇 than。

(A) 比起 ... (B) 就如同 (C) 反之 (D) 雖然

3. Anyone can become a YouTuber or Vlogger with the right personality, message, and style.

「任何人都能成為一名 YouTuber 或是 Vlogger，只要有適當的個性、訊息以及風格。」此題由上下文推測，成為一名 YouTuber 或是 Vlogger 必須提供合適的訊息跟風格之外，必須也要有合適的個性，在網路世界上傳播能達到有效且正面中肯的訊息。

(A) 人 (B) 人格 (C) 作家 (D) 框架

4. That's because it's easier to get on YouTube than on TV or in movies.

「這是因為要出現在 YouTube 上比電視或是電影簡單多了。」依據文章，比起上電視，以 YouTube 方式錄製影片讓別人認識自己比起上電視或電影簡單。

(A) 進展 / 應對 (B) 逃跑 / 洩漏 (C) 挑選 (D) 偶遇

5. Anyone with a video camera and a YouTube account can sign up and build their online presence.

「任何擁有攝影機與 YouTube 帳號的人都能登入並創造自己的網路形象。」所以，只要「建立、註冊」一個帳號，即可讓自己的影片上傳到網路。

(A) 著手 / 處理   (B) 登出 * log in 登入

(C) 註冊 / 報名 / 參加   (D) 打開 / 取決於

Ann's notes

Vlogger 是 video 與 blogger 混合而成的網路新用語，也就是以錄影方式來記錄生活與網友們分享不同的資訊。

Victory belongs to the most persevering. / Napoleon Bonaparte
勝利屬於不屈不饒、堅忍不拔的人。(拿破崙)

≫ **Part 3**：**Reading Comprehension**
閱讀理解

說明

閱讀測驗常常是考生容易放棄的考題，但其實本類型應該是較易拿分的考題才是。很多考生缺乏耐心把全文看完，或者因為詞彙量不夠，就容易亂了頭緒而放棄。除了了解文章大意之外，細節部分當然也是考試重點，包含內容單字在文章裡面須以上下文定義某些單字的含義（很多學習者常常只背單字的第一個意思，或是沒有例句或是情境上下文的狀態之下，容易誤用，導致中英語言文化上很大的隔閡）與文章有提到什麼或是沒有提到什麼，然後最困難的部分在於請讀者判斷以文章作者的寫作語氣來推論文章最可能想傳達什麼想法。以下有幾個建議：

第一，閱讀文章時速度不要太快，應著重於整篇文意的了解，對於不懂的字詞不要浪費時間猛想，建議由上下文瞭解或猜測意思；第二，考題常依人、事、物、時、地等重點出題，因此，在閱讀文章時，可用筆 underline 劃記文章的這些重點；第三，作答時不可依個人主觀認知來作答，一切以文章所提供的資訊作答；第四，作答時間若不夠時，可先看題目，利用邏輯判斷或是背景知識認知判斷答案，再看文章內容，以確認答案正確性。

切記，增進閱讀能力不是努力一兩天就能一蹴可幾，如果常常強迫自己看一些艱澀文章，那必定是反效果。建議學習者以自己有興趣的文章或是讀物開始培養英文閱讀的思考邏輯。那麼，我們就先從較容易的生活應用英語開始吧！

Unit 1：Airport English 機場英文

Ann is at the airport to catch her flight to London.

A Ann Wang S Airline Staff I Immigration Officer

1. Checking Baggage

    S: Good morning! May I have your passport, please? Can you tell me where you're headed today?

    A: Sure. I am flying to Heathrow Airport in London. I have a question. While checking in online, I couldn't select my seat. Is there any chance I could possibly have an aisle seat?

    S: Yes, we still have some available. How many items of baggage do you have?

    A: One carry-on and one checked bag.

    S: OK. Please place the bag on the scale. Are you carrying forbidden items?

    A: No.

    S: Here is your boarding pass. Please be at gate D4 by 12.05.

    A: Cheers.

2. Going through Immigration

    I: Passport, please. What is the purpose of your visit?

    A: Tourism. I'm here on vacation.

    I: How long will you be staying in the country?

    A: I'll be here for five days.

    I: Do you have the address that you will be staying at and a return ticket to your point of origin?

    A: Yes, I have the information here. I'll be staying at two hotels during my stay, and both addresses are listed. Later, I'll be departing from Edinburgh.

    I: I see. All right, Ms. Wang. Welcome to the UK! Enjoy your stay.

    A: Thank you very much.

Questions:

1. What is the first conversation about?

   (A) Asking for food on the plane
   (B) Looking for the passport
   (C) Checking in at the airport
   (D) Avoiding sleeping during the journey

2. Where do you think the second conversation takes place?

   (A) At school
   (B) At the checking point of the customs
   (C) At the tube station
   (D) At the hospital

Answers: 1. C   2. B

翻譯

Ann 在機場要搭機飛往倫敦

Ａ Ann Wang Ｓ Airline Staff 機場人員 Ｉ Immigration Officer 移民署官員

1. Checking Baggage 推運行李

   機場人員：早安。麻煩護照。請問您今天要飛往何處？

   Ann：　　嗯，我將飛往倫敦希斯羅機場。我有一個問題。我在網路上作登機報到時，沒辦法選擇我的座位。請問我是否可以選擇走道位子？

   機場人員：可以的，我們還有一些位子。您有幾件行李？

   Ann：　　一件手提行李和一件托運行李。

   機場人員：好的，請將托運行李放到磅秤上。您是否要帶走在磅秤上的任何一物件？

   Ann：　　沒有。

   機場人員：這是您的登機證。請在十二點零五分之前到 D4 登機門。

   Ann：　　謝謝。

2. Going through Immigration 辦理入境手續

   移民署官員：麻煩護照。您此次旅遊的目的為何？

   Ann：　　　觀光。我來渡假的。

   移民署官員：您會在我們國家待多久？

Ann： 我會待上五天。

移民署官員：您有您在這裡居住的地址跟您出發地的回程機票嗎？

Ann： 有的，這裡是我準備的資料。此行，我將會住在兩個旅館，兩個旅館資料列在我提供資料上。之後，我會從愛丁堡離境。

移民署官員：好的，我瞭解了。王小姐，歡迎到英國，也祝您旅途愉快。

Ann： 非常感謝您。

問題

1. 這個對話主旨為何？

   (A) 要求機上食物。
   (B) 尋找護照。
   (C) 機場報到。
   (D) 避免在旅程中睡覺。

2. 第二個對話應該是在哪裡？

   (A) 學校。
   (B) 海關報到處。
   (C) 地鐵站。
   (D) 醫院。

Give it a try on the "Crosswords"！

Game: Crosswords for the search of following words

Across:	Down:
Easy to get something (9)	An important item of going abroad (8)
About travelling (7)	The opposite seat of window seat (5)
Measuring weights (5)	The other word of the Internet (6)

4.							
1.		5.					
	6.						
		3.					
		2.					

The words you need to know:

1. passport (n.) 護照

   E.g. Don't forget to have the passport with you all the time when you are abroad.
   在國外的時候，別忘記隨身帶著你的護照。

2. available (adj.) 空的；可得到的；可利用的

   E.g. The British Museum is especially available on Friday evening.
   大英博物館在星期五晚上特別開放。

3. scale (n.) 秤；磅秤；天平

   E.g. You should keep in mind before putting your luggage on the scale you should check out your luggage is well packed.
   你應該牢記將行李放到磅秤上之前，確認你有將你的行李打包完整。

4. tourism (n.) 觀光；觀光業

   E.g. Italy is famous for its classical architecture and history.
   義大利以古代建築與歷史聞名。

Notes

online (adj., adv.) 網路上（的）；線上（的）

aisle (n.) 走道（aisle seat 指的是靠走道的座位）

take place (v.) 發生 / 舉行

tube station (n.) 地鐵站

Ann's notes

Tube/Underground vs. Subway vs. Metro

1. Tube/Underground：tube 原意是水管，在英國也可以用 tube 這個字來指地鐵，因為地鐵就像水管一樣埋在地底下。underground 是英式用語，一般特指倫敦地鐵，要說得更清楚，也可以用 underground railroad。你會發現 underground 這個字其實很常出現在生活中，但要注意，它不僅指地鐵，也有地下、地底的意思。

2. Subway：subway 是美式用法，但要注意，subway 這個字在英式用法的情況下大多指你要過街的地下通道，完全不是地鐵的意思！不過，在美國，也不是所有城市的地鐵都叫 subway。像亞特蘭大有 MARTA，而波士頓有 The T，這時候 subway 就只是一個口語上的稱法，不代表絕對的交通運輸名稱。

3. Metro：這個字源自法文，巴黎最初的地鐵就叫作「Chemin de Fer Métropolitain」。這個字後來被縮減成「métro」，從法語進入英文後變成 metro。

   Metro 同時有「都會區」的意思，另外，它不僅可以用來指地鐵，在某些地區也概括了大眾交通工具。

The Answer to the Crosswords

4.p								
1.a	v	5.a	i	l	a	b	l	e
s	6.o	i						
s	n	3.s	c	a	l	e		
p	l	l						
o	i	e						
r	n	2.t	o	u	r	i	s	m
t	e							

Ever tried and failed? No matter. Try again and fail better./ Samuel Beckett

你曾經嘗試過卻面臨失敗嗎？沒關係。再試一次，失敗得更好一點。（山爾·貝克特）

Unit 2：Beauty and the Beast 美女與野獸

Fans of Disney's 1991 animated musical Beauty and the Beast should gear up for the release of its live-action adaptation. The beloved story features Bell, a bright and independent young woman who sacrifices her own freedom for the sake of her father's. Kept prisoner in the Beast's castle, Belle befriends the castle's enchanted staff and comes to see past the Beast's brutish exterior, discovering the true, kind-hearted Prince hidden deep within. It is a French story about a girl who is well-read, intelligent and courageous to live her own life.

Included in the all-star cast are Emma Watson, of Harry Potter fame, as Belle, Dan Stevens as the Beast, and Luke Evans as Gaston, Belle's egotistical suitor. In addition, A-list actors Ewan McGregor, Sir Ian McKellen and Emma Thompson lend their voices to some of the castle's endearing staff. Don't miss the opportunity to see this bewitching tale come to life. Check out Beauty and the Beast in the cinema.

Questions:

1. What is the article about?

   (A) An animated film 'Beauty and the Beast' is released.
   (B) Many famous actors perform in the film 'Beauty and the Beast'.
   (C) The Beast is a well-read, intelligent and courageous character in the film.
   (D) The film was a live-action adaptation in 1991.

2. Which of the following statement is NOT true?

   (A) Emma Watson previously starred in *Harry Potter*.
   (B) Many actors sing for some of the castle's endearing staff.
   (C) Belle would not like to sacrifice her freedom for her father because she wants to gain more knowledge.
   (D) The film is adapted from a French story.

| Answers: | 1. B 2. C |

翻譯

1991 年動畫音樂劇「美女與野獸」的粉絲們應該準備好迎接真人動畫版的上映。這個受大家喜歡的故事描寫貝兒 -- 一位美麗與獨立的年輕女孩 -- 為了父親，願意犧牲自己的自由。貝兒被困在野獸的城堡中，她與城堡中的被施了魔法的人員當朋友，並看

透在野獸殘暴的外表之下，發現善良的王子隱藏在其中。這是個描寫關於一名飽讀詩書、聰明而且勇敢活出自我的女性的法國故事。

這部真人版電影包含了巨星卡司，《哈利波特》中的明星艾瑪華森演出貝兒，丹史蒂芬斯演出野獸，路克伊凡斯演出自我中心主義、貝兒的追求者賈斯頓。除此之外，大咖演員伊旺麥奎格，伊恩·麥克連爵士還有艾瑪·湯普遜，都在此劇中替這些可愛的城堡角色獻出他們的歌聲。你絕對不能錯過觀看這個迷人故事真人版的機會，現在就去電影院觀賞「美女與野獸」吧！

問題

1. 這篇文章主旨為何？

　　(A) 動畫電影「美女與野獸」將上映。

　　(B) 許多有名卡司演出電影「美女與野獸」。

　　(C) 在這部電影野獸是一個飽讀詩書、聰明與勇敢的角色。

　　(D) 這部電影在 1991 年改編成真人版電影。

Ann's notes

根據選項給予的答案，「Included in the all-star cast are Emma Watson, of Harry Potter fame, as Belle, Dan Stevens as the Beast, and Luke Evans as Gaston, Belle's egotistical suitor.」是選項中有提到的。而 A、C、D 選項的意思不正確。

2. 下列敘述何者不正確？

　　(A) 艾瑪華森以前演過「哈利波特」。

　　(B) 許多演員為城堡可愛的人員獻聲。

　　(C) 貝兒不想為她的父親犧牲她自己的自由因為她想要學更多知識。

　　(D) 這部電影「美女與野獸」是改編自一個法國故事。

Ann's notes

根據選項，只有 C 答案錯誤。文中「The beloved story features Bell, a bright and independent young woman who sacrifices her own freedom for the sake of her father's.」清楚說明貝兒犧牲自己的自由來換取她父親的生命。

The words you need to know:

1. gear up (v.) 促進 / 增加；gear up for 準備

   E.g. The company gears up their sales by inviting a Korean movie star to promote their products.

   這間公司邀請一位韓國電影明星來代言他們的產品以促進他們的銷售。

2. adaptation (n.) 改編作品；adapt (v.) 適應 / 改編

   E.g. The film is adapted from a real story in Denmark.

   這部電影是一個丹麥的真人故事改編的。

3. sacrifice (v.) 犧牲

   E.g. You can't sacrifice your health as it is the most important in your life.

   因為健康是你生命中最重要的，你不能犧牲自己的健康。

4. brutish (adj.) 如禽獸的 / 殘酷的

   E.g. The man was so brutish that he killed many people in the music festival held in Las Vegas.

   這個人非常殘酷，他在拉斯維加斯的音樂會殺了很多人。

5. egotistical (adj.) 自我中心的

   E.g. Don't be too egotistical. Sometimes you should think of others.

   不要太過自我中心。有時候你應該替別人著想。

6. bewitch (v.) 施魔法於 / 著迷 / 蠱惑

   E.g. J. K. Rowling is like bewitching the readers into Harry Potter's fantasy world.

   羅琳像是對讀者們施魔法帶他們進入哈利波特的魔幻世界。

7. for the sake of somebody = for someone's sake 為了（某人）

   E.g. He moved his family to a warmer place for the sake of his wife's health.

   為了妻子的健康，他把家搬到一個更暖和的地方。

8. cinema (n.) 電影院 = theatre（英式英文）/ theater（美式英文）

   E.g. She has worked in the cinema all her life.

   她一生從事電影事業。

Success consists of going from failure to failure without loss of enthusiasm. / Winston Churchill

從失敗中站起來且保有熱情才是最棒的成功。（溫斯頓·邱吉爾）

Unit 3：Matilda 瑪蒂達

Matilda, which is produced by the Royal Shakespeare Company (RSC), is widely known as a great and outstanding musical. If you have never seen a musical before or you are a faithful fan of The Phantom of the Opera, you will be addicted to this show of being adapted from a children's book of the same name *Matilda*. Also, if you hope to challenge the text of Matilda with critical thinking or experience the life being a child differently, you shouldn't miss it. Matilda originated from a famous children's author called Roald Dahl. Most children in the UK haven't read it but at least they have heard about it. In 1996, the book was made into a film.

In this story, Matilda is a little girl who was born in a complicated family in England. Her parents not only make money illegally but also gamble it away. However, this little girl is so talented that she could read a great number of books when she was just three. Before she goes to primary school, she studied well to gain all kinds of knowledge. Nevertheless, her mean parents unbelievably think their little girl is a weird child and read these useless books. When she reached school age, not only do her parents mistreat her mentally, but school also bullies her. The trickiest thing is that the person who bullies her is not her classmate but the school principle. Miss Trunchbull hates kids and treats students badly. Therefore, Matilda starts to use her talents and intelligences to fight with her parents and the school principle. Luckily, she meets a peaceful and thoughtful teacher, Miss Jennifer Honey, who notices her magic and extraordinary abilities and intelligence. At the end of the story, Matilda overcomes her struggles at both home and at school, and succeeds to drive Miss Trunchbull away. Her efforts make teachers at the school happy because they were under pressure from Miss Trunchbull. Matilda can finally escape from her parents' control and live a happy life with Miss Honey.

1. The point of this article is _____.

    (A) to prove that Matilda is a popular girl

    (B) to prove that Matilda is a complicated story of an English family

    (C) to give information about the story of Matilda

    (D) to give many examples of British funny stories

2. Who firstly tries to stop Matilda from learning?

    (A) Miss Honey

    (B) Matilda's parents

    (C) Miss Trunchbull

    (D) Roald Dahl

3. Which of the following is NOT true?

   (A) Matilda makes efforts to keep Miss Trunchbull away.

   (B) Matilda's parents finally become nice and they live a happy life.

   (C) Miss Honey finds Matilda is talented and intelligent.

   (D) In 1996, the book was adapted into a film and then became a notable English story.

Answers:　　1. C　2. B　3. B

翻譯

「瑪蒂達」是由皇家莎士比亞劇團製作的一部廣受歡迎且傑出的音樂劇。如果你第一次看音樂劇,或者是「歌劇魅影」的忠實觀眾,那你一定會被這部由兒童故事「瑪蒂達」所改編的戲劇吸引。還有,如果你希望以批判思考提出對「瑪蒂達」的異義,或是以不同的方式經歷小孩的生活,那麼你更不能錯過這個音樂劇。「瑪蒂達」來自於知名兒童文學作家羅爾德·達爾(Roald Dahl)。在英國,很多小孩就算沒讀過這本書,他們也都聽過這本書。在 1996 年,這個故事被改編成電影。

故事中，瑪蒂達是一個出生在英格蘭複雜家庭的小女孩。她的父母親不僅賺不義之財還把全部的錢都賭光了。然而，這個小女孩非常聰明，從她三歲開始就閱讀非常多的書籍。在她上小學之前，她已經學習到很多不同知識。但是，她的卑鄙爸媽不可置信地認為這個小女孩是個怪異的小孩，而且還念了很多沒用的書籍。在她達到學齡後，除了她的父母在心理上虐待她之外，學校也霸凌她。最莫名其妙的事情是霸凌她的人不是她的同學而是學校校長。莊博老師（Miss Trunchbull）討厭小孩而且對學生很壞。因此，瑪蒂達開始用她的才智跟聰穎來對抗他的父母跟校長。很幸運的是，她遇到很平和又體貼的老師，珍妮弗·霍尼（Jennifer Honey）老師，她發現她魔幻又非凡的能力跟才智。故事的結尾，瑪蒂達克服了學校及家庭的抗爭，成功趕走莊博老師。她的努力讓學校的老師都很開心，因為莊博老師讓他們備感壓力。瑪蒂達最後擺脫了父母的掌控，跟霍尼老師過著快樂的生活。

1. 文章主旨是？
   (A) 證明瑪蒂達是一個受歡迎的女生。
   (B) 證明「瑪蒂達」是一個複雜的英國家庭的複雜故事。
   (C) 提供瑪蒂達故事的資訊。
   (D) 提供英國有趣故事的例子。

Ann's notes

文章第一段介紹「瑪蒂達」這部劇，改編自英國兒童文學小說作家 Roald Dahl，鼓勵觀眾可以進到劇院去看這部音樂劇或是電影。第二段簡單介紹「瑪蒂達」故事內容，依據提供的資訊，選項 (A) (B) (D) 錯誤，答案選擇 (C)。

2. 誰是第一個阻止瑪蒂達從書本中學習知識的人？
   (A) 霍尼老師。
   (B) 瑪蒂達的父母。
   (C) 莊博老師。
   (D) 羅爾德·達爾

Ann's notes

依據「Nevertheless, her mean parents unbelievably think their little girl is a weird child and read these useless books.」可以推測出，瑪蒂達的爸媽是第一個阻止她從書本學習知識的人。

3. 下列哪一個敘述錯誤？

   (A) 瑪蒂達很努力把莊博老師趕走。

   (B) 瑪蒂達的父母最後變得善良而且他們過著快樂的生活。

   (C) 霍尼老師發現瑪蒂達有天份又聰穎。

   (D) 在 1996 年，這本書被改編成電影，成為有名的英文故事。

Ann's notes

依據文章最後一句話「Matilda can finally get rid of her parents' control and live a happy life with Miss Honey.」，瑪蒂達跟霍尼老師過著幸福快樂的日子。

Let's have fun doing the Crosswords!!

Across

1. to like doing something a lot (6)
2. the opposite to simple things (11)
3. a person eating a bicycle? (5)
4. abuse (8)
5. a problem being hard to deal with (6)

Down

1. to break the law (7)
2. being very smart (6)
3. the opposite to noise (8)
4. being capable to do some things (7)
5. working hard (6)

Answers:

The words you need to know:

1. addict (n.) 上癮的人 (v.) 使沉溺

   E.g. Ann is a coffee addict because she needs coffee every morning.
   Ann 算是咖啡上癮者，因為她每天早上都需要喝咖啡。

2. complicated (adj.) 複雜的

   E.g. The puzzle is to complicated to solve.
   這個謎題太複雜了而無法解出答案。

3. weird (adj.) 怪異的

   E.g. She is considered weird, so many people are scared of talking to her.
   她看起來很怪所以很多人都不敢跟她說話。

4. autistic (a.) 孤獨的 / 孤僻的 / 自我中心的

   E.g. A way of getting rid of being autistic is to try to get along with people.
   擺脫孤僻的方法就是跟人群相處。

5. mistreat (v.) 虐待

   E.g. People who are autistic sometimes find it hard to get along with people.
   孤僻的人常發現自己很難跟人們相處。

6. tricky (adj.) 狡猾的 / 機警的

   E.g. The question is quite tricky so we can't easily find the correct answer.
   這個問題相當棘手，所以我們找不到正確答案。

7. illegal (adj.) 非法的

   E.g. You should be aware of avoiding carrying illegal items when you go through the security at the airport. the airport.
   當你在機場安檢時，你應該知道避免攜帶非法的物品。

8. talent (n.) 才能 / 天賦

   E.g. He has many talents so he has many options to choose which job to engage in.
   他很有才華，所以有很多選擇可以決定想要從事哪一項工作。

   When you look long into an abyss, the abyss looks into you. / Friedrich Nietzsche
   當你凝視深淵時，深淵也在凝視你。（尼采）

9. peaceful (adj.) 和平的 / 寧靜的

E.g. That song is so peaceful that the baby soon falls asleep.

這首歌非常平靜，所以這個嬰兒很快就睡著了。

10. ability (n.) 能力

E.g. English ability is considered as a requirement to study at a British university.

英文能力是進入英國大學的一個條件。

11. effort (n.) 努力 / 成就

E.g. If you are sure of what you want, you need to make every effort to achieve your goal.

如果你很清楚自己想要什麼，現在你需要努力去完成你的目標。

Unit 4：A Real and Local British 道地英國人生

There are many things associated with 'Britishness', for example, a love of fish and chips or an obsession with the royal family. But perhaps, more than anything else, British people have a unique fondness for discussing the weather. Even when no other topic of conversation exists, common ground and comfort with a British person can always be found by talking about the current state of the weather.

Being British however, the current state of the weather is often rather wet. This, when combined with British people's love of talking about it, has led to some vivid expressions for rain. Here are a few interesting examples.

Raining cats and dogs – This is quite a common expression and is used to describe very heavy rain. Many previously thought that the expression derived from a desire to portray the raindrops as particularly large (i.e. the size of cats and dogs). It turns out however, that the more likely origin is from a tendency in the past for heavy rain showers to wash cats and dogs into the street.

Raining stair-rods – Stair-rods are thin metal rods used to hold a carpet in place upon each step of a staircase. This expression therefore, is used to describe rain that is so heavy and constant. It takes on the appearance of upturned stair-rods. Now stair-rods are no longer commonly found in modern homes.

Nice weather for the ducks – This expression can, generally speaking, be used to describe any sort of rain. It's a lovely expression, since it attempts to put a positive spin on what most people would describe as miserable weather (a very British thing to do). Although origin about its expression is unclear, the expression is suggesting that, if anyone is to be happy about the rain, it should be the ducks. After all, they are used to being wet. Rain to a duck is like water off a duck's back.

Questions:

1. Which of the following statements cannot be associated with Britishness according to the article?

   (A) Fish and chips.
   (B) The royal family.
   (C) Crosswords.
   (D) Weather discussion.

2. Which of the following explanation is NOT true?

   (A) British people like to talk about weather in diverse and fun ways.
   (B) Raining cats and dogs means light raindrops.
   (C) Raining stair-rods is from the expression of thin metal rods used to hold carpet in place on a staircase and thus is used to describe heavy and constant rain.
   (D) Nice weather for the ducks is an adorable expression.

3. According to the passage, ducks are used to being wet. Rain to a duck is like water off a duck's back, which refers to _____.

(A) rain having little effect on ducks.

(B) duck's trembling with fear.

(C) playing with ducks.

(D) paying attention to ducks.

4. What can readers infer from the passage about what the author would like to express?

(A) The British educational system.

(B) British people's dislike of the weather.

(C) The British obsession with the royal family.

(D) The sharing of British culture.

Answers: 1. C 2. B 3. A 3. D

翻譯

有很多事情跟「英國形象」很相關，例如熱愛炸魚薯條或是津津樂道皇室家庭。但或許相較於其他，英國人更獨鍾於討論天氣。甚至沒有其他話題可以對話時，也可以透過談論目前天氣，和英國人找到共同點及慰藉。

然而，在英國，天氣狀況常常很潮濕。結合與英國人熱愛談論這個話題的喜好，這個情況產生了許多生動且和雨相關的措辭。以下有幾個有趣的例子。

➡ 傾盆大雨：這是相當常見的一個措辭，用來形容下很大的雨。之前很多人以為這個說法是來自於雨滴大小的描述（即落下的雨滴與貓狗一樣大）。然而結果出爐，更可能的起源傾向於因為過去的大雨會將貓狗沖到街上。

➡ 一輪強風暴雨：樓梯桿是用來支撐地毯與每一階樓梯的薄金屬桿。因此，這個說法用來形容與下得很大或是來的急促。看起來像往上的樓梯桿。現在這種樓梯桿在現代家庭中已不再常見了。

➡ 適合鴨子的天氣：大致上而言，這個說法是用來形容任何類型的雨天。這是一個很可愛的說法，因為它試著對大多數人們所描述地糟糕的天氣發揮正面的影響（非常英國人的行為）。雖然有關於這個說法的來源並不清楚，不過這個說法意味著，如果要說誰喜歡雨天，那應該就是鴨子了。畢竟鴨子很習慣潮濕。下雨對鴨子來說，就像是鴨背上的水 -- 毫無影響罷了。

問題

1. 根據本文章，下列敘述何者跟「很英國」無關？

   (A) 炸魚薯條。

   (B) 皇室家族。

   (C) 填字遊戲。

   (D) 討論天氣。

Ann's notes

文中沒有談論到 crosswords 填字遊戲。

2. 下列解釋何者不正確？

   (A) 英國人喜歡用不同方式聊天氣。

   (B) Raining cats and dogs（傾盆大雨）指的是下毛毛雨。

   (C) 一輪強風暴是從蓋樓梯用的棍薄的金屬片狀物來的，而因此用來形容大跟突如其來的雨。

   (D) 適合鴨子的天氣是一種可愛的說法。

Ann's notes

根據文章「Many previously thought that the expression derived from a desire to portray the raindrops as particularly large (i.e. the size of cats and dogs).」說明了雨滴下得特別大。

3. 根據這篇文章，鴨子習慣潮濕。下雨對鴨子來說沒什麼大事，代表 ＿＿＿＿＿＿？

   (A) 對鴨子沒什麼影響。

   (B) 鴨子害怕抖動。

   (C) 跟鴨子玩樂。

   (D) 注意鴨子。

Ann's notes

「water off a duck's back」是一俚語用法，指的是「不起作用、毫無影響」的意思。water 意指水，back 意指背後；water off a duck's back 是指押背羽毛光滑，沾不住水，淋上去的水都滴了下，喻指對某人的忠告全當耳邊風，吹過去就如同水落在鴨背上一樣毫無作用。

E.g. The teacher keeps telling her students that they should study hard, but however it's like water off a duck's back.

老師一直告訴她的學生要努力用功讀書，但是，絲毫不起任何作用。

4. 依據這篇文章，讀者可以推測出作者想表達什麼？

    (A) 英國的教育系統。

    (B) 英國人討厭天氣。

    (C) 英國人迷戀英國皇室。

    (D) 英國文化分享。

Ann's notes

此文中沒有討論到英國教育系統；雖然天氣很讓人惱怒，但此文沒說到英國人如何討厭天氣；文章有討論到英國皇室家庭確實另人津津樂道，但沒有特別提出英國皇室歷史的演進。而從三種形容天氣的方式，可以得知作者想跟讀者分享英國文化，因此文章開頭及提到 Britishness，可以翻作「英國大小事」或是「很英國人」，可以推論這篇文章跟文化分享很有關係。

PS. Ann 的英國友人常常覺得 Ann 特愛研究英國文化，所以覺得 Ann 有時候比英國人還要英國人。

The words you need to know:

1. obsession (n.) 念念不忘 痴迷

    E.g. Charles has great obsession with chocolate.

        Charles 對巧克力強烈的痴迷。

2. fondness (n.) 喜好；be fond of +N. 喜歡做 ...（某事）

    E.g. Candy's fondness for playing volleyball is well known.

        大家都知道 Candy 喜歡打排球。

3. expression (n.) 表達 / 說法 / 表情

    E.g. Freedom of expression is a basic human right.

        言論自由是基本的人權。

4. vivid (adj.) 生動的 /（顏色）栩栩如生的 / 鮮豔的 / 明亮的

    E.g. I have a very vivid picture of the first time I met Irene.

        我對於第一次見到 Irene 有非常鮮明的印象。

5. portray (v.) 描寫 / 描繪 / 刻畫

   E.g. The mother in the film is portrayed as a fairly unpleasant character.

   影片中的父親被塑造成一個很不討喜的角色。

6. particularly (adv.) 特別 / 尤其

   E.g. I didn't particularly want to go, but I had no choice.

   我並不是特別想去,但我沒得選擇。

7. tendency (n.) 趨勢 / 傾向;tend to + V (v.) 傾向 ...

   E.g. There is a growing tendency to regard money more highly than quality of life, so more and more people tend to have practical attitude.

   越來越多人傾向把金錢看得重於生活品質,所以越來越多人傾向功利態度。

8. attempt (v.) [attempt to + V.] 努力 / 嘗試 / 企圖

   E.g. James attempted a joke, but no one laughed.

   James 開了個玩笑,試圖調和氣氛,但沒有一個人笑。

Nothing is so common as the wish to be remarkable. / William Shakespeare

沒有什麼比希望不平凡而更平凡的了。(莎士比亞)

· 閱 · 讀 · 練 · 習 ·

Unit 5：Robin Hood and the Golden Arrow 羅賓漢與金劍

Robin Hood was a famous thief who lived in Sherwood Forest in England. He was the leader of a band of thieves called the Merry Men, who stole from the rich and gave to the poor. The Sheriff of Nottingham wanted to catch Robin Hood. So, Robin Hood's companion Little John had once tricked the Sheriff into coming to Robin's or the Merry Men. The Sheriff failed to succeed arresting Robin Hood. He did not forget this indeed. Instead, he kept thinking of ways to bring Robin Hood to swift justice.

The Sheriff discussed the matter with his friend the Abbot. 'If I cannot harm Robin Hood,' said the Sheriff, 'then I shall do him no harm as I capture and imprison him!' He tried to think of a way to lead Robin Hood into a trap, but the Abbot reminded him that Robin was too smart to fall for simple tricks. The Sheriff thought about it some time and came up with a brilliant plan: he would hold an archery contest, and the winner would receive a prize that Robin Hood could not resist—an arrow made of gold.

When Robin Hood heard about the contest, he was very excited. He was quite sure that he would win, and he wanted to receive the Sheriff's prize. The Merry Men warned him that it was probably a trap, but Robin reminded them of the Sheriff's oath. On the day of the contest, Robin Hood disguised himself as an old man and set off with his men. When it was Robin's turn, he aimed and shot an arrow at the furthest target—it struck the very centre. With this, Robin won the contest. He approached the Sheriff and collected his prize when suddenly, a horn sounded, and the guards attacked. The Sheriff had seen through Robin's disguise.

The Merry Men found themselves in a heated battle to protect Robin. They took aim with their arrows and swung their swords with all their might, but they were outnumbered. All hope seemed lost, when out of the crowd, Little John—who had the strength of 10 men—leaped to Robin's side and joined the fight. With that, the men pushed back the guards and made their escape. Robin Hood got away from the Sheriff once again—with the golden arrow in tow.

Questions:

1. What is the text mainly about?

   (A) It is a story about a legendary leader of thieves in Nottingham.
   (B) It is a story about a sheriff arresting a criminal in Nottingham.
   (C) It is a report about an abbot winning an archery contest.
   (D) It is a report about how to make a golden arrow.

2. According to the story, Merry Men_____.

   (A) are a mob who steal from the poor and the rich.
   (B) are a group of thieves who like to help the poor by robbing from the rich.
   (C) are happy persons who lived in Sherwood Forest.
   (D) are natives of Nottingham.

3. Which of the following is NOT true?

   (A) Robin Hood became a thief because he helped the poor by stealing from the rich.
   (B) The Sheriff of Nottingham at last arrested Robin Hood.
   (C) Robin Hood decided to attend the archery contest because he was excited with it no matter how likely he was to be caught.
   (D) There were 10 men and Little John helping Robin Hood in the fight.

Answers:　　1. A　2. B　3. B

翻譯

羅賓漢是一個住在英格蘭雪伍德森林的一個義賊。他是一支稱作「綠林好漢」專門劫富濟貧的一幫義賊的首領。諾丁漢的警長想要抓羅賓漢。但是，羅賓漢的同伴小約翰曾經設計過警長找到綠林好漢或是羅賓漢的家。警長沒有成功抓住羅賓漢，他不曾忘記這件事情，但，他仍然不斷想辦法把羅賓漢繩之以法。

警長跟他的朋友修道院院長討論過這件事情。「如果我不能傷害到羅賓漢」，警長這麼說著，「那麼，當我抓住並將他關進牢裡時，我不會傷害他！」。他試著想出一個辦法引羅賓漢到陷阱處，但是修道院院長提醒他，羅賓漢太聰明了不會落入簡單的陷阱。警長想了一會兒，想出一個高明的計畫：他想舉辦一個弓箭比賽，而且贏家可以獲得一個羅賓漢無法抗拒的獎項 -- 也就是黃金箭。

當羅賓漢得知這個比賽消息，他非常興奮。他確定他一定會贏，而且他想得到警長的獎品。綠林好漢警告他這可能是一個陷阱，但是羅賓漢提醒他們警長說過的誓言。比賽當天，羅賓漢裝扮成一個老人而且和綠林好漢們出發去比賽。到了羅賓漢的時候，他瞄準而且用一支箭射中最遠的靶 -- 正中紅心。因此，羅賓漢贏了比賽。他接近警長準備拿他的獎品時，突然間當號角響起，侍衛們開始圍攻。警長早就看穿了羅賓漢的偽裝。

綠林好漢不由自主為了保護羅賓漢而展開激烈的戰鬥。他們拿起弓箭設法用他們的力量瞄準，但他們人數不夠。看似一切沒有希望的時候，就在群眾中，小約翰有著一抵十人的力量，跳到羅賓漢旁邊，加入這場戰役。有了他的加入，好漢們擊退了侍衛們，而且將他們趕跑了。羅賓漢再次從警長手中脫逃，而且拖著金箭離開。

問題

1. 這個文章主旨為何？
   (A) 這是一個有關發生在諾丁漢義賊們的領導者的傳奇故事。
   (B) 這是一個有關發生在諾丁漢一位警長逮捕一位罪犯的故事。
   (C) 這是一個有關一位修道院長贏得射箭比賽的報導。
   (D) 這是一個有關如何製造黃金劍的報導。

Ann's notes

根 據「Robin Hood was a famous thief who lived in Sherwood Forest in England. He was the leader of a band of thieves called the Merry Men, who stole from the rich and gave to the poor.」，正確答案選擇 A。

2. 根據這個故事，綠林好漢是 _____。
   (A) 一群去偷竊有錢人與窮人的暴民。
   (B) 一群喜歡偷有錢人的錢去幫助窮人的義賊。
   (C) 一群住在雪伍德森林的快樂人們。
   (D) 諾丁漢的當地人。

Ann's notes

根據「a band of thieves called the Merry Men, who stole from the rich and gave to the poor」他們是一群劫富濟貧的義賊。

3. 下列何者錯誤？
   (A) 羅賓漢成為小偷，因為他喜歡劫富濟貧。
   (B) 諾丁漢警長最後逮捕了羅賓漢。
   (C) 羅賓漢決定參加射箭比賽，不管他多麼可能被抓，對於這個比賽仍然感到非常興奮。
   (D) 在這場戰役中，十個綠林好漢跟小約翰幫助羅賓漢脫逃。

Ann's notes

根據「All hope seemed lost, when out of the crowd, Little John—who had the strength of 10 men—leaped to Robin's side and joined in the fight. With that, the men pushed back the guards and made their escape. Robin Hood got away from the Sheriff once again—with the golden arrow in tow.」由這段內容可以得知，最後羅賓漢從諾丁漢警長的包圍中逃脫。

Background knowledge:

羅賓漢 (Robin Hood) 是中世紀英國民間傳說（folklore）中一位劫富濟貧的俠盜，以英格蘭中部的諾丁漢 (Nottingham) 為根據地。現存相關的民謠 (ballad) 可以追朔到十五世紀後半，數百年來還有許多戲劇 (play) 及文學作品傳頌羅賓漢的故事，使他成為家喻戶曉的英雄人物，跟台灣知名義賊廖添丁故事有異曲同工之妙。此外，文中的 Merry Men 指的是羅賓漢的夥伴們，常翻譯為「綠林好漢」。原本的 merry 是指「快樂的、快活的」意思，但 merry men 原意指的是騎士 (knight) 或是逃犯 (outlaw) 的隨從或是夥伴的通稱。

（照片拍攝於英國中部城市諾丁漢 Nottingham）

The words you need to know:

1. harm (n.) (v.) 傷害

    E.g. Vicky meant no harm (= did not intend to offend); she was only joking.
    Vicky 並無惡意，只是在開玩笑。

    E.g. Thankfully no one was harmed in the accident.
    謝天謝地，沒有人在事故中受傷。

2. swift (adj.) 迅速的；立即的

    E.g. The police took swift action against the mob.
    當地警方對擅暴民採取了迅速的行動。

3. remind (v.) 提醒；使想起

    （remind somebody of something 提醒某人 ...... 使某人想起 ......）

    E.g. Please remind me of the meeting this morning.
    請提醒我今天早上的會議。

4. brilliant (adj.) 傑出的；聰明的；高明的

    E.g. Her mother was a brilliant writer.
    她母親是一位才華橫溢的作家。

5. come up with (v.) 想出

    E.g. The creator of the Post-It had come up with an idea to make strong glue in the beginning, but he failed and then made the Post-It.
    便利貼的創作者最早想出製造強力膠水，但之後失敗後而創造了便利貼。

6. resist (v.) 克制（誘惑）；抵抗

    E.g. The party leader resisted demands for his resignation.
    該黨領導人拒不答應他辭職的要求。

7. trick (n.) 騙局 詭計 惡作劇 / 訣竅 秘訣 技巧

    E.g. Children like to go trick-or-treating on Holloween.
    小孩喜歡在萬聖節那天去玩搗蛋要糖活動。

    E.g. What's the trick to getting this chair to fold up?
    把這張椅子摺疊起來有什麼訣竅？

8. disguise (v.) (n.) 喬裝 / 偽裝

    E.g. He disguised himself by wearing a false beard.
    為了偽裝自己，他剃了光頭還粘著假鬍鬚。

9. leap (v.) 跳躍

    E.g. The cat leaped over the gate into the field.
    這隻貓越過大門朝田野跑去。

10. oath (n.) 發誓 / 誓言；詛咒 / 咒罵

    E.g. Medieval knights took an oath of loyalty to their lord.
    中世紀騎士宣誓效忠於君主。

Note

sheriff (n.) 警長

abbot (n.) 男修道院院長

imprison (v.) 囚禁；監禁

archery (n.) 劍術；射箭運動

Let's have fun doing the Crosswords!!

Across

2. hide (8)

4. soon(5)

6. bright (9)

9. get an idea (4, 2, 4)

Down

1. think of something (6)

3. swear (4)

5. cheating (5)

7. difficult to say no (6)

8. jump (4)

10. damage (4)

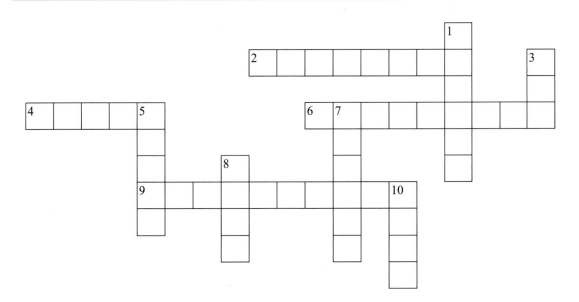

★答案就在上一篇的 words you need to know 喔！加油！

Go as far as you can see; when you get there you'll be able to see farther/ Thomas Carlyle

走到你能看到最遠之處，當你到那，你將能夠看到更遠。（湯瑪斯‧卡萊爾）

Unit 6：Young Adult Readers Prefer Printed to Ebooks in the UK
紙本魅力不敗 英國年輕人愛實體書勝過電子書

According to a newspaper survey of the Guardian in the UK, Luke Mitchell of agency Voxburner, who researched questions about buying and using content of printed books with 1,420 young adults, says that 'It is surprising that 16 to 24-year-old people are known as the online super-connected generation, obsessed with snapping selfies or downloading the latest mobile apps. Thus it comes as a surprise to learn that 62% of 16 to 24-year-old prefer traditional books over their digital equivalents from a survey. Regarding preferences for physical products versus digital content, printed books jump out as the media most desired in material form, ahead of movies (48%), newspapers and magazines (47%), CDs (32%), and video games (30%) respectively.

This outcome leads us to think of 16-24 year-old people as being attached to their smartphones and digital devices, so it does shout out amazingly. The two biggest reasons for preferring printed ones are value for money and an emotional connection to physical books. On questions of ebook pricing, 28% think that ebooks should be half their current price, while just 8% say that ebook pricing is right. Besides, there are some qualitative comments like 'I like to hold the product' (51%), 'I am not restricted to a particular device' (20%), 'I can easily share it' (10%), 'I like the packaging' (9%) and 'I can sell it when when it is used. ' (6%). Moreover, Mitchell also finds that young people prefer physical books included things like 'I collect books', 'I like the smell', and 'I want full bookshelves'. Books are status and symbols and you can't really see what someone has read on their Kindle or pads.

Questions:

1. Which of the following is NOT correct?

    (A) Young people are not that stuck to ebooks on the mobile.
    (B) Young people prefer a copy including things like collecting.
    (C) Young people smell the books.
    (D) Young people enjoy bookshelves filled with many books.

2. What is the reason for young people preferring printed books to ebooks?

    (A) They can have films, newspapers, music and online games.
    (B) They can sell ebooks after they are used.
    (C) Printed books are cheaper than ebooks.
    (D) They value for money and an emotional connection to physical books.

翻譯

根據英國衛報調查，Voxburner 數據調查公司的盧克米切爾 (Luke Mitchell)，在 1,420 位年輕人當中進行關於買實體書或是使用紙本書籍問題的調查，令人驚訝的是，16 到 24 歲的人士是大眾所知與網路有超級強烈連結的世代，愛自拍或是下載最新的手機應用軟體。然而，從調查中意外得知有 62% 的 16 到 24 歲之間人士偏好傳統書籍勝過於數位產品。關於實體產品對比數位內容，紙本書籍一躍到最令人喜愛的媒體形式，分別超越電影 48%，報紙與雜誌 47%，CD 32% 還有電玩遊戲 30%。

我們思考到 16 到 24 歲的人應該沉迷於智慧型手機和電子產品，所以這個結果讓我們大為驚奇。選擇紙本書兩個最大原因是物有所值和與對實體書的情感聯繫。關於電子書價錢的問題，有 28% 的讀者認為電子書應該是實體書的半價，而只有 8% 的讀者認為價錢合理。除外，還有一些性質上的評論像是 51% 的讀者認為「我喜歡手握實體書」，20% 的讀者「我不想被特定的設備限制住」，10% 的人認為「我可以容易地分享」，9% 的人「我喜歡外包裝」還有 6% 的人認為「我使用過後可以賣出」。除此之外，米切爾也發現年輕人偏好實體書的評價包含「我想收集書」、「我喜歡書籍的味道」還有「我想要擁有滿滿的書架」。書籍是種身份象徵，你無法真正了解人們用他們的 Kindle 或是平板所閱讀到的東西。

問題

1. 下列哪個敘述不正確？
    (A) 年輕人不那麼受制於手機上的電子書。
    (B) 年輕人偏好實體書，包含像是收集事物。
    (C) 年輕人會聞書的味道。
    (D) 年輕人喜歡有滿滿書的書架。

Ann's notes

根據「I like the smell」跟「Young people smell the books.」是不同的。一個是喜歡書味道（這是某些人的評論跟偏好），而另一個是年輕人會聞書的味道意思是不同的。

2. 什麼原因使得年輕人偏好印製書而非電子書？

(A) 他們可以看電影、報紙、聽音樂跟玩線上遊戲。

(B) 他們會在使用電子書後將它賣出。

(C) 印製書籍比電子書便宜。

(D) 他們珍惜錢同時對於實體書有情感的連結。

Ann's notes

根據文中「The two biggest reasons for preferring printed ones are value for money and an emotional connection to physical books.」可以得知 D 選項為正確答案，其餘答案皆非。

The words you need to know:

1. content (n.) 內容 / 容量；(adj.) 滿足的 / 甘願的

   E.g. They're content to socialize with a very small circle of people.
   他們滿足於只和一小群人交往。

2. obsess [with] (v.) 迷住 / 佔據心思

   E.g. She used to obsess about her weight so she seldom had proper diet.
   她過去總是過分在意自己的體重所以很少正常飲食。

3. equivalent (n.) 同等物 / 等價物；(adj.) 相等的 / 同意義的

   E.g. Is $50 equivalent to about £30?
   50 美元是不是大約相當於 30 英鎊？

4. outcome (n.) 結果 = result / income (n.) 收入

   E.g. It's too early to predict the outcome of the election.
   現在預言選舉的結果還言之尚早。

5. attach [to] (v.) 貼上 / 使附屬於 / 依附於 / 連接

   E.g. In the UK, packets of cigarettes come with a government health warning attached to them, and so do they in Taiwan.
   在英國，香煙的包裝盒上都印有政府的健康警告，台灣的也一樣。

6. restrict [to] (v.) 限制 / 約束

   E.g. Her parents' activities were restricted by old age.
   她父母親的活動因年事已高而受到限制。

Unit 7：Stop Learning by Rote 別再死讀書了

Taiwanese students are good at memorizing long articles or even entire lessons. The students say that this 'special skill' takes time to learn. For the past five decades, Taiwanese students have been memorizing things. They keep doing this to pass tests. However, they don't pay a lot of attention to the meaning of what they memorize.

Over the last ten years in the United Kingdom, fewer and fewer students have been memorizing things. They have been paying more attention to being original. Originality in the classroom allows students to make new things and think in new ways. For example, some teachers no longer just ask simple questions about something students read. Instead, they might tell the students to write a new ending to a story. Or they might tell them to think up a new subject to write about. Students might even be told to change a piece of Shakespeare's writing into modern English. This is done to make sure they understand the meaning of what they read. The new idea is to teach a student how to think and work out problems. Moreover, it's a good way to strengthen what has already been taught in the classroom. One thing is certain:we should stop learning by memorizing.

Questions:

1. According to the article, what are Taiwanese students good at?

   (A) Understanding the meaning
   (B) Listening in class
   (C) Solving problems
   (D) Memorizing articles

2. What are British students taught to do?

   (A) Think originally
   (B) Memorize things
   (C) Pass tests
   (D) Learn 'special skills'

3. What do some teachers in the United Kingdom no longer do?

   (A) Telling students to write a new ending
   (B) Making students think up a new subject
   (C) Asking students simple questions
   (D) Having students recreate Shakespeare

4. What is the new idea of teaching?

    (A) To get students to pass tests
    (B) To get students to memorize articles
    (C) To ask students many questions
    (D) To instruct students how to think

Answers:　　1. D　2. A　3. C　4. D

翻譯

台灣學生擅長背誦長篇文章甚至是整課內容。學生說這個「特殊技巧」需要時間習得。在過去五十年來，台灣學生一直背誦許多東西。他們持續這麼做是為了要通過考試。然而，他們並沒太注意他們背誦東西的意義是什麼。

在英國過去十幾年之間，越來越少學生做背誦的事情。他們一直專注於原創。教室裡的創意使得他們製造新事物並用新的方式思考。例如，一些老師不再只問學生閱讀過的一些簡單問題。反而，他可能會要求學生替一個故事寫一個新的結局。或者要求學生想新的主題來寫。學生甚至會被要求把莎士比亞的文章改成現代英文。這樣做是用來確認學生了解到他們所閱讀到的內容意義。這個新的想法是為了教導學生如何思考還有怎麼解決問題。除此之外，這是一個很好的方式來加強在教室中所學到的東西。很確定的一件事就是：　　　我們應該停止用背誦的方式來學習。

問題

1. 根據這篇文章，台灣學生擅長什麼？

    (A) 理解意義。
    (B) 課堂上課。
    (C) 解決問題。
    (D) 背誦文章。

Ann's notes

所以開門見山法，文章內容第一句話說明「Taiwanese students are good at memorizing long articles or even entire lessons.」台灣學生善於背誦。

2. 英國的學生被教導如何做？

(A) 創意思考。

(B) 背誦事物。

(C) 通過考試。

(D) 學習「特殊技巧」。

Ann's notes

根據文中「They have been paying more attention to being original.」可以得知英國老師們鼓勵學生創意思考。

3. 英國的老師不再做什麼東西來鼓勵學生學習？

(A) 告訴學生寫新的結局。

(B) 讓學生想出新的主題。

(C) 問學生簡單的問題。

(D) 要學生重新創作莎士比亞的寫作

Ann's notes

根據文中「some teachers no longer just ask simple questions about something students read.」所以答案選擇 (C)。

4. 教學的新旨意是什麼？

(A) 要求學生通過考試。

(B) 要求學生背誦文章。

(C) 問學生很多問題。

(D) 引導學生如何思考。

Ann's notes

從文中「The new idea is to teach a student how to think and work out problems.」和「One thing is certain: we should stop learning by memorizing.」可以得知希望新的教學方式可以引導學生思考。

The words you need to know:

1. rote (n.) 死背（learn... by rote 靠著背學習 ...）

   E.g. You'll never acquire knowledge if you learn things by rote.
   如果你用死背的方式學習，那麼你永遠無法獲得知識。

2. memorize (v.) 背誦；memorization (n.) 背誦

   E.g. The first thing we communicate with English speakers is to memorize some English words so that we have some vocabulary to talk with them.
   與英語人士溝通的第一件事就是背誦一些英文單字以便有單字量可以跟他們聊天。

3. entire (adj.) 全部的；entirely (adv.) 全然地 = completely, totally

   E.g. You should not tell strangers the entire information of yours.
   你不應該告訴陌生人有關你所有一切的資訊。

4. original (adj.) 創意的 / 原始的；(n.) 原文

   originality (n.) 創意 = creativity

   E.g. I deeply believe that everyone has his or her own originality to show the potential he or her has.
   我深信每個人都有自己的創意能夠表現出自己的潛力。

5. strengthen (v) 加強

   E.g. Ann strengthened her English writing by writing a lot of essays constantly.
   Ann 藉由不斷地寫英文作文來增強她的英文寫作。

6. work out (v.) 解決 / 使（事物）有效 / 鍛鍊（身體）/ 發展

   E.g. Let's hope this new job works out well for Kate.
   希望這項新工作會非常適合 Kate。

Let's have fun doing the Crosswords!!

Across

2. feeling pleased (7)
4. complete (6)
5. creativity (11)
6. learning things from memory rather than from understanding (4)
10. the same (10)

Down

1. developing in a particular way (4, 3)
3. remember (8)
7. becoming stronger (10)
8. limit (8)
9. not an income (7)

★答案就在 Unit 6 & 7 的 words you need to know 喔！加油！

Living without an aim is like sailing without a compass./ Alexandre Dumas

生活沒有目標就像航海沒有指南針。（大仲馬）

Unit 8：Moods and Weather 天氣影響心情

When people are in a bad mood, we sometimes say that they must have gotten up on the wrong side of the bed. We usually say this when we don't know why they are in such a foul mood. Have you ever gotten up in a bad temper for no apparent reason and wondered why? Don't be puzzled. There is an explanation for this phenomenon.

Some people say that one's mood is greatly affected by seasonal changes. The time of year can have a big influence upon how you feel. In the winter, it is common for people to easily become depressed. During this time of the year, there aren't as many daylight hours and the sun is out for a shorter period of time. Others even believe that the motion of the moon can affect one's mood. For example, some mental patients have been known to behave more bizarrely than even when there is a full moon. Researchers who hope to help these patients during these difficult times have noticed this behavior. Strange as it may seem, there must be some basis for this argument. Why else do we often say, 'I'm under the weather', when we aren't feeling well?

Questions:

1. The expression 'people are in a bad mood' means

   (A) they are too heavy to move.
   (B) they got up on the right side of the bed.
   (C) that the climate is very mild.
   (D) they are unhappy, irritable or angry.

2. Some think that_____

   (A) seasonal change and the moon have a lot of influence on one's mood.
   (B) people easily lose their temper because they have to get up angry.
   (C) you had better get up early to be in a better mood.
   (D) there is no explanation for the reason why people like to go shopping.

3. Why have researchers studied mental patients when there is a full moon?

   (A) To make them ignorant of their own health.
   (B) To learn how to help their patients during this time.
   (C) So they can better understand the change of seasons.
   (D) They can only study them during a full moon.

4. Why do people become depressed during the winter months?

    (A) There is too much sunshine for them to go outdoors.

    (B) There aren't as many hours of daylight.

    (C) Their doctors are unable to figure out why.

    (D) Depression is natural when it is hot outside.

Answers: 1. D   2. A   3. B   4. B

翻譯

當人們心情不好的時候，我們有時候會說：他們起床時下錯邊了（意指心情不好）。當我們不知道為什麼他們心情那麼差的時候，通常都用這個說法來表示。你曾經起床後毫無理由的心情不佳而且納悶著為什麼嗎？別困惑了。有一個解釋可以說明這個現象。

有人說，人的心情會受季節變化的影響很大。一年中的時間對於你的感受有很大的影響。在冬天，人們普遍容易感到沮喪。一年裡的這個時間中，日照時間不像別的時間有那麼多，而且太陽出現的時間也比較短。也有人甚至相信月亮的移動會影響一個人的心情。例如，有些精神疾病病人在月圓的時候，行為更加怪異。協助嚴重病狀情況的病人的研究學家已經發現有這樣的行為。雖然看似奇怪，不過對於這個論點必定有一些基礎說法。那麼又為什麼我們常常在感覺不舒服的時候常說「我心情不好」。

問題

1. 「心情不好」的說法意味著 ＿＿＿＿＿＿。

    (A) 他們太重而無法移動。

    (B) 他們起床下錯邊了。

    (C) 天氣非常溫和。

    (D) 他們不快樂、憤怒或是生氣。

Ann's notes

雖然答案 B 有隱喻心情不好的意思，但 B 選項是一種「心情不好的說法」，並非是一種解釋，因此答案選擇 D。

2. 有人說 _____ 。

(A) 季節的變化跟月亮對人的心情有很大的影響。

(B) 人們容易憤怒是因為他們必須早起。

(C) 你最好早起能有好心情。

(D) 沒有原因可以解釋為什麼人們喜歡購物。

> **Ann's notes**
>
> 文章第二段第一行「Some people say that one's mood is greatly affected by seasonal changes.」清楚說明季節變化影響人們的心情。

3. 為什麼研究學家在月圓時候研究精神疾病病人？

(A) 讓他們忽略自己的健康。

(B) 學習如何在這段時間照顧他們的病人。

(C) 所以他可以更理解季節的變化。

(D) 他們可有在月圓的時候做研究。

> **Ann's notes**
>
> 根據文中「Researchers who hope to help these patients during these difficult times have noticed this behavior.」研究學者是希望透過季節變化這段期間，更瞭解他們的病人並給予他們適當的協助。

4. 為什麼在冬天月份期間人們會比較沮喪？

(A) 有很多陽光讓他們可以出外活動。

(B) 沒有很多日照時間。

(C) 他們的醫師無法找出為什麼。

(D) 當外面天氣熱的時候，憂鬱症是很自然的。

> **Ann's notes**
>
> 根據文中「In the winter, it is common for people to easily become depressed. During this time of the year, there aren't as many daylight hours and the sun is out for a shorter period of time.」清楚得知因為冬天時間日照時間短，以至於容易讓人的心情受影響或沮喪。

The words you need to know:

1. mood (n.) 心情；moody (adj.) 心情低落的

   E.g. She doesn't have good mood because of the frustrating test result.
   因為令人挫折的成績，她現在心情很差。

2. foul (adj.) 惡劣的 =bad

   by fair means or foul 不擇手段

   E.g. We have had foul weather these days in London, like sometimes heat wave and freezing rain.
   這幾天倫敦天氣不好，有時熱浪或是冰冷的雨天。

   E.g. I vowed to attain my goals by fair means or foul.
   我絕不會為了達到目標不擇手段。

3. apparent (adj.) 顯而易見的 = clear, obvious

   E.g. It is apparent that we can understand his sadness from his face.
   顯然的是，我們可以從他的臉上體會到他的悲傷。

4. puzzled (adj.) 困惑的 = confused

   E.g. Don't be puzzled too much because the problem is not that hard to solve.
   別太困擾，因為這個問題不沒那麼困難解決。

5. phenomenon (n.) 現象（單數）; phenomena (n.) 現象（複數）

   E.g. It is a quite common phenomenon that if you don't have your own ID with you, then you will be refused to get in the library.
   相當普遍的現象是，如果你沒有帶自己的學生證，那麼你將遭到拒絕進入圖書館。

6. affect (v.) 影響 = influence

   E.g. Don't get affected by others. What you need to do is focus on your task.
   別受別人影響。你需要做的事情就是專注在你的任務上。

7. depressed (adj.) 感到沮喪的；depressing (adj.) 令人沮喪的

   depress (v.) 使沮喪

   用法：S（人）+ be-V. + depressed with + N. 某人因為某事感到沮喪

   S（物）+ be-V. + depressing... 某事物令人沮喪

   E.g. Henry seems depressed with his parents because they don't care for him at all.
   Henry 似乎對他的父母感到失望因為他們一點也不在乎他。

E.g. It is depressing that Henry's parents don't care for him at all.

令人沮喪的是，Henry 的父母一點也不在乎他。

8. motion (n.) 移動

E.g. Every motion in his great soul was entirely reflected in his face and form.

他心裡所想到的動作完全反映在他的臉上及外表。

9. mental (adj.) 精神的 = psychological

E.g. Mental illness is usually the hardest one to get cured.

精神疾病通然是最困難治癒的。

10. bizarrely (adv.) 怪異地 / bizarre (adj.)

E.g. If you just arrive in a bizarre place, try to keep calm so that people there would not regard you a fool and try to steal things from you.

如果你到了一個很怪異的地方，試著保持冷靜，那麼那邊的人就不會認為你是傻子或是想偷你的東西。

11. argument (n.) 論點 / argue (v.) 爭論

E.g. It is nice to provide the audience in the conference with your precious argument, which can lead to people's thinking and discussing.

在這場會議中提供給觀眾你的寶貴論點是很棒的，可以引導人們思考和討論。

The Idioms you need to know:

1. be in a good/bad mood 心情好 / 不好

E.g. Laura was in a bad mood because her boyfriend, D, fought with her without reasons.

Laura 心情很差，因為她男朋友 D 在沒有原因的情況下跟她吵架。

2. get up on the wrong side of the bed 起床下錯邊（比喻：心情不好）

E.g. The manager looked like getting up on the wrong side of the bed this morning. Please be careful that don't annoy him today.

經理今天早上看起來心情不怎麼好。請小心不要去惹他。

3. have an influence/impact/effect on... 對 ...... 有影響

E.g. Will's in-depth speech had a great influence on my way of thinking.

Will 有深度的演場對我的思考方式有很大的影響。

Unit 9：A Meeting Schedule 演講活動

Welcome, doctors, nurses, clinical scientists and other health care workers. King's College Hospital NHS Foundation Trust is pleased to have you join us at our annual conference. This year we are focusing on making the children of our nation stronger and healthier. We are dedicating the day to discussing the issues around healthcare for children and new medical devices that can be applied in children's illness on solutions to the problems.

Our nation's youth are in danger of ruining their health. It is our duty to discuss these problems and to come up with solutions to help solve this crisis. As healthcare workers, we see how children are becoming more and more unhealthy and we must put an end to it. We at King's College Hospital NHS Foundation Trust hope that as a team, we can all work together to help our nation.

The following is a schedule of events for your reference.

Schedule of Events
The 28th of June, 2017
Conference Room A
08.00　Breakfast and tea meeting
09.00　Opening speech, delivered by Ms Hannah Zhang, Chief of Nutrition and Pharmacy in the University of Southampton
09.40　Break Time
Conference Room A
10.00　'Encouraging Young People to Exercise' by Dr Emma Davis, Head of Children's Medicine at the National Medical Center
Conference Room B
10.00　'Myopia' by Dr Poulami Chaudhuri, Chief of the International Vision Project, Hyderabad, India
Conference Room C
10.00　'Development of a Model for the Determination of Replacement Priority for Medical Devices towards Youth's Controlling Diabetes' by Dr Michael Peter Ayers, Head of the Department of Medical Equipment Management, King's College Hospital, London, Great Britain
Conference Room A
12.00　Lunch
Schedule continued on next page

Questions:

1. Who will attend the conference?

    (A) People who work with children
    (B) Sick children and their parents
    (C) Young people with vision problems
    (D) The head of the hospital

2. Where will the speech about youth's diabetes take place?

    (A) In the emergency room
    (B) In conference room A
    (C) In conference room B
    (D) In Conference room C

3. What will Dr Poulami Chaudhuri talk about?

    (A) She will speak after lunch.
    (B) Eye problems in young people
    (C) Diabetes in young people
    (D) Getting children to exercise

4. The purpose of the conference is to _____ .

    (A) meet other doctors and scientists
    (B) get more money for a special hospital
    (C) eventually help the health of children
    (D) eat lunch with famous doctors

5. Which speech isn't being given by a doctor?

    (A) The one on diabetes
    (B) The one about vision problems
    (C) The opening one
    (D) The speech about exercising

Answers:　　1. A　2. D　3. B　4. C　4. C

翻譯

歡迎醫師、護理師、臨床科學家還有其他護理工作者的到來。國民保健署基金信託國王學院醫院很高興有你們的參與我們年度會議。今年我們將目標設定在讓我們國家的

孩童越來越健壯。我們將在這天著重於探討孩童健康議題還有應用在解決孩童們疾病的新醫療器材。

我們國家的年輕人目前面臨到健康危機。討論這些問題並想方設法來解決這個危機是我們的職責。作為健康護理工作者，我們看到孩童們越來越不健康，所以我們必須杜絕這個狀況。在這裡，國民健康署基金信託國王學院醫院希望作為一個團隊，我們可以一起努力來幫助我們國家。

以下提供您參考的會議時間表。

議程時間

2017 年 6 月 28 日

A 會議廳

08.00　早餐點心餐敘

09.00　開幕演講，由南安普敦大學營養與醫療主席張漢娜女士主講

09.40　休息時間

A 會議廳

10.00　「鼓勵年輕人運動」，由國家醫學中心兒童醫療主任艾瑪達衛斯博士主講。

B 會議室

10.00　「近視問題」，由印度海得拉巴國際視力專案主席波納密丘杜利博士主講。

C 會議室

10.00　「控制青少年糖尿病的醫療器材替換優先權決策發展」，由英國倫敦國王學院醫院醫療器材管理科主任邁可彼得艾爾斯博士主講。

A 會議室

12.00 午餐餐敘

議程表接續下一頁

問題

1. 誰可以參與這個會議？

　　(A) 跟孩童工作相關的工作人員。

　　(B) 生病的孩童還有他們的家長。

　　(C) 有視力問題的人。

　　(D) 醫院的主席。

Ann's notes

這個研討會一開始就以「Welcome, doctors, nurses, clinical scientists and other health care workers.」開頭，說明了此次與會人士是哪些人。

2. 有關青少年糖尿病的演講在哪裡舉行？

(A) 急診室。

(B) A 會議室。

(C) B 會議室。

(D) C 會議室。

Ann's notes

根據「Development of a Model for the Determination of Replacement Priority for Medical Devices towards Youth's Controlling Diabetes」關鍵字「Diabetes」可以得知答案是 (D) C 會議室。

3. 波納密丘杜利博士的演講將探討什麼？

(A) 他將在午餐之後演講。

(B) 年輕人的視力問題。

(C) 年輕人糖尿病。

(D) 鼓勵孩童運動。

Ann's notes

根　據「'Myopia' by Dr Poulami Chaudhuri, Chief of the International Vision Project, Hyderabad, India」可以得知 Dr Poulami Chaudhuri 演講內容是「Myopia」近視，如果不知道這字的意思，可以從 Dr Poulami Chaudhri 的職稱得知她是國際視力專案主席得知，她的演講與視力有關。

4. 這個會議的主旨是 _____。

(A) 認識其他醫生還有科學家。

(B) 為一間特殊醫院募得更多錢。

(C) 最後可以幫助孩童的健康問題。

(D) 跟有名的醫生博士吃午餐。

Ann's notes

根據議程表上方的最後一段話「We at King's College Hospital NHS Foundation Trust hope that as a team, we can all work together to help our nation.」清楚知道這個會議希望可以幫助孩童的健康問題。

5. 下列哪一個演講不是由博士所主講？

(A) 糖尿病演講。

(B) 視力問題演講。

(C) 開幕演講。

(D) 運動相關演講。

Ann's notes

根據議程表上早上九點時間「Opening speech, delivered by Ms Hannah Zhang, Chief of Nutrition and Pharmacy in the University of Southampton」開幕演講部分是由張漢娜女士主持的。

The words you need to know:

1. pleased (adj.) 高興的

   be pleased to V. 樂於 = be glad to V.

   E.g. I am pleased to deliver a speech to you.

   　　我很高興可以跟你分享這個演講。

2. conference (n.) 會議

   E.g. They frequently hold conferences at that hotel.

   　　他們常在那家飯店舉辦會議。

3. focus (v.) (n.) 焦點 / 注意

   focus on... = aim at... = concentrate on... 專注於 ......

   E.g. I tried to focus on the lecture but in the end I fell asleep.

   　　我試著專注上課，但最後我還是睡著了。

4. dedicate (v.) 奉獻

   E.g. The new president said she would dedicate herself to protecting the rights of the sick and the homeless.

   新任總統説她將致力於保護老人、病人和無家可歸者的權利。

5. issue (n.) 議題

   E.g. It is a management issue as well as a technology issue.

   這既是一個技術問題，也是一個管理問題。

6. solution (n.) 解答（與 to 並用）

   E.g. There's no easy solution to this problem.

   這個問題沒有容易的解決辦法。

7. ruin (v.) 破壞

   E.g. Cheap imported goods are ruining many businesses.

   廉價的進口商品使　多公司正走向破　。

8. crisis (n.) 危機（單數）；crises (n.) 複數

   E.g. Food crisis, energy crisis, the financial crisis are besetting the world.

   糧食危機、能源危機、金融危機困擾著當前世界。

9. event (n.) 大事 / 活動

   E.g. This year's Olympic Games will be the biggest ever sporting event.

   今年的奧林匹克運動會將是歷史上規模最大的體育盛事。

10. encourage (v.) 鼓勵

    E.g. My parents have always encouraged me in everything I've wanted to do.

    不論我想做什麼，我爸媽總是會鼓勵我。

11. eventually (adv.) 終究

    E.g. I really hope that you can turn the corner and make it eventually.

    我真心希望你能克服難關，並最終取得成功。

常見的醫學單字：

myopia (n.) 近視 vision (n.) 視力 diabetes (n.) 糖尿病 insomnia (n.) 失眠

fever (n.) 發燒   fatigue (n.) 疲倦 faint (n.) 頭暈 anxiety (n.) 焦慮

diarrhea (n.) 腹瀉 heat stroke (n.) 中暑 symptom (n.) 症狀 cancer (n.) 癌症

The idioms you need to learn:

1. focus on 專注

   E.g. Tonight's programme focuses on the way that homelessness affects the young.
   今晚的節目著重討論無家可歸的現象如何影響年輕一代。

2. dedicate A to B 將 A 奉獻給 B

   E.g. I'd like to dedicate this book to Simon, without whose help this book wouldn't have been printed out.
   我想要把這本書送給 Simon，如果沒有他的幫忙，這本書不會出版。

3. work on... 研究

   E.g. We spent about half a day working on the problem, but unfortunately we couldn't come up with any idea.
   我們花了半天的時間解決這個問題，但很遺憾的是，我們沒能想出任何方法。

4. come up with... = think up 想出 ......

   E.g. Finally, he came up with the solution to the tough problem.
   最後，他想出這個擾人問題的解決之道。

5. put an end to... 終止 ......

   E.g. Let's do something to put an end to the dispute.
   讓我們終止這個爭論吧！

Let's have fun doing the Crosswords!!

Across

2.　making efforts (4,2)

4.　thinking of an idea (4,2,4)

5.　destroying something completely (4)

6.　pay attention to something (5,2)

7.　making someone more likely to do things (9)

8.　at last (10)

9.　special activity (5)

Down

1.　the answer to a problem (8)

3.　confusion or suffering (6)

4.　a meeting (10)

★答案就在上一篇的 words and idioms you need to know 喔！加油！

Stay hungry, stay foolish. / Steve Jobs

求知若飢，虛心若愚。(賈伯斯)

Unit 10：An Invitation Letter 邀請函

Flat 39,

Carmel House,

1 Church Road,

London,

SW16 8HQ

1st July 2017

To whom it may concern,

Regarding Vicky Zhang,

I am writing to confirm that Vicky Zhang is my friend and that I have invited her to visit me in London from 01/07/2017. The purpose of her visit is for a holiday and to attend several writing workshops. I enclose an email from the British Library confirming payment for one such workshop.

I am currently working full-time as a Clinical Scientist at King's College Hospital. I enclose a recent payslip confirming both my employment in this capacity and my salary of £3,500/month. I will be fully supporting Vicky during her stay in the UK.

I can confirm that Vicky will be staying with me in my flat during her visit. The flat is owned by myself. I enclose a recent gas statement as evidence that I live at the address provided above.

I have enclosed the following evidence:

1. Copy of my British passport

2. Email confirming payment for a course at the British Library

3. Copy of payslip as evidence of employment and ability to fully support Vicky during her visit

4. Copy of gas bill as evidence of living at stated address

Yours faithfully,

Dr Richard Heirs

1. According to the letter, what is it about?

   (A) Ms Zhang is going to attend a conference.

   (B) Ms Zhang is going to read books at the British Library.

   (C) It is an invitation letter for proving support for Ms Zhang's visit to the UK.

   (D) Dr Richard Heirs will go for holidays in the UK.

2. Who is the letter addressed to?

   (A) The waiters and waitresses in the restaurant

   (B) The people who work in the department stores

   (C) Customs officers at the airport

   (D) Doctors at King's College Hospital London

3. Which of the following is not provided with the letter?

   (A) A real copy of a British passport

   (B) An email confirming a course at the British Library

   (C) A copy of gas bill

   (D) Evidence of employment

Answers:　1. C　2. C　3. A

翻譯

39 號

卡麥爾莊園

教堂一路

倫敦 (郵遞區號 SW16 8HQ)

2017/07/01

敬啟者

關於張維琪的來訪

我寫這封信是為了確認張維琪小姐是我的朋友，我邀請她 2017 年 7 月 1 日來倫敦度假。此次她旅行目的是度假還有參加幾個寫作研討會。隨信附上大英圖書館研討會的費用單據。

我目前在倫敦國王學院醫院為全職的臨床科學家。隨信附上我最近的薪資單確認我的薪資能力與月收入為 3,500 英鎊。我將全力支持維琪在英國停留的費用。

我確認維琪在她停留英國期間會住在我的公寓。這個公寓是由我本人持有。隨信附上瓦斯收費單據作為我住在以上所提供的地址的證據。

附上以下單據：

1. 我的英國護照影本

2. 大英圖書館的研討會已付費電子信件

3. 支持維琪停留期間的工作薪資單與薪資能力影本

4. 以上所列的地址瓦斯費用單據影本

謹上

理查艾爾斯博士

問題

1. 根據這封信，這封信是有關什麼？

    (A) 張小姐將參加一個會議。

    (B) 張小姐將在大英圖書館閱讀書籍。

    (C) 這是一封邀請函提供支持張小姐在英國停留期間的證明。

    (D) 理察艾爾斯博士將前往英國度假。

Ann's notes

信中內容的第一句話「I am writing to confirm that Vicky Zhang is my friend and I have invited her to visit me in London from 01/07/2017.」很清楚表明是一封邀請函。

2. 這封信是寫給誰？

    (A) 餐廳的服務生們。

    (B) 在百貨公司工作的人。

    (C) 機場的海關人員。

    (D) 倫敦國王學院醫院的博士們。

Ann's notes

依據內容（有關到英國參與研討會跟度假），因此這封信是要給機場入境時給海關人員查看的。

3. 下列何者是這封信沒有提供的資訊？

    (A) 英國護照正本

    (B) 大英圖書館的課程確認信

    (C) 瓦斯費用單據影本

    (D) 工作證明

Ann's notes

依據信的內容所提供的項目是「Copy of my British passport」英國護照影本而非「A real copy of a British passport」英國護照正本。

The words you need to know:

1. concern (n.) (v.) 關心 / 顧慮 / 涉及

   E.g. The documentary concerns a woman who goes to China as a missionary.
   這部紀錄片講述的是一位去中國傳教的女子的故事。

2. confirm (v.) 確認 / 肯定

   E.g. Flights should be confirmed 48 hours before departure.
   應該在起飛前 48 小時確認航班。

3. purpose (n.) 目的 / 企圖 [on purpose 故意地]

   E.g. The purpose of a trap is to catch and hold animals.
   陷阱是用來捕捉野獸的。

4. enclose (v.)（隨信）附上；包圍

   E.g. Please enclose a curriculum vitae (CV) with your application.
   請在求職信中附上一份簡歷。

5. workshop (n.) 研討會；車房 / 工作坊

   E.g. Ann likes to attend different workshops to learn knowledge.
   Ann 喜歡參加一些研討會學習知識。

6. payslip (n.) 薪資單

   E.g. You need to provide the bank with your payslip if you want to apply for a credit card.
   如果你想申請一張信用卡的話，你需要提供銀行你的薪資單。

Knowledge will give you power, but character respect. / Bruce Lee
知識給你力量，品格給你別人的尊敬。(李小龍)

Unit 11：Paddington 柏靈頓熊

Paddington Bear is a fictional and famous character in children's literature. He first appeared on the 13rd of October 1958 and has been featured in more than twenty books written by English author Michael Bond and illustrated by Peggy Fortnum and other artists. The friendly bear from deepest and darkest Peru—with his old hat, battered suitcase, duffel coat and love of marmalade—has become a classic character from English children's literature. Michael Bond created Paddington books, which have translated into 30 languages across 70 titles and sold more than 30 million copies worldwide. The story is also adapted into two films, Paddington and Paddington 2.

Paddington is a human-like and spectacled bear. He is always polite – addressing people as "Mr", "Mrs" and "Miss", barely by first names – and kindhearted, though he imposes hard stares on those who offer his disapproval. He has an endless capacity for innocently getting into troubles, but he is known to 'try so hard to get things right'. He was discovered in Paddington Station, London, by the Brown family who firstly rejected to offer him a home but at last adopted him, and thereby he was given his full name as "Paddington Brown". He has typical British habits, like decent greetings, enjoying tea and talking about the weather. For example, he says 'nice weather for the ducks' when the weather is so bad. He enjoys it. Besides, there are some interesting traditional British sayings like 'use the facilities' or 'freshen up', meaning going to the toilet or bathroom especially after a long journey.

In addition to being polite, however, seldom does he have bad emotion. He sometimes gives a 'hard stare' when no one tries to listen to him. He's such an impressive bear in the fictional world. In June 2016, Vivendi's StudioCanal owns Paddington Bear and its copyright and trademark across the world. Bond continued to own the publishing rights to his series. However, it is sad that Bond passed away on the 27th of June 2017. After all, he is one of the important children's literature authors, giving both children and adult pleasure on reading.

Questions:

1. What is a key point of this text?

    (A) Paddington Bear is a real bear from Peru, shipped to the UK.

    (B) Paddington Bear is a renowned British children's literature written by Michael Bond.

    (C) Paddington is a story illustrating the busy station in Paddington.

    (D) Paddington likes to be polite by addressing people's first names.

2. What does 'human-like' refer to in Paddington?

(A) Paddington is a real person.
(B) Paddington likes humans.
(C) Paddington acts like a human.
(D) Paddington is created by humans.

3. Which of the following is not the feature of Paddington?

(A) Paddington is a polite bear and has great love of marmalade.
(B) Paddington is a real story, which is adapted by Michael Bond.
(C) Paddington has typical British culture and character.
(D) Paddington offers reading pleasure and fun to many children and adults.

Answers: 1. B   2. C   3. B

翻譯

柏靈頓熊是兒童文學中一個虛構的著名角色。他首次出現於 1958 年的 10 月 13 日，出自英國作家邁可龐德筆下撰寫的二十多本書籍，以及佩姬福南還有其他的藝術家的共同繪畫。這隻友善的熊來自於又深又黑的秘魯，帶著他的舊帽子、破舊的手提箱，厚尼大外套還有對柑橘醬的愛好，成為英國兒童文學中的經典著名的角色。邁可龐德創作柏靈頓熊的書籍，在全世界已經被翻譯成三十多種語言與七十個書名，賣超過三千萬本書。目前也已經改編拍成兩部電影，「熊愛趴趴走」與「柏靈頓熊熊出任務」。

柏靈頓是一隻像人類且特別的熊。他總是有禮貌地稱呼人「先生」「太太」還有「小姐」，很少直接稱呼別人的名字，而且心地善良，雖然有時候他會怒瞪那不認同他的人。他不停的大意犯錯，但大家都知道他一直「盡力把事情做好」。他在倫敦的柏靈頓火車站被伯朗一家人發現，他們剛開始拒絕給他一個家但最後收養他，還因此給他一個全名「柏靈頓伯朗」。他有著典型的英國人習慣，像是禮貌跟人打招呼、喜歡喝茶、聊聊天氣。例如，他會在天氣糟的要命的時候依然說著「天氣真好」。除此之外，還有一些有趣的傳統英國說法，例如「使用設備」或是「盥洗」，都是代表著去上廁所或是使用浴室，特別是在長途旅行之後。

然而，除了有禮貌之外，他幾乎不會有心情不好的時候。當沒有人聽他說話時，他有時會給個「凶狠的眼神」。他在虛擬世界裡是一個那麼令人印象深刻的熊。2016 年六月，Vivendi's Studio Canal 擁有全世界柏靈頓熊的智慧財產權還有註冊商標權。龐德依然繼續出版他寫的系列。然而，令人遺憾的是，龐德在 2017 年 6 月 27 日過世。畢竟，他是重要兒童文學中作家的其中一位，同時帶給小孩與大人在閱讀上的樂趣。

· 閱 · 讀 · 練 · 習 ·

問題

1. 本文主旨為何？

 (A) 柏靈頓熊是一個來自於秘魯的真熊，被運送到英國。

 (B) 柏靈頓熊是由邁可龐德所寫的知名英國兒童文學。

 (C) 柏靈頓是一個書寫在柏靈頓繁忙車站的故事。

 (D) 柏靈頓喜歡禮貌地稱呼別人名字。

Ann's notes

根據第一段第二句「He first appeared on the 13rd of October 1958 and has been featured in more than twenty books written by English author Michael Bond and illustrated by Peggy Fortnum and other artists.」可以得知柏靈頓熊是由邁可龐德所寫的知名英國兒童文學故事。

2. 「像人類般」在柏靈頓熊裡面是指什麼？

 (A) 柏靈頓是一個真人。

 (B) 柏靈頓喜歡人類。

 (C) 柏靈頓表現得很像人類。

 (D) 柏靈頓是由人類創造的。

Ann's notes

「human-like」指的是「像人類一般」的意思，可以從「human-like」後面的句子「He is always polite – addressing people as "Mr", "Mrs" and "Miss", barely by first names – and kindhearted, though he imposes hard stares on those who offer his disapproval.」得知這隻熊會做一些人類做的事情，例如有禮貌跟人打招呼或是心地善良，或是生氣也有情緒。

3. 下列何者不是柏靈頓的特色？

 (A) 柏靈頓是一隻有禮貌的熊而且非常喜歡柑橘醬。

 (B) 柏靈頓是一個真實的故事，由邁可龐德所改編的故事。

 (C) 柏靈頓有著典型的英國文化跟特質。

 (D) 柏靈頓帶給很多兒童與大人閱讀的樂趣。

Ann's notes

根據文章內容答案 A, C, D 為正確選項，而 B 選項的答案在「Paddington Bear is a fictional and famous character in children's literature.」和「He's such an impressive bear in the fictional world.」可以得知這是一個虛擬的故事，非改編故事，是由邁可龐德所創作的兒童文學故事。

Background knowledge:

Paddington Bear 柏靈頓熊，是英國兒童文學中的一個虛構角色。他第一次出現是在 1958 年，Michael Bond 麥可·邦所寫的書是以柏靈頓為主角，由 Peggy Fortnum 佩姬·佛特南繪製的柏靈頓熊圖像獲得獨家銷售權。圖畫中的柏靈頓熊比較像是一隻泰迪熊，也就是小熊維尼的原型，而非是一隻真正的熊。柏靈頓熊的靈感來自於邦德與妻子在聖誕節期間在一家店內所看到的泰迪熊，因為那隻泰迪熊是貨架上最後一隻小熊，他們覺得它會感到孤獨因此把它買了回家。

柏靈頓熊是一隻擬人化的熊，說英語，總是戴著一頂舊帽子，無論到哪裡都帶著一個裝有他私人物品的舊皮箱（後來打開才知道裡面有一個秘密隔間，柏靈頓熊在內放置一些他認為最重要的東西，例如：他的護照）。在初創及較早的版本中，他穿著一件厚呢風衣，及一雙威靈頓長統靴。他總是有禮貌地以「先生」、「女士」或「小姐」來稱呼他人，很少直接用名字。他也總是心懷善意（雖然他會瞪他不同意的人），喜歡柑橘醬三明治及可可，雖然大家知道他「非常努力想把每件事情做對」，但是他卻不斷惹出許多麻煩。在倫敦柏靈頓車站可以見到他可愛的身影，而作者於 2017 年 6 月 27 日過世，很多人到柏靈頓車站來紀念他，感謝 Michael Bond 創造了 Paddington，為大家的生活增添不少兒時回憶與閱讀之樂。

（照片拍攝於英國倫敦 Paddington Station）

The words you need to know:

1. feature (v.) 特寫 / 放映；(n.) 特色

   E.g. Paddington Bear has many attractive features, such as good manners and cute looking.

   柏靈頓熊有很多吸引人的特色，例如有禮貌還有可愛的外表。

2. battered (adj.) 破舊的

   E.g. He put on his battered trousers to show his special life style.

   他穿著破舊的褲子來顯示他特別的生活風格。

3. translate (v.) 翻譯

   E.g. Jenny works for the UN, translating from English into French.

   Jenny 在歐盟工作，擔任英譯法翻譯。

4. address (v.) 稱呼 / 演講；(n.) 地址

   E.g. He likes to be addressed as "Sir" or "Mr Brown".

   他喜歡被稱為「先生」或「伯朗先生」。

5. disapproval (n.) 反對 / 不贊成

   E.g. After two hours of discussion, they are still in disapproval of the topic of their science project and feel hard to make a decision.

   討論兩個小時後，他們依然無法贊同他們的科學報告標題，覺得很難做決定。

6. capacity (n.) 容量 / 才能 / 能力

   E.g. Annie has a great capacity for hard work.

   Annie 特別能吃苦耐勞。

7. adopt (v.) 收養 / 採納；adapt (v.) 適應 / 改編

   E.g. They have no children of their own, but they're hoping to adopt.

   他們沒有親生子女，但是他們希望能領養。

8. adapt (v.) 適應 / 改編

   E.g. The play had been adapted for children.

   這個劇本已被改編成兒童劇。

8. facility (n.) 設施

   E.g. British people sometimes have this expression 'using the facilities' which means to go to the toilet.

   英國人有時候用「使用設備」這個説法表示使用廁所。

9. freshen up (v.) 梳洗 / 使清潔

   E.g. She opened a window to freshen up the room.

   她打開一扇窗戶給屋裡換換空氣。

10. publish (v.) 出版 / punish (v.) 處罰

   E.g. She was only 19 when her first novel was published.

   她的第一部小説出版時她年僅 19 歲。

Unit 12：Pasty in Cornwall 康沃爾餡餅

Cornwall is the most westly part of Great Britain. The pasty is not only a traditional food of the UK but it is also the national symbol of Cornwall. Pasty myths and legends are all around. Nobody can quite pinpoint when pasties were originated, but there is a letter in existence from a baker to Henry VIII's Jane Seymour, saying that hopefully this pasty reaches the guests in better condition than the last one.

Before the eighteenth century, pasty is offered to the rich. In the eighteenth and nineteenth centuries, pasty is convenient for labours to bring up their families on a diet of vegetable baked in barley dough in the ashes of the fire. A West Briton report in 1867 shows the subsistence in the pasty is what the miners lived for and reveals their great dependence on flour. Many of these early writers expressed surprise that both children and adults looked reasonably well nourished rather looked like what they considered a very poor diet. Then, as now, the pasty had its detractors, but as a complete meal in itself it found a place in the hearts and stomachs of the Cornish who are proud to claim firmly that the pasty 'belongs' to them.

Over the centuries pasties played an important roll in the diet of the Cornish. However fishermen never took them to sea because they assumed it's bad luck to take a pasty on board. When fishermen set sail, they left their pasties ashore. Miners would leave a little piece of pastry for the spirits in the mine, which would lead them to a road back home. It is said that the Devil stays out of Cornwall because he's afraid of being baked in one.

Nowadays pasties are an important part of the Cornish economy. Tourism, here, is big business and nearly all visitors want to sample the iconic dish. Many tourists find their way to Ann's Pasties as they have been told they offer the most delicious pasties in Cornwall. If you have a chance to visit Cornwall, never forget to explore and taste the real Cornish pasty.

Questions:

1. What is a pasty?

    (A) It is a national landmark in Cornwall.

    (B) It is a poor diet in Cornwall.

    (C) A pasty is a traditional food and has many myths and legendary stories.

    (D) It was created to honour Henry VIII

2. Detractors refer to _____.

    (A) shareholders

    (B) critics

    (C) rumors

    (D) writers

3. Which of the following is not correct?

    (A) Pasties played an important part in the diet of the Cornish over centuries.

    (B) Pasties are one of main parts of the Cornish economy.

    (C) Ann's Pasties attracts many visitors.

    (D) Fishermen never went to sea without pasties.

Answers:　　1. C　2. B　3. D

翻譯

康沃爾是大英國協最西邊的區域。餡餅不僅是英國的傳統食物也是康沃爾的地域象徵。餡餅的神話跟傳說一直都存在著。沒有人可以真正指出餡餅是出自何處，但現存一封來自於亨利八世的皇后珍希穆爾寫給烘焙師的信，信寫著希望這次的餡餅跟上一次的比起來，能以更好的狀態送到客人手中。

十八世紀以前，餡餅是給有錢人吃的食物。在十八跟十九世紀時，用火爐烘烤麵粉裹上蔬菜的餡餅對勞工來說，方便攜帶給家人食用。1867 年的西頓日報表示餡餅就是礦工工人賴以維生的東西，也透露他們對於麵粉有絕對的依賴。很多早期的作家表示驚訝，因為孩童跟大人們看起來都得到合理的營養，而並非像外表所見，被認為非常糟糕的食物。到現在，餡餅有許多惡意的批評者，但在康沃爾人的心中及胃裡，餡餅被視為完整的一餐，可以驕傲地向別人宣稱這是「屬於」他們的餡餅。

在過去幾世紀以來，餡餅在康沃爾人的飲食中扮演一個重要的角色。然而，漁夫從來不會帶著餡餅出海，因為他們認為帶著餡餅出海是厄運的代表。當漁夫出海的時候，他們只會把餡餅放在岸邊。礦工工人會帶著一些餡餅作為他們的精神代表，因為這會引領他們回家的道路。據說，魔鬼會待在康沃爾外面，因為他害怕自己會被烤成餡餅。

如今，餡餅是康沃爾經濟的重要部分。這裡的觀光是一個重要的生意，大部分所有的遊客們想來這裡嘗試這個象徵性的食物。許多旅客找到「Ann's Pasties」這家店，因為遊客們聽說這裡提供康沃爾最美味的餡餅。如果你有機會來到康沃爾，絕對別忘了探索與品嚐康沃爾的餡餅。

問題

1. 餡餅是什麼？

   (A) 它是康沃爾的國家地表。

   (B) 它是康沃爾缺乏營養的飲食。

   (C) 餡餅是一種傳統食物，而且有著許多神話跟傳奇故事。

   (D) 它用來榮耀亨利八世。

Ann's notes

> 文章第一段「The pasty is not only a traditional food of the UK but it is also the national symbol of Cornwall. Pasty myths and legends are all around.」說明了康沃爾的餡餅是傳統英國美食，同時也有許多神話傳奇故事。

2.「Detractor」（惡意批評者）代表著 _____。

    (A) 股東。

    (B) 評論者。

    (C) 謠言。

    (D) 作家。

Ann's notes

根據文章內容「the pasty had its detractors, but as a complete meal in itself it found a place in the hearts and stomachs of the Cornish who are proud to claim firmly that the pasty 'belongs' to them.」在「detractors」後面的說明，可以知道不管別人說什麼，康沃爾人很堅定地說明這是屬於他們的東西，由此可以猜測這個字跟「評論或是惡意相向」有關（如果不知道這個字的意思情況下）。

3. 下列何者敘述不正確？

    (A) 幾世紀以來餡餅在康沃爾飲食中扮演一個重要的角色。

    (B) 餡餅是康沃爾經濟主要來源之一。

    (C)「安妮餡餅」(Ann's Pasties) 吸引很多遊客。

    (D) 漁夫沒有餡餅就不出海。

Ann's notes

根據文章內容「Fishermen never took them to sea because they assumed it's bad luck to take a pasty on board.」可以得知因為漁夫認為餡餅是一種厄運的象徵，所以他們不帶餡餅出海，即便這是他們賴以為生的食物。

Background knowledge:

餡餅（康沃爾語：Pasti, 英語：Cornish pasty）是與英國康沃爾有關的傳統烤製肉餡餅。圓形酥皮上包入生肉和蔬菜做的餡料，對折起來做成半圓形餃子狀，餅皮邊緣打摺封好後烘烤。

傳統的康沃爾肉餡餅餡料有：牛肉、馬鈴薯絲或馬鈴薯塊、蕪菁甘藍（也叫黃蕪菁或 "rutabaga"，在康沃爾地區稱作蕪菁）和洋蔥，以鹽和胡椒調味後烤製。至今，已經成為以康沃爾命名的一道名菜，也是公認的國民食物。餡餅有各種餡料，一些店鋪也以販賣多種口味的餡餅聞名。

儘管有很多古文件和小說都有相關紀錄，但起源仍然不明。到各地採礦的康沃爾的礦工們，讓這道菜成為全球知名的菜餚，而在澳洲、美國、阿根廷、墨西哥、阿爾斯特等，各地都有變化版的康沃爾肉餡餅。

Ann 在英國期間曾經到訪 Cornwall 康沃爾郡，這個傳統食物在英國的超市或是商店很常見，不過我覺得真正好吃的 pasty 真的是在 Cornwall，而且 Cornwall 的「Ann's Pasties」賣的 pasty 真的特別美味！英國朋友們都笑說，這一定是我來投資的店！有機會前往英國旅遊的人，可以考慮英國西南部的 Cornwall（康沃爾郡），體驗一下英國冷得要命的海還有傳統美食。

The words you need to know:

1. traditional (adj.) 傳統的

    E.g. The school uses a combination of modern and traditional methods for teaching reading.

    該校採用傳統與現代方式相結合的方法教授閱讀。

2. myth (n.) 神話故事；mythology (n. uncountable) 神話總集

    E.g. The children enjoyed the stories about the gods and goddesses of Greek and Roman myth.

    那些孩子都喜歡聽希臘、羅馬神話中諸神的故事。

3. legend (n.) 傳奇

E.g. Ann is writing a thesis on Taiwanese legend and mythology.
Ann 正在寫一篇關於台灣民間故事和神話的論文。

4. condition (n.) 條件 / 狀況

E.g. The hospital say her condition is improving slowly.
醫院說她的健康狀況正在慢慢好轉。

5. labour (n.) 勞工 / 勞力 / 努力 [英式英文]；labor [美式英文]

E.g. Retirement is the time to enjoy the fruits of your labours.
退休就是享受辛勤工作成果的時候。

6. subsistence (n.) 生存 / 賴以維生的東西

E.g. The family was living at subsistence level.
這家人過著勉強餬口的生活。

7. mine (n.) 礦地；miner (n.) 礦工

E.g. My grandfather used to work in the mines.
我祖父以前在礦井裡工作。

8. detractor (n.) 惡意批評者 / 誹謗者

E.g. The parties' detractors claim that his fierce temper makes him unsuitable for leadership.
這個政黨批評者聲稱他脾氣暴躁，不適合做政黨領導。

9. tourism (n.) 旅遊 / 觀光

E.g. Tourism is Paris' main industry.
旅遊業是巴黎的主要產業。

10. sample (v.) 品嚐 / 抽樣；(n.) 樣本 / 試用品

E.g. As the pasty looked so good, Ann decided to sample some from Ann's Pasties.
餡餅看起來很誘人，於是 Ann 決定嚐嚐「安妮餡餅」。

11. explore (v.) 探索

E.g. The children have gone exploring in the woods.
孩子們去樹林裡觀察大自然了

Reading Module 1
閱讀模擬測驗

本測驗分三部分，全為四選一之選擇題，共 40 題，作答時間 45 分鐘。

Part 1：詞彙與結構

共 15 題，每題含一個空格。請由試題冊上的四個選項中選出最適合題意的字或詞作答。

1. My grandparents prefer to live in a(n) _____ little house rather than in a big mansion.

   (A) cozy   (B) cultural   (C) vivid   (D) accurate

2. The white doves are usually used to _____ peace. We can easily see them in some movies.

   (A) remove   (B) prevent   (C) represent   (D) thank

3. For a college graduate, renting a flat is more _____ than buying a house.

   (A) casual   (B) affordable   (C) experimental   (D) doubtful

4. The tainted oil will make a great _____ to our bodies.

   (A) chance   (B) solution   (C) key   (D) injury

5. To my mother's _____ , my dad forgot their wedding anniversary.

   (A) arrangement   (B) appointment   (C) disappointment   (D) surprise

6. This movie is _____ the haunted house.

   (A) concerned with   (B) weeded out   (C) pulled over   (D) turned into

7. It is impolite of you to _____ the speech.

    (A) label   (B) tug   (C) interrupt   (D) leak

8. The class was designed to help us_____ the beauty of classical music.

    (A) stuff   (B) appreciate   (C) offset   (D) repair

9. There are many_____to traveling, including releasing yourselves.

    (A) discounts   (B) decks   (C) canyons   (D) benefits

10. Happiness is subjective. Everyone has different _____ of it.

    (A) complaints   (B) definitions   (C) structures   (D) cycles

11. _____ a homeless dog is better than buying a puppy from a pet store.

    (A) Adopting   (B) Adopt   (C) Adopted   (D) To adopting

12. Smoking _____ our health, not to mention our lives.

    (A) threatens   (B) announces   (C) restricts   (D) reassures

13. I don't like Jenny. She is talkative and likes to _____ .

    (A) pause   (B) swear   (C) destroy   (D) gossip

14. My mother grows some lovely rose _____ in her garden.

    (A) flushes   (B) bushes   (C) territory   (D) trend

15. In her traveling book, the writer _____ the history of the cathedral.

    (A) fastens   (B) hug   (C) traces   (D) dip

Part 2：段落填空

共 10 題，包含二個段落，每個段落各含 5 個空格。請由試題冊上的四個選項中選出最適合題意的詞或詞作答。

Questions 16~20

Every day, a lot of people travel on the underground in and around London. The London underground is the oldest tube for 150 years over the world. The system is smooth and convenient, and rivals any other transit system in the world. Riding on the underground is now easier than __(16)__ before with the Oyster Card. The Oyster Card is fast replacing the old ticket system and is also find its place into the wallets and hearts of underground passengers everywhere.

Why you should __(17)__ from the stored-valued tickets to the Oyster Card is of one word—speed. All it takes is one quick swipe across the sensor at the turnstile. The card can even be read through leather, which saves you the __(18)__ of taking it out of your bag or wallet. __(19)__ , you can add money to it by using your ATM card. This is really great if you don't have any cash __(20)__ . There are sometimes a few bugs in the system, but Oyster Card makes it easier to experience the comfort of traveling in London.

16. (A) long   (B) once   (C) ever   (D) even

17. (A) commute   (B) switch   (C) refrain   (D) escape

18. (A) habit   (B) nerve   (C) trouble   (D) pain

19. (A) In addition   (B) Otherwise   (C) Instead   (D) As a result

20. (A) in person   (B) on hand   (C) before your eyes   (D) under control

Questions 21~25

Many Taiwanese and Chinese parents do not expect their children to do housework. They think that children should spend all their time __(21)__ , instead of doing house chores. However, in the Western thinking, children should be responsible for keeping a house neat and __(22)__ and share family things.

For one thing, doing house chores will prepare young people to assume the role of a good parent in the future. If you've never cleaned a house, how can you suddenly know how to do it? __(23)__ , some chores can be shared by more than one member of a household. For instance, when one person washes the dishes, another dries them., or when one __(24)__ the floor, another mops them. Finally, by doing regular housework, children can learn a sense of responsibility and a sense of __(25)__ . For the reasons above, it is highly suggested that even children should participate in keeping their home clean and in order.

21. (A) study   (B) be studied   (C) studying   (D) to study

22. (A) tiny   (B) tender   (C) tidy   (D) tame

23. (A) For some   (B) For others   (C) For the other   (D) For another

24. (A) sheds   (B) sweeps   (C) shaves   (D) drifts

25. (A) achievement   (B) punctuality   (C) guilt   (D) shame

Part 3：閱讀理解

共 15 題，包含數篇短文，每個短文後有 2~4 個相關問題。請由試題冊上四個選項中選出最適合者作答。

Question 26-27

Claiming Compensation for a Delayed Flight

Please read EU Airlines' Compensation Policy carefully to find out whether you are eligible for compensation and how you can claim it.

1. You can claim compensation for a delayed flight if you arrive at your final destination more than three hours after the scheduled time AND if issues within EU Airlines' control caused the delay.

   (A) Issues with our control include technical problems, plane component failure, and other mechanical issues that are related to the airplane, airport machinery, or EU Airlines' computer systems. For a full list of issues deemed within our control, check out more information below.

   (B) Issues NOT within our control include natural disasters, weather conditions, security issues, airport traffic congestion, and airline staff strikes. For a full list of issues deemed outside our control, check out more information below.

2. In the case of overnight delays, the airline will arrange for hotel rooms for passengers, in addition to transportation to and from the hotel. Passengers can also choose to return their home. In this case, all transportation costs will be met.

3. Passengers delayed by more than three hours as described above are entitled to cash payments of:

* € 215 for flights shorter than 1,500 kilometers.

* € 357 for flights between 1,500 and 3,500 kilometers.

* € 357 for flights loner than 3,500 kilometers if the delay is three to four hours.

* € 530 for flights longer than 3,500 kilometers if the delay is more than four hours.

26. What does EU Airlines say about paying compensation?

    (A) The airline promises to refund the whole price of flights delayed by three hours.

    (B) The airline will compensate people for all delays greater than four hours.

    (C) The airline will pay compensation if flights are delayed due to bad weather.

    (D) The airline will only pay compensation within its control.

27. What will EU Airlines do if passengers' flights are delayed overnight?

    (A) It will arrange new flights immediately if this situation occurs.

    (B) It will ask people to remain in the airport but compensate them for this.

    (C) It will arrange and pay for all necessary transportation and accommodation.

    (D) It will ask all passengers to return home until new flights are organized.

Questions 28~29

June 14, 2017

Dear Julia,

   I received your mail that you're going to visit the UK this month. If you would like, you can stay at my place for your journey. I'd also be more than happy to show you around Cornwall, the place I live in. We could start to arrange some plans going around Cornwall. If you would like to visit any place, please let me know so I can suggest some special attractions that many tourists may not know.

   There are plenty of things to do in Cornwall. First, I think we can visit Truro, which is a major city in Cornwall. We can visit the cathedral there and see the houses which are made of rock. It's quite special view. Secondly, after Truro, we can drive to Coverack and Lizard. Coverack is a lovely village and we can consider to for one night. Then, Lizard is the most south-westerly point of the British mainland and boasts its own unique landscape and stunning views. Besides, the most famous pasty in the UK is available in Ann's Pasties. We can give it a try. If we still have time, I highly suggest that we visit and St. Michael's Mount and St. Ives. Oh dear, now I have many ideas about places we can visit in Cornwall. Let met know what plan you are thinking about. Later I can give you more proper suggestions.

   I am looking forward to seeing you soon.

All the best,

Tamsin

28. When will Julia go to the UK?

    (A) July

    (B) June

    (C) The 14th of June

    (D) This month

29. What is NOT mentioned in Tamsin's letter?

    (A) They can go to Coverack staying for one night.

    (B) St. Michael's Mount and St. Ives are good options if they have time during their trip.

    (C) Lizard has the most famous boats around the UK.

    (D) Julia can stay at Tamsin's place during her stay in the UK.

Questions 30~33

There are many famous inventors who have come from the USA. However, Benjamin Franklin is probably one of the most famous American inventors. Although he was also a writer and a philosopher, Franklin is best remembered today for his many inventions.

Franklin invented a lot of useful things, often because he needed them. For example, Franklin wore glasses, but as he got older, he began to need another pair that worked better to read books. Because he got tired of using two sets of glasses, Franklin decided to invent one pair that would allow him to see clearly both things near and far. So, he cut two kinds of the lenses in half, and piece them together into one pair of glasses. These glasses are now known as bifocals.

Moreover, you may have heard the story of Franklin's famous kite flight, but it is not true that Franklin invented electricity. However, from this experience, Franklin gained the knowledge to invent the lightning rod, which is a device that protects buildings and ships from lightning.

Franklin also invented a special iron stove, which was called the Franklin stove. It allowed people to heat their homes less dangerously and with less wood than using traditional fireplaces. In addition, he even invented a simple machine to measure distances. As his town's postmaster, Franklin had to know how long the roads were, so he invented this tool to help him **keep track of** these distances.

Without a doubt, Benjamin Franklin invented many useful things, many of which are still used today. Though he had a success in politics, wrote several famous books, and was even put on the U.S. hundred-dollar bill, Franklin remains best known for his inventions.

30. The passage is mainly about _____.

    (A) Franklin as a well-known inventor

    (B) Franklin's comfortable life

    (C) Franklin's view on the United States

    (D) Franklin's struggle with difficulties

31. Which is true about the bifocals Franklin invented?

    (A) They had two different lenses in one pair of glasses.

    (B) They were mainly used to see far things clearly.

    (C) They were designed only for reading.

    (D) They were helpful in measuring distances.

32. According to the passage, which is NOT true about Franklin?

    (A) He used to work for the post office.

    (B) He invented electricity.

    (C) He invented the lightning rod.

    (D) He worked hard to improve his quality of life.

33. To **'keep track of'** something is similar in meaning to '_____'.

    (A) travel (B)   select (C)   know (D)   improve

Questions 34~37

When you were young, your parents and teachers taught you how to act properly. Most of the behavior is so natural to you that you can't imagine people behaving differently. However, each culture has its own set of expectations for how people behave. If you travel to another country, it is important that you learn that country's cultural practices so that your behavior won't be insulting to your hosts.

One cultural rule includes body language. In America, for example, you may hold your fist out with your thumb raised in the air as a way to say 'good job!' or 'I approve'. In other places, this gesture might not be acceptable.

If you go to an Arab country, you should be careful to keep your feet on the floor because it is extremely rude to point the bottoms of your feet at people. In Indonesia, you should never use your left hand to give something to someone because the left hand is considered unclean.

The use of eye contact varies greatly from culture to culture as well. In some places, such as the U.S., looking someone in the eye means that you are showing respect, paying attention, and that you are being open and honest. A student in the U.S. may get into trouble if he or she refuses to look the teacher in the eye when the teacher is talking to him or her. In other countries, lowering the eyes is the way to show respect. In parts of Africa, if a child meets the teacher's eyes, he or she may be punished for being disrespectful.

These examples show how simple movements could cause great conflict between people if they are unaware of the meanings of the behavior. If you visit another culture, be sure to learn some of that culture's norms to avoid conflict.

34. The word 'norms' in the last paragraph is closest in meaning to '_____'.

    (A) expressions   (B) gestures   (C) standards   (D) locals

35. According to the passage, who are more likely to be interested in this passage?

    (A) Travelers   (B) Chefs   (C) Farmers   (D) Principals

36. According to the passage, what will happen if an African child looks the teacher in the eye?

    (A) Be supported   (B) Be admired   (C) Be praised   (D) Be punished

37. According to the passage, which of the following is suggested by the author?

    (A) Always buy airline tickets one month earlier before your trip.
    (B) It's better to understand the meanings of gestures of the country you are going to visit.
    (C) Don't forget to carry your personal belongings with you during a trip.
    (D) Learn some basic phrases of the country you are planning to travel to.

Questions 38~40

Have you ever been to America? If so, you may have noticed some special things in American life. If you haven't, then maybe you should try to understand more about American culture just in case you visit the country one day. Here are some good things to remember.

When Americans see a friend or greet someone for the first time, they normally shake hands. It is polite to shake hands with both men and women. Make sure you give a firm handshake as this will show you are friendly and sincere.

Americans are very patriotic people. Independence Day on the fourth of July and Thanksgiving in November are what they call national celebrations. On these days, never start eating until everyone is seated and ready. Sometimes a person at the dinner table will say a short prayer before a meal to thank God for the food. This prayer is called 'grace'.

In America, equality is very important. If you talk about people being different or having to do different jobs or treat people unequally, you will be considered rude and old-fashioned. In America, men, women, and children are all expected to clean the house and do the cooking. In the kitchen, Americans are generally aware of the importance of recycling, so make sure you know about separating trash.

One last thing to keep in mind is tipping. When you catch a taxi or go to a restaurant, you must always leave a tip when you pay. A tip is an extra fifteen percent of the total on your bill. Waiters and taxi drivers need these tips because their regular pay is very low.

Most visitors find Americans very friendly. Make sure you visit their country one day and learn more about their culture.

38. According to the passage, in America, people greet each other by _____ .

    (A) having hugs   (B) kissing heeks   (C) eating dinner   (D) shaking ands

39. According to the passage, which is NOT polite to do in American culture?

    (A) Giving a firm handshake to both men and women.
    (B) Treating people unequally.
    (C) Not starting eating until everyone is seated on Thanksgiving.
    (D) Saying grace before eating.

40. What's the best title for this passage?

    (A) American Culture
    (B) Cultural Shock
    (C) Travel in America
    (D) Life in Different Cultures

Part 1：詞彙與結構

1. 我的祖父母比起住在大房子偏好住在溫暖的小房子。

   (A) 溫暖的　　　　(B) 文化的　　　　(C) 活躍的　　　　(D) 正確的

2. 白鴿通常用來代表和平。我們常常可以在電影中看到。

   (A) 移除　　　　(B) 避免　　　　(C) 代表　　　　(D) 感謝

3. 對一個大學畢業生來說，租一個公寓比起買房子較負擔得起。

   (A) 休閒的　　　　(B) 負擔得起　　　　(C) 實驗性的　　　　(D) 懷疑的

4. 那個有問題的油對我們的身體造成很大的傷害。

   (A) 機會　　　　(B) 解決　　　　(C) 關鍵　　　　(D) 傷害

5. 令我媽媽失望的是，爸爸忘記他們的結婚紀念日。

   (A) 安排　　　　(B) 預約　　　　(C) 失望　　　　(D) 驚訝

6. 這部電影有關於這棟鬧鬼的房子。

   (A) 有關於　　　　(B) 淘汰　　　　(C) 行駛道路旁　　　　(D) 變成

7. 你這樣打斷演講是不禮貌的。

   (A) 貼標籤　　　　(B) 猛拉 / 用力拉　　　　(C) 打斷 / 中斷　　　　(D) 洩漏

8. 這門課的設計是要幫助我們欣賞古典音樂之美。

   (A) 填塞　　　　(B) 欣賞　　　　(C) 補償 抵銷　　　　(D) 修理

9. 旅遊有許多好處，包括放鬆你們自己。

   (A) 折扣　　　　(B) 甲板　　　　(C) 峽谷　　　　(D) 好處 / 利益

10. 快樂是主觀的。人人都有不同的定義。

    (A) 抱怨　　　　(B) 定義　　　　(C) 結構　　　　(D) 循環

11. 領養流浪狗比到寵物店買狗來得好。

    答案選擇 (A)，以動名詞 (Ving.) 作為主詞，句子的動詞使用第三人稱單數 is。

12. 吸菸對健康造成威脅，更別說是生命了。

    (A) 威脅　　　　(B) 宣布　　　　(C) 限制　　　　(D) 安慰

13. 我不喜歡 Jenny。她既多嘴又喜歡説閒話。

(A) 暫停 / 中止　　(B) 發誓　　　　(C) 破壞　　　　(D) 説閒話

14. 我媽媽在花園裡種了一些漂亮的玫瑰花叢。

(A) 臉紅　　　　(B) 花叢　　　　(C) 領土　　　　(D) 趨勢

15. 那位作者在她的旅遊書中追蹤這座教堂的歷史。

(A) 鎖住 / 繫緊　　(B) 擁抱　　　　(C) 追蹤　　　　(D) 浸泡

Part 2：段落填空

每天都有許多人搭乘地鐵穿梭大倫敦地區。倫敦地鐵是世界上有 150 年歷史最久的地鐵。地鐵系統平穩又方便，可媲美世界上其他的大眾運動系統。現在有牡蠣卡，搭乘地鐵就比以前更方便了。牡蠣卡現在正迅速取代儲值票卡。它不僅入主乘客的皮夾，也在他們心中佔有一席之地。

為什麼你應該把儲值卡換成牡蠣卡，就只有一個字：快。現在只要在入口處將牡蠣卡放在感應器上很快刷一下即可，甚至隔著皮革也能讀取，如此一來可免去乘客從手提包或是皮夾將卡拿出來的麻煩。不僅如此，你還可以利用提款卡來加值你的牡蠣卡。如果你手上剛好沒有現金，那這項服務實在棒極了。雖然目前這項系統有時候有小缺點，但牡蠣卡能讓你更輕鬆自在地悠遊大倫敦地區。

單字提示

1. rival (v.) 比得上 / 媲美
2. stored-valued ticket 儲值卡
3. reader (n.) 讀卡機
4. swipe (v.) 刷（卡）
5. sensor (n.) 感應器
6. turnstile (n.) 入口處的旋轉式柵門
7. leather (n.) 皮革
8. bug (n.)（機器或是體系等）毛病 / 缺點
9. comfort (n.) 舒適 / 愉快

答案解析

16. 此題空格根據語意跟用法應選 (C) ever。

含比較級形容詞或副詞的主要字句 + than ever before

意指「比以前任何時候更 ...」

E.g. There are now more people using the Internet than ever before.
現在世界上使用網路的人口比起以前任何時候都要來得多。

17. 此題空格應選 (B) switch。

(A) commute from A to B「在 A 和 B 之間通勤」

E.g. Michael uses the tube to commute from his home to work.
Michael 搭地鐵通勤上班。

(B) switch from A to B「從 A 轉換到 B」

E.g. Simon's discussion group switched from Monday to Thursday.
Simon 星期一的小組討論會調到了星期四。

(C) refrain from + N/Ving. 克制 / 抑制 ... ，不要 ...

E.g. Would you please refrain from speaking so loudly in the museum?
能不能請你不要在博物館裡大聲喧嘩？

(D) escape from... 從 ... 逃脫

E.g. A few criminals escaped from the prison last night.
數名罪犯昨夜自監獄逃脫。

18. 此題因文意應選 (C) trouble。

(A) habit (n.) 習慣

(B) nerve (n.) 勇氣 / 神經 / have the nerve to + V. 有勇氣（做）...
= have the courage/guts to + V.

E.g. Anny doesn't have the nerve to ask Alan out on a date.
Anny 不敢問 Alan 是否願意跟她約會。

(C) save sb. the trouble of + Ving 替某人省下 ... 的麻煩

E.g. AI can save people the trouble of dong so much work.
人工智慧機器人可以幫人們做很多工作，省下不少麻煩。

(D) pain (n.) 痛苦

take pains to + V 煞費苦心 / 費盡心思（做）...

19. 此題根據上下文語氣用語答案選 (A) In addition。

    (A) In addition (adv.) 不僅如此 / 除此之外 = Besides, Additionally

        In addition to + N. 除了 ... 之外

        E.g. You need money and time. In addition, you need diligence.

            你需要金錢與時間，此外你還需要努力。

        E.g. In addition to his apartment in New York, he has a villa in Italy and a castle in Scotland.

            除了在紐約擁有一套公寓外，他在義大利還有一座鄉間別墅，在蘇格蘭有一座城堡。

    (B) Otherwise (adv.) 否則 / 不然

        E.g. Come in now, otherwise you'll get wet. 改快進來，不然你會淋濕。

    (C) Instead (adv.) 作為替代 / 反而 / Instead of + N 作為替代 ...

        E.g. I'm going to drop yoga and do aerobics instead.

            我準備把瑜珈退掉，去上有氧舞蹈課。

        E.g. Instead of complaining, why don't we try to change things?

            與其抱怨，不如我們來做改變？

    (D) As a result (adv.) 因此 = Therefore, Thus

        As a result of + N 由於 ... 因為 ... = Because of, Due to, Thanks to, In consequence of

        E.g. Emma ate too many donuts and gained weight as a result.

            艾瑪吃太多甜甜圈，因此胖了不少。

        E.g. As a result of dietary changes, Jerry reduced his blood pressure to healthy levels.

            由於飲食改變，傑瑞的血壓降至健康標準了。

20. 此題根據題意答案選 (B) on hand。

    (A) in person 親自

        E.g. The Prime Minster greeted the Queen in person.

            總理親自招呼女王。

    (B) on hand 在手頭 / 在近旁

        E.g. My cellphone is never on hand when I really need it.

            我總是在需要手機時沒把它帶在身上。

(C) before one's eyes 當著某人的面

    E.g. The thief stole Jack's wallet before his eyes.

        這個小偷當著 Jack 面前偷他的皮夾。

(D) under control 在控制 / 掌控之中

    E.g. Keep calm and don't panic. Everything is under control.

        保持冷靜不要驚慌。一切都在掌握之中。

很多台灣跟華人父母不期望小孩做家事。他們認為小孩子應該花時間讀書，而不是做家事。然而，在西方的想法中，小孩應該負起保持家裡整齊清潔的責任還有分擔家裡的事情。

從一方面來說，做家事可使年輕人做好準備，以便將來承擔父母的角色。如果你從未打掃過房子，怎麼可能突然知道怎麼做？另一方面，有些家事可以由多位家中成員一起分擔。例如，一個人洗碗，另一個人就負責擦乾，或是一個掃地，另一個就拖地。最後，藉由做家事可以讓小孩學習責任感與成就感。因為上述原因，非常建議即使是小孩，也應該參與保持家中整齊清潔的任務。

單字片語提示

1. chore (n.) 雜事（常用複數） E.g. do house/household chores 做家事
2. household (n.) (adj.) 家庭（的）
3. mop (v.) 拖（地）
4. a sense of responsibility 責任感
5. instead of ... 而不 ... = rather than...
6. be responsible for... 為 .. 負責
7. participate in 參與 參加
8. keep... in order 保持 ... 整齊有條理

答案解析

21. 此題因為 spend 的用法，所以答案應選 (C) studying。

    spend + money/time + (on) + Ving... 花時間做 ...

    E.g. Charles spent the whole day doing his project.

        Charles 花了一整天的時間做他的報告。

22. 此題因為文意，答案選擇 (C) tidy。

(A) tiny (adj.) 微小的

(B) tender (adj.) 溫柔的 /（身體上）疼痛的、一觸即痛（例如感冒或是身體不舒服時的疼痛）

(C) tidy (adj.) 整潔整齊的 / neat and tidy 乾淨整齊

E.g. It's easy to find the thing you want if your desk is tidy.

如果你的書桌整齊，那麼就很容易找到你要的東西。

(D) tame (adj.) 馴服的

E.g. Don't get close to the money. It's not tame.

別靠近那隻老虎。牠還沒被馴服。

23. 此題為固定用，答案選擇 (D) For another。

For one thing... For another (thing)... 一則 ... 二則 ...

E.g. This colour looks awful on you. For one thing, it's a quite different colour from your colour of your hair. For another, the shirt is too tight.

這顏色穿在你身上很難看。一來，它跟你頭髮的顏色非常不同。二來，這件衣服也太緊了。

24. 此題依據語意，可知 (B) sweeps 為正確答案。

(A) shed (v.) 流（淚）；使脫落

E.g. She sheds tears whenever she watches that TV drama.

她每次看那齣電視劇都會流眼淚。

(B) sweep (v.) 打掃 / 清掃

E.g. I help Mum sweep the floor last weekend.

我上週幫媽媽掃地。

(C) shave (v.) 刮（毛 / 鬍子）

E.g. Connie shaves the hair on her legs every morning in order to make her look nice.

Connie 每天早上刮腿毛為了讓她看起來漂亮。

(D) drift (v.) 飄落 / 飄移

E.g. A mist drifted in from the marshes.

一陣霧氣從沼澤地裡飄過來。

25. 此題依據語意應選 (A) achievement。

    (A) achievement (n.) 成就 / a sense of achievement 成就感

        E.g. It was a hard work of writing a book, but the sense of achievement is huge.

            雖然寫一本書是一件辛苦的事，卻很有成就感。

    (B) punctuality (n.) 準時 / punctual (adj.) 準時的

    (C) guilt (n.) 罪惡 / a sense of guilt 罪惡感

    (D) shame (n.) 恥辱 / a sense of shame 羞恥心

Part 3：閱讀理解

班機延誤賠償辦法

請詳閱 EU 航空公司賠償政策以釐清您是否符合賠償條件以及如何要求賠償。

1. 如果您比預定時間晚三小時抵達最後目的地，並且該延誤是由 EU 航空公司控制範圍內的問題所造成，那麼您可以因班機延誤要求賠償。

    (A) 我方控制範圍內的問題包括技術問題、飛機零件故障，以及其他有關飛機、機場機器或 EU 航空公司電腦系統的機械問題。被視為我方控制範圍內的完整清單，請查閱下方資訊。

    (B) 不在我方控制範圍內的問題包括天災、天氣狀況、安全問題、機場交通壅塞，以及航空公司員工罷工。被視為我方控制範圍外的完整清單，請查閱下方資訊。

2. 隔夜延誤的情況中，除了往返旅館的交通之外，航空公司還會為旅客安排旅館住宿。旅客也可以選擇返家。在此情況下，所有的交通費用將由航空公司支付。

3. 如上述延誤被三小時以上的旅客有權獲得現金款項：

    搭乘里程少於 1,500 公里的航班獲得 215 歐元。

    搭乘里程介於 1,500 公里跟 3,500 公里之間的航班獲得 357 歐元。

    搭乘里程超過 3,500 公里且延誤超過三到四小時的航班獲得 357 歐元。

    搭乘里程超過 3,500 公里且延誤超過四小時的航班獲得 530 歐元。

---

26. 下列何者為 EU 航空公司敘述的賠償？

    (A) 班機延誤三小時，航空公司將賠償所有的班機費用。

    (B) 航空公司將賠償旅客延誤比超過四小時更多的費用。

    (C) 如果因為天氣狀況班機延誤的話，航空公司將賠償費用。

    (D) 航空公司只在控制範圍內賠償費用。

在此聲明書在一開始「Please read EU Airlines' Compensation Policy carefully to find out whether you are eligible for compensation and how you can claim it.」就説明在以下敘述的情況之下有該賠償,所以答案選擇 (D)。

27. 如果旅客班機延誤超過隔夜,EU 航空公司會怎麼處理?

    (A) 如果有這樣的情況發生,立刻安排新的航班。

    (B) 航空公司會要求旅客留在機場,但是也會賠償他們。

    (C) 航空公司會安排且付需要的交通或是住宿的費用。

    (D) 直到安排新的航班前,航空公司會要求所有旅客回家。

答案解析

賠償聲明第二點有説到「In the case of overnight delays, the airline will arrange for hotel rooms for passengers, in addition to transportation to and from the hotel. Passengers can also choose to return their home. In this case, all transportation costs will be met.」所以,正確答案選擇 (C)。

2017 年 6 月 14 日

Julia 你好,

    我收到你的信,得知你這個月將到英國旅行。如果你願意的話,你在英國的時間可以住在我家。我也非常樂意帶你到我住的康沃爾走走。我們可以開始安排在康沃爾的旅行計畫。如果你有想去的地方,讓我知道一下,以便我可以建議你一些很多旅客不知道的特別景點。

    在康沃爾有很多好玩的地方。首先,我想我們可以先去「特魯羅」,那是康沃爾的一個重要城市。我們可以參觀那裡的大教堂還有那裡的石頭房子。那是相當特別的一個景象。接下來,參觀完特魯羅後,我們開車去「科爾瑞克」還有「麗澤」。柯爾瑞克是一個很漂亮的村莊,我們可以考慮住在那邊一個晚上。之後,麗澤是英國本土跟最西南邊的景點,還有獨特的鄉村風景還有令人驚艷的景色。除外,英國最有名的餡餅就在「安的餡餅」。我們可以去吃吃看。如果還有時間,我非常建議應該去聖麥克山還有聖艾弗小城走走。天啊!現在我有好多可以康沃爾哪些地方的想法。讓我知道你有什麼想法,之後我再給你更多適合的建議。

    期待很快見到你。

祝好

Tamsin

28. Julian 什麼時候去英國？

    (A) 七月。

    (B) 六月。

    (C) 六月十四日。

    (D) 這個月。

答案解析

依據信內容給的資訊，Julia 在六月十四日收到 Tamsin 的信，說明了「這個月」指的是「六月」要去英國，所以可以得知 Julia 六月出發到英國。而 (D) 的答案不夠清楚以示六月到英國去，因此答案選擇 (B)。

29. 下列是 Tamsin 信中沒有提到的？

    (A) 他們可以在柯爾瑞克待一個晚上。

    (B) 在旅行中還有時間的話，聖麥克山還有聖艾弗小城是很不錯的選擇。

    (C) 麗澤有英國最出名的船隻。

    (D) Julia 在旅英期間可以住在 Tamsin 的家。

答案解析

依據信內容，只提到「Lizard is the most south-westerly point of the British mainland and boasts its own unique landscape and stunning views.」並沒有提到有最出名的船隻。另外，「boast」(v.) 吹噓 / 有（值得自豪的東西）的意思，因此答案選擇 (C)。

美國有許多有名的發明家。然而，班傑明富蘭克林大概是美國最有名的發明家之一。雖然他是一個作家也是一個哲學家，但至今他最令人難以忘懷的是他的發明。

富蘭克林發明很多有用的東西，常常是因為他需要這些東西。例如，富蘭克林戴眼鏡，但當他年紀越來大時，他開始需要一副更好的眼鏡讓他可以閱讀書籍。因為他對於使用的兩副眼鏡感到厭煩了，富蘭克林決定發明一副可以讓他清楚看遠或是看近的眼鏡。所以，他把兩種鏡片各切一半，然後把它們拼湊在一起。這就是廣為大家所知的雙光眼鏡（遠近視兩用的眼鏡）。

除此之外，你可能聽過富蘭克林風箏飛機的故事，但富蘭克林發明電力這件事不是真的。然而，從這個經歷，富蘭克林獲得發明避雷針的知識，這個裝備可以保護大樓與船隻觸電。

富蘭克林也發明特別的鑄鐵火爐，被稱為富蘭克林火爐。它可以讓人們用比較不危險的方式讓家變暖和，而且比起使用傳統的壁爐用還要少的木材。除外，他甚至發明一個簡單的機械來測量距離。身為他的城鎮的郵政局長，他必須知道路的距離多長，所以他發明這個器材來幫他追蹤距離。

無疑地，班傑明富蘭克林發明許多有用的東西，到今日很多人還在使用的東西。雖然他在政治上、寫作還有被放在美國錢幣上成功讓人記得許久，不過富蘭克林依然以他的發明而聞名。

單字提示

1. philosopher (n.) 哲學家
2. piece (n.) 片狀物；(v.)（片狀物）湊成 ...
3. bifocals (n.) 雙光眼鏡（遠近視兩用的眼鏡）
4. lightening rod (n.) 避雷針
5. device (n.) 器材 / 設備 / 裝置

答案解析

30. 這篇文章主要關於 _____。

    (A) 富蘭克林是一名知名的發明家

    (B) 富蘭克林舒適的生活

    (C) 富蘭克林在美國的想法

    (D) 富蘭克林對抗困難

依據文章第一段「Benjamin Franklin is probably one of the most famous American inventors. Although he was also a writer and a philosopher, Franklin is best remembered today for his many inventions.」可以得知他是一個知名的發明家。所以答案選擇 (A)。

31. 下列有關富蘭克林發明的雙光眼鏡是正確的？

(A) 這副眼鏡有兩個不同的鏡片。

(B) 眼鏡主要用在可以清楚看遠物。

(C) 眼鏡設計僅為閱讀用。

(D) 眼鏡對於測量距離常有幫助。

依據文章「Because he got tired of using two sets of glasses, Franklin decided to invent one pair that would allow him to see clearly both things near and far. So, he cut two kinds of the lenses in half, and piece them together into one pair of glasses.」可以得知，眼鏡使用不同兩個鏡片而且可以看遠物跟近物，雖然一開始是因為他覺得就眼鏡讓他在閱讀上面很困擾所以發明新的眼鏡，但雙光眼鏡的發明最後不是僅為閱讀所用，因此答案選 (A)。

32. 根據這篇文章，有關富蘭克林下列何者不正確？

(A) 他過去在郵局工作。

(B) 他發明電力。

(C) 他發明避雷針。

(D) 他很努力生活來改善他的生活品質。

依據文章內容提到「Moreover, you may have heard the story of Franklin's famous kite flight, but it is not true that Franklin invented electricity.」清楚說明，電力不是他發明的，因此答案選擇 (B)。

33.「keep track of」意思是 _____。

(A) 搭乘

(B) 選擇

(C) 知道

(D) 改善

根據文章「As his town's postmaster, Franklin had to know how long the roads were, so he invented this tool to help him keep track of these distances.」提及他必須知道距離多遠，所以發明此工具讓他可以追蹤了解距離。所以答案選擇 (C)。

當你還年輕時，你的父母跟老師教導你合宜的行為舉止。對你來說大部分的行為都很自然，所以你無法想像人們有不同的行為表現。然而，每個文化都有其不同人們的期許。如果你到另外一個國家旅行，學習那個國家的文化習俗是重要的，以免你的行為污辱到招待你的人。

文化規則包含肢體語言。例如在美國，你可能以握拳舉起大拇指來表示「做得好」或是「我認同」。在其他地方，這個姿勢可能不被接受。

如果你到阿拉伯國家去，你應該要注意把雙腳放在地上，腳底向著人的話是非常無禮的。在印尼，你不可以用左手拿東西給人，因為左手被視為是不乾淨的。

每個文化中的眼神接觸也非常不同。在一些地方，例如美國，看著別人的眼睛表示你對別人的尊重、關注，並且表示你敞開心胸也誠摯。在美國，如果老師跟他／她說話時，學生拒絕看著老師的眼睛，那學生就會有麻煩了。在其他國家，眼神往下是一種顯示尊重的方式。在非洲一些地方，如果一個小孩直視老師的眼睛，他或她就會被以不尊重的態度而受處罰。

這些例子都顯示簡單的動作可能造成人們之間很大的衝突，如果他們沒有意識到一些行為的意義的話。若你去別的國家，確認好清楚那個國家的規範，避免衝突。

答案解析

34. 最後一段的「norm」意思最接近 _____。

(A) 說法　(B) 姿勢　(C) 標準　(D) 當地人

根據整篇文章談論到不同姿勢和手勢有不同的意思，代表不同國家的文化，所以 norm (n.) 規範，最接近 (C) standard (n.) 標準。

35. 根據這篇文章，誰對這篇文章最可能感到興趣？

(A) 遊客　(B) 廚師／主廚　(C) 農夫　(D) 校長

根據文章第一段「If you travel to another country, it is important that you learn that country's cultural practices so that your behavior won't be insulting to your hosts.」更清楚得知，到一個國家旅行前，了解一個國家的文化習俗是很重要的，因此答案選擇 (A)。

36. 根據這篇文章，如果一個非洲小孩直視老師的眼睛會發生什麼事情？

    (A) 得到支持。

    (B) 備受崇拜。

    (C) 得到讚許。

    (D) 受到處罰。

    根據文章「In parts of Africa, if a child meets the teacher's eyes, he or she may be punished for being disrespectful.」答案選擇 (D)。

37. 根據這篇文章，下列是作者的建議？

    (A) 切記在你的旅行前一個月買好航空公司的機票。

    (B) 最好了解你準備去旅行的國家的一些手勢的意思。

    (C) 不要忘記在你的旅程中隨身將個人物品待在身旁。

    (D) 學一些你準備前往國家的基本用語。

    根據文章，答案 (A) 、(C) 、(D) 都沒有提及，正確答案選擇 (B)。

你曾經去過美國嗎？如果有，你可以有發現美國生活中一些特別的事情。如果你還沒有，那麼你應該試著更了解美國文化，以防有一天你會到訪這個國家。這裡有些值得記住的事。

當美國人看到朋友或是第一個跟人打招呼時，他們通常都會握手。跟男士或是女士握手都是禮貌的。確保你做出一個堅定的握手禮，這表示你對待人友善與誠懇。

美國人是非常愛國的人士。七月四日美國獨立日跟十一月份的感恩節他們都稱之為國慶假日。在這些日子，在每個人坐下並準備好之前，切勿開始進食。有時候在餐前會有人先做一個短的禱告來感謝神賜予食物。這種禱告稱之為「謝飯禱告」。

在美國，平等是非常重要的。如果你用不同的態度對人談話、或做出不同的行為，或是不平等地對待人，你會被認為無禮或是老土。在美國，男人、女人和小孩都應該打掃房子及煮飯。在廚房裡，美國人通常都知道回收的重要性，所以要確保你知道怎麼做垃圾分類。

最後一件需要注意的事情就是小費。當你搭計程車或是去一間餐廳，付帳單時，一定要記得留小費。小費是你餐費總額再加 15%。服務人員或是計程車司機需要小費，因為他們平常薪水都很低。

大部分遊客會發現美國人都很友善。確保有一天你去這個國家時，能學習他們的文化。

答案解析

38. 根據這篇文章，在美國，人們打招呼方式是 _____。

(A) 擁抱　(B) 親臉頰　(C) 吃晚餐　(D) 握手

根據文章第二段「When Americans see a friend or greet someone for the first time, they normally shake hands.」所以答案選擇 (D)。

39. 根據這篇文章，在美國文化中，下列何者是不禮貌的？

(A) 跟男士還有女士握手。

(B) 不公平對待別人。

(C) 在感恩節時，直到大家都坐好時才開始吃飯。

(D) 飯前禱告。

根據文章內容「In America, equality is very important. If you talk about people being different or having to do different jobs or treat people unequally, you will be considered rude and old-fashioned.」答案選擇 (B)。

40. 最適合最篇文章的主題是？

(A) 美國文化。　　　　(B) 文化衝擊。

(C) 美國旅遊。　　　　(D) 生活文化差異。

根據文章一開頭「Have you ever been to America? If so, you may have noticed some special things in American life.」清楚可以得知探討美國文化，所以答案選擇 (A)。

Your time is limited, so don't waste it living someone else's life./ Steve Jobs
你的時間有限，不要浪費時間過別人的生活。（史提夫‧賈柏斯）

Reading Module 2
閱讀模擬測驗

本測驗分三部分，全為四選一之選擇題，共 40 題，作答時間 45 分鐘。

Part 1：詞彙與結構

共 15 題，每題含一個空格。請由試題冊上的四個選項中選出最適合題意的字或詞作答。

1. No one could exactly explain why he radar of the airplane _____.

   (A) inspected   (B) vanished   (C) hurt   (D) floated

2. This movie made many people believe in the _____ of the aliens.

   (A) mission   (B) response   (C) exit   (D) existence

3. Patrick _____ not _____ see Amy. That made her mad.

   (A) prepared / for   (B) attached / to
   (C) affected/ to   (D) compared / with

4. Every _____ tradition has its origin. You should respect it.

   (A) relieved   (B) responsible   (C) religious   (D) reliable

5. I grew up with many _____. I have three brothers and two sisters.

   (A) siblings   (B) spouses   (C) spikes   (D) tides

6. To expand the company, it _____ over 100 workers this year.

   (A) has employed   (B) have employed
   (C) was employed   (D) has to employ

7. The celebration was already _____, and the next sow was the highlight.

   (A) underway   (B) scarce   (C) mighty   (D) weird

8. Andy _____ his jeans to clean off the mud.

   (A) handled   (B) translated   (C) tore   (D) scrubbed

9. These _____ explored the jungle and found some rare species.

   (A) magicians   (B) linguists   (C) biologists   (D) firefighters

10. A great number of citizens _____ building a nuclear power plant in the country.

    (A) are isolated from   (B) are exempted from

    (C) are opposed to   (D) are checking up

11. The company's founder retired to devote his time _____ charities.

    (A) with   (B) to   (C) as   (D) for

12. The audience were very motivated after this writer's _____ speech.

    (A) inspiring   (B) automatic   (C) industrial   (D) mess

13. It is _____ that by 2026 three working people have to support an old person.

    (A) paved   (B) sprained   (C) obtained   (D) estimated

14. Your _____ attitude is not good for your study.

    (A) active   (B) passive   (C) realistic   (D) tolerant

15. Emily found it easy to _____ herself to studying in the UK.

    (A) adjust   (B) adopt   (C) adhere   (D) attempt

Part 2：段落填空

共 10 題，包含二個段落，每個段落各含 5 個空格。請由試題冊上的四個選項中選出最適合題意的詞或詞作答。

Questions 16~20

For many people, flying a kite is an enjoyable way to spend an afternoon. If the wind is right and the sun is shining, what __(16)__ do you need? But have you ever considered flying a kite in the evening __(17)__ the sun isn't shining? If you can __(18)__ see the kite, your sense of touch reads the kite's position in the sky by the way the wind pulls on the line. You can also hear the kite much more clearly as it cuts through the air. You can

(19) night flying anytime. Just close your eyes and carry on (20) normal. This works especially well when you wear sunglasses as no one can tell what you are doing. How interesting!

16. (A) other   (B) else   (C) many   (D) less

17. (A) where   (B) how   (C) when   (D) why

18. (A) no longer   (B) not more   (C) more or less   (D) so long

19. (A) stimulate   (B) simulate   (C) simplify   (D) stand

20. (A) if   (B) until   (C) since   (D) as

Questions 21~25

I have been a nurse in the emergency room for several years, and I really like my job most of the time. To become a nurse, I needed five years of specialized training. I (21) a certificated program at the nursing school. During my studies, I learned a lot, but school couldn't prepare me completely for the life of a nurse, which is exciting, valuable and stressful.

One thing I really like about my job is that it can help many people. We treated all kinds of medical emergencies. For me, working at the hospital is quite challenging. The major difficulty of the job is the stress. Nurses, just like doctors, have to (22) life and death situations all the time. (23) it is rewarding to help someone, we aren't always successful. Sometimes patients die, and we will face the (24) from their family. We also have to work extremely quickly, and that can be stressful, too. We help people (25) are hurt and in trouble, and we can feel that they are very stressed, too.

21. (A) competed   (B) completed   (C) contested   (D) contended

22. (A) deal with   (B) put up with   (C) come up with   (D) equip with

23. (A) So   (B) Although   (C) When   (D) Since

24. (A) complain   (B) to complain   (C) complaints   (D) complained

25. (A) they   (B) what   (C) whom   (D) who

Part 3：閱讀理解

共 15 題，包含數篇短文，每個短文後有 2~4 個相關問題。請由試題冊上四個選項中選出最適合者作答。

Questions 26~27

Attention

Due to a great number of incidents in the school gym, the General Office has announced some changes.

1. All students must use their gym lockers to store all their personal belongings. No personal items are allowed to be left on the gym benches or floors.

2. If a student has any personal belongings of value, the item must be registered with one of the Physical Education teachers. That item will be placed in a secure location for safekeeping.

3. All students must take home the attached official school form. A parent or guardian should read and then sign the form. This form makes clear how parents can contribute to a safer school environment. These forms must be signed and returned no later than Friday, December 1.

Alex Wang

General Office

---

26. What is the purpose of the notice?

    (A) To advise students of changes in PE classes

    (B) To inform students of security policy changes

    (C) To warn students of improper behavior

    (D) To announce new storage facilities

27. When should student return the forms?

    (A) November 30

    (B) December 2

    (C) January 23

    (D) January 1

Question 28~30

Freelancer Translation Services

Flat 45, Shaftesbury Avenue,

Southampton, SO17 1HQ

TEL:(44)07823118809 Fax:(44) 07823618909

Freelancetranslationservices.com

Hans Import and Export Company

1 Greenwich Road

London, SW14 5JQ

March 10, 2017

Dear Mr Snow,

In response to your inquiry of the fifth of March, we are sending you two of our company drafts, one of which is the translation, and the other of which is the interpretation. Besides, we also attach the pamphlet to the mail, including price lists with our services and services fees. We also sending you a sample contract in the event that you would like to have a short-tern or a long-term service agreement with us rather than a one-time arrangement.

Freelancer Translation Services has assisted over one hundred companies in the British Museum and the British Library for many years. We offer translation services in 20 languages and interpretation services in 15.For business, government or educational work, international conferences or workshops, see us first. We are ready to serve you and your clients anytime. Please call, fax, or email us at your earliest convenience.

Rebecca Wright

Customer Service

Freelance Translation services

28. To whom is Rebecca Wright responding?

(A) To a university or college

(B) To a trading company

(C) To a government office

(D) To a travelling agency

29. What is NOT enclosed in Rebecca Wright's mail?

    (A) A sample contract

    (B) An application form for a Visa

    (C) A pamphlet on translation fees and services

    (D) Drafts on interpretation and translation

30. Which of the following statements is true about Freelance Translation Services?

    (A) It has been in business for many years.

    (B) It has branch offices in 15 countries.

    (C) Its employees speak 20 languages.

    (D) Its headquarter is in Southampton.

Questions 31~34

Each Spring, an unconventional contest takes place in Aproz, Switzerland, called the Battle of the Queens. It involves Hérens cows, a breed known for its high aggression. The Battle of the Queens is different from Spanish bullfighting, in which humans fight bulls in a violent ritual. In the Swiss event, the cows fight each other. Another difference between the two types of bullfighting is that blood is rarely shed at the Battle of the Queens. In fact, the fighting at this event is relatively tame. The cows mostly lock horns and push each with their foreheads. The cow that turns around and walks away first loses the fight. According to records, some of the fighters have lost horns, but none have been seriously injured.

31. What does the passage mainly discuss?

    (A) A popular tradition in Spain

    (B) A contest in which cows fight

    (C) People's reactions to bullfighting

    (D) The different types of cows in Switzerland

32. How is the Battle of the Queens different from Spanish bullfighting?

    (A) In the Battle of the Queens, the two cows fight to the death.

    (B) In the Battle of the Queens, the cows are not likely to be injured.

    (C) In the Battle of the Queens, humans fight cows.

    (D) In the Battle of the Queens, only one cow appears at a time.

33. What can we see at the Battle of the Queens?

   (A) A cow that lost its horns receiving a prize
   (B) Serious fighting that causes lots of bloodshed
   (C) Two cows locking horns with each other
   (D) A cow winning the contest by walking away first

34. What do we know about Spanish bullfighting?

   (A) It is popular in Switzerland.
   (B) It always involves Hérens cows.
   (C) It typically results in bloodshed.
   (D) It is relatively tame.

Question 35~37

Background music, visual displays, and product samples work together to make a shop a pleasant place. Some businesspeople also believe that pleasant smells could help increase sales.

This concept of 'scent marketing' aims to attract consumers through their sense of smell. Shopkeepers use artificial aromas to create a mood or to reinforce the odor of the product the shop sells. These smells can be distributed by a simple spray system, but shoebox-sized machines also exist to allow shops to vary scents.

Martin Lindstrom, author of the book Brand Sense, explains that for 80% of men and 90% of women, smells bring back strong, emotional memories. This is because olfactory memories are stored in the brain's 'limbic system', which is also the neurological home of emotions. Thus, if smells are associated with a positive memory, they could encourage customers to buy a product, or at least stay longer.

However, not everyone accepts the principle of using smells to sell. Some shop managers also worry about polluting the air and even causing breathing problems for customers with medical conditions. But with signs, colors, and music everywhere, certain shops will certainly continue to try this method—if only to be different.

35. Which of the following is NOT the purpose for shop owners to use aromas?

   (A) To bring back emotional memories.
   (B) To make customers buy more.
   (C) To make their products more impressive.
   (D) To attract more children.

36. _____ may be one of the negative points of using scents to increase sales.

    (A) More osts

    (B) Health problems

    (C) Bad emories

    (D) Inconvenience

37. According to the last paragraph, _____.

    (A) signs, colors, and music are all too common for stores

    (B) scent marketing is no longer here to stay

    (C) all people and stores embrace the idea of using smells to sell

    (D) marketing strategies are the best solution for all the businesspeople

Questions 38~40

It is hard to imagine that people would have poisonous shots on themselves to look more beautiful. Yet, today, people all over the world are paying hundreds of dollars to be injected with botulinum toxin—a bacterial poison popularly called "Botox."

Botox weakens and paralyzes human muscles. Therefore, when injected into facial muscles, it reduces the appearance of wrinkles. Similarly, Botox injections can solve the problem of excessive sweating by paralyzing nerves that activate the sweat glands. Thus, Botox is largely used for cosmetic purposes, to help people look younger and more attractive.

These benefits have made Botox increasingly popular. In 2002 alone, 1.1 million Americans paid to receive Botox injections. Botox is a chemical favored by celebrities across the world and is well-loved by Oscar nominees who do not wish to break into a nervous sweat on stage!

Unfortunately, it is used rather irresponsibly. Often, Botox injections are carried out at beauty salons and even in people's homes, without the approval of medical advisors. People also store it in their refrigerators, in close contact with food, which may cause food poisoning. This is dangerous, considering the toxin is so strong that it has been used as a weapon in warfare. Botox injected to pregnant women harms the unborn child, and it is also dangerous for people above the age of 65. Since its effects last only for a few months, it needs to be used repeatedly, which only increase its harm.

Given these risks, one must wonder whether the dangers that might result from the careless use of Botox are preferable to the signs of aging. In a world obsessed with the mythical "fountain of youth," however, people continue to believe that looks eclipse health. The improper use of the poison of youth, Botox, continues.

38. What is the passage mainly about?

    (A) A medical discovery about bacteria.
    (B) A popular way of looking younger.
    (C) An effective pill for removing wrinkles.
    (D) A longstanding belief in staying young.

39. According to the passage, what is true about Botox?

    (A) It can ease nervousness.
    (B) It strengthens the muscles.
    (C) It is mostly injected by famous people.
    (D) It helps solve the problem of over-sweating.

40. What does 'looks eclipse health' mean?

    (A) Looks are valued above health.
    (B) Looks come second to health.
    (C) Better looks improve mental health.
    (D) Both looks and health are important.

The important thing is not to stop questioning. / (Einstein)
重要的事是永遠不要停止發問。(愛因斯坦)

Part 1：詞彙與結構

1. 沒有人能確實解釋為何那架飛機的雷達訊號消失了。

   (A) 檢查　　　　(B) 消失　　　　(C) 傷害　　　　(D) 漂流

2. 這部電影使許多人相信外星人的存在。

   (A) 任務　　　　(B) 回應　　　　(C) 出口　　　　(D) 存在

3. Patrick 假裝沒看見 Amy。這讓她很生氣。

   (A) 準備 prepare for + N.　　　　　(B) 附加 / 附著 attach to + N.
   (C) 假裝 affect to + V.　　　　　　(D) 比較 compare with + N.

4. 每個宗教傳統都有它的起源。你應該尊重它。

   (A) 放寬心的　　(B) 負責任的　　(C) 宗教的　　(D) 可靠的

5. 我和許多兄弟姊妹一起長大。我有三個哥哥和兩個姊姊。

   (A) 手足　　　　(B) 配偶　　　　(C) 尖刺　　　　(D) 潮汐

6. 為了擴大公司，今天已經雇用了超過 100 名員工。

   此題為文法結構題型，因為有明確的時間「今年」，表是今年「已經」雇用了超過 100 名員工，以「現在完成式 have/has + Vpp.」敘述此句話比較合適。所以答案選擇 (A) has employed「已經雇用了」符合句子的時間與句意。

7. 慶祝活動已經在進行中，下一場表演將是高潮。

   (A) 進行中的　　(B) 罕見的　　　(C) 強大的　　　(D) 怪異的

8. Andy 用力擦洗他的牛仔褲，以將泥土清掉。

   (A) 處理　　　　(B) 翻譯　　　　(C) 撕裂　　　　(D) 擦掉 / 刷洗

9. 這群生物學家勘查了叢林並發現一些罕見的物種。

   (A) 魔術師　　　(B) 語言學家　　(C) 生物學家　　(D) 消防員

10. 很多市民反對在國內興建核能電廠。

    (A) 隔離　　　　(B) 免除 / 豁免　(C) 反對　　　　(D) 檢查

11. 該公司創辦人退休後將時間奉獻在慈善事業上。

    devote (v.) 奉獻，這個單字的用法是 devote + O. + to + N/Ving 奉獻於 / 致力於某事。因此答案選擇 (B) to。

12. 觀眾聽完這個作家鼓勵人心的演講後，感到激勵。

    (A) 鼓勵人心的　　　(B) 自動的　　　　(C) 工業的　　　　(D) 雜亂的

13. 據估計到 2026 年，三位工作人口必須扶養一個老年人。

    (A) 鋪上　　　　　(B) 扭傷　　　　　(C) 獲得　　　　　(D) 估計

14. 你消極的態度對你的學習不好。

    (A) 主動的　　　　(B) 消極的　　　　(C) 實際現實的　　(D) 包容的

15. Emily 發現自己很容易就適應在英國讀書。

    (A) 適應　　　　　(B) 領養 採納　　　(C) 黏著　　　　　(D) 企圖

Part 2：段落填空

對許多人而言，放風箏是度過一個愉快下午的好方法。假如風速適中陽光又燦爛的話，你還需要什麼呢？但你有沒有想過在一個沒有陽光的晚上放風箏呢？當你看不到風箏時，你的觸感會由風牽動線的方向告訴你風箏的位置，你也能更輕地聽見風箏劃破夜空的聲音。你也可以隨時模擬夜間放風箏。只要閉上眼中像平常那樣進行就可以。戴著太陽眼鏡進行這種練習最好，因為沒有人能分辨出你在做什麼。真有趣！

片語解析

1. sense of touch/sight/hearing/smell/taste 觸 / 視 / 聽 / 嗅 / 味覺

    E.g. My grandfather had lost his sense of sight. It was rather hard time before he passed away.

    我爺爺以前失去視覺。在他過世之前，那真是一段痛苦的時間。

2. carry on 繼續 / 進行

    E.g. Well goes a saying from the UK 'Keep calm and carry on'.

    英國一句諺語說得好「保持冷靜繼續走下去」。

答案解析

16. 此題空格應選 (B) else，此為固定用法。

    else (adj.) 別的 / 其他的

    E.g. Is there anything else I can do for you?

    還有其他需要幫忙的嗎？

else 常用於疑問代名詞及不定代名詞 (anything, anyone, something, somebody, no one) 等之後，為固定用法，所以答案選擇 (B)；另外，沒有「what otehr/many/less」的用法，因此 (A)、(C)、(D) 皆為錯的選項。

17. 此題答案應選 (C) when。

(A) 關係副詞 where 引導的形容詞子句，只能以修飾其表示的地方的先行詞（名詞），空格前是「the evening」並非例如像是「the place」，所以不得選 (A)。

E.g. Liz used to often play in the factory where her mother had worked before.

Liz 以前常常在她媽媽工作的工廠玩。

(B) 關係副詞 how 引導的形容詞子句，用來修飾 the way，但 the way 在有 how 的時候必須省略，或者保留 the way 省略 how。

E.g. I am not sure the way he looks like.

= I am not sure how he looks like. 我不確認他的樣子。

(C) 關係副詞 when 所引導出的形容詞子句，可用來修飾前面表示的時間，本句空格前的先行詞是 the evening，所以 when 放在其後符合其句意。

E.g. I got home at 6pm when it became dark.

我晚上六點鐘回家時，那時天色已經暗。

(D) 關係副詞 why 所引導的形容詞子句用來修飾 the reason，作為解釋原因。

E.g. The reason why I overslept this morning was that I had stayed up late last night.

我今天早上睡過頭的原因是因為我昨夜熬夜了。

18. 此空格應選 (A) no longer 不再 ... 的意思。

(A) no longer = no more... 不再 ...

no longer 可放於句首、句中或是句尾修飾，而 no more 通常放於句首或句尾。

E.g. We will no longer have dinner at this restaurant.

= We will have dinner at this restaurant no more.

我們再也不會在這個餐廳吃晚餐了。

(C) more or less 多少 / 有幾分

E.g. Josh is more or less a nice guy.

Josh 可以算是一個好人了。

(D) so long = goodbye 再見

19. 此題依語意選擇 (B) simulate。

(A) stimulate (v.) 刺激 / 使興奮

(B) simulate (v.) 模擬

(C) simplify (v.) 簡化

(D) stand (v.) 位於 .../ 忍受 ...

20. 此題為 (D) as normal「照平常一樣」的固定用法。

＊ as normal 照平常一樣

E.g. She was very ill last night, but she is at work today as normal.
她昨天晚上病得很嚴重，但今天她仍照常上班。

我在急診室當護理師已經好幾年了，大致上來說，我還是非常喜歡我的工作。為了成為一名護理師，我需要五年的專業訓練。我在護理學校完成合格訓練課程。在學習過程中，我收穫良多，但學校沒辦法完全幫助我面對護理師的生活，這是一個非常刺激、珍貴而且壓力大的生活。

我真心喜歡我工作的一件事是因為可以幫助很多人。我們治療所有醫療急診。對我來說，在醫院工作相當具挑戰性。這工作主要的難處是壓力大。護理師就跟醫師一樣，總需要處理所有生與死的情況。雖然幫助人是有意義的，但我們不可能都成功救人。有時候病人過世，我們需要面對家屬的抱怨。我們也必須工作迅速，這樣的工作壓力也很大。我們幫助受傷或是有困難的人，我們也能體會他們壓力很大。

單字提示

1. emergency room (n.) 急診室
2. specialized (adj.) 專門的 / 專科的
3. certificated (adj.) 合格的 / 有證明書的
4. valuable (adj.) 珍貴的
5. rewarding (adj.) 有意義的
6. patient (n.) 病人；(adj.) 有耐心的

21. 依據文意答案選擇 (B) completed。

    (A) compete (v.) 競爭　　　　　(B) completed 完成

    (C) contest (v.) 爭取 / 比賽　　(D) contend (v.) 滿足

22. 依據文意答案選擇 (A) deal with。

    (A) deal with 處理　　　　　　(B) put up with 忍受

    (C) come up with 想出　　　　(D) equip with 裝備 / 配備有 ...

23. 依據上下文的前因後果，答案選擇 (B) although。

    (A) so 所以　(B) although 雖然　(C) when 當 ...　(D) since 自從 / 因為

24. 空格前面是動詞 face「面對」，因此答案選擇 (C) complaints (n.)。

    ＊ complain (v) 抱怨

25. 此題依據文法結構，空格前面是 people，修飾先行詞所連接的關係代名詞子句，關係代名詞選擇 who（主格，代表人），答案選擇 (D) who。

    (A) they 他們

    (B) what（疑問詞）

    (C) whom 關係代名詞受格

    (D) who 關係代名詞主格

Part 3：閱讀理解

注意

因為校園體育館內發生了幾起事件，總務處下令進行一些更變。

1. 所有學生必須使用體育館置物櫃存放所有私人物品。私人物品不得留在體育館椅凳上或地上。

2. 如果學生有任何貴重私人物品，必須向體育老師登記該物品。該物品會被放置在安全的地方保管。

3. 所有學生必須將所附的學校正式表格帶回家。家長或是監護人應閱讀該表格並在上面簽名。該表格可讓家長更明白要有何作為才能讓校園環境更安全。這些表格最晚必須在 12 月 1 日星期五以前簽署並繳回。

王艾力克斯

總務處

---

26. 這份公告的目的是什麼？

    (A) 告知學生體育課變更。

    (B) 通知學生安全政策的改變。

    (C) 警告學生不當的行為。

    (D) 公告新的儲藏設施。

    根據本公告第一段「Due to a great number of incidents in the school gym, the General Office has announced some changes.」得知此公告是通知學生安全政策有所變更，所以答案選 (B)。

27. 學生應該要何時歸還表格？

    (A) 11 月 30 日

    (B) 12 月 2 日

    (C) 1 月 23 日

    (D) 1 月 1 日

    根據本公告「These forms must be signed and returned no later than Friday, December 1.」這些表格最晚要在 12 月 1 日前繳回，所以答案選擇 (A)。

自由工作翻譯服務公司

南安普敦市 歐福斯瑞大道 45 號 F

郵遞區號：SO17 1HQ

電話 :(44)07823118809 傳真 :(44) 07823618909

Freelancetranslationservices.com

漢斯進出口貿易公司

倫敦 格林威治 1 號

郵遞區號：SW14 5JQ

March 10, 2017

史諾先生您好

茲回覆您在三月五日的來信詢問，我們將寄給您本公司的兩個文件稿，分為別翻譯跟口譯稿件。除外，我們也在信附上一本冊子，包含本公司的服務項目與費用清單。我們也將寄給您一份合約樣本以便如果您想與本公司簽署短期或長期的服務協議，而非僅一次性的安排。

自由工作翻譯服務公司在大英博物館與大英圖書館協助過超過一百多家公司長達數年。本公司提供 20 種語言的文字翻譯與 15 種口譯服務。凡是您有商務、政府或是教育相關工作、國際會議或是研討會的需求，請與我們接洽。本公司隨時準備好要為您與你的客戶服務。請儘速以電話、傳真或是電子郵件的方式與本公司聯繫。

自由工作翻譯服務公司

客服部

瑞貝卡懷特

單字片語提示

1. in response to... 回應

    E.g. I am applying for this job in response to your ad in Monday's paper.

    針對貴公司週一在報上刊登的廣告，我想應徵這份工作。

2. inquiry (v.) 詢問 (+about)

    E.g. I've been making inquires about the cost of a programme of astronomy.

    我一直在詢問有關天文學課程的課程費用。

3. pamphlet (n.) 廣告小冊

4. interpretation (n.) 口譯

5. in the event that 如果 ... / in the event of + N. 如果發生某事

    E.g. In the even of an accident, please call this number.

    如果發生意外事件，請撥打這個電話。

6. short-term 短期的 / long-term 長期的

7. assist (v.) 協助 = help (v.)

8. at one's earliest convenience 在某人方便儘早

    E.g. Can you send me a mail at your earlier convenience to arrange your plan?

    你方便時可否寄封郵件給我安排您的計劃？

答案解析

28. 瑞貝卡懷特是回應誰的來信？

    (A) 某大學

    (B) 某貿易公司

    (C) 某政府辦公室

    (D) 某旅行社

    從與收件人對話，可以得知「Hans Import and Export Company」（漢斯進出口貿易公司），得知此為貿易公司，因此答案選 (B)。

29. 瑞貝卡懷特信中別為附上什麼文件？

    (A) 合約樣本

    (B) 簽證申請表

    (C) 有關翻譯費用和服務的小冊

    (D) 口譯與翻譯的文件稿。

    信中並沒有提及簽證申請表格，所以答案選擇 (B)。

30. 有關自由工作翻譯服務公司的陳述下列哪一項是真的？

    (A) 該公司已經在業界服務多年。

    (B) 該公司在 15 個國家有分公司。

    (C) 該公司的員工會説 20 種語言。

    (D) 該公司總部在南安普敦。

    信件第二段「Freelancer Translation Services has assisted over one hundred companies in the British Museum and the British Library for many years.」得知

    在業界服務多年，答案選擇 (A)，其他選擇的資訊錯誤。

每年春天，在瑞士愛彭斯會舉辦一個非傳統的比賽，女王之戰。這個比賽包含了艾宏斯的牛，一種具高度侵略性的品種。女王之戰，與人用殘暴儀式對抗公牛的西班牙鬥牛比賽非常不同。在瑞士的活動中，只有牛跟牛的比賽。兩者之間不同的方式是，在女王之戰，幾乎沒有流血事件。事實上，這個活動的比賽是相當溫馴的。牛隻們大部分的牛角都被綁住，並且以牠們的前額互推彼此。牛會轉來轉去然後第一個走掉的牛就輸了比賽。根據紀錄，有一些參賽者失去了牛角，但沒有人受傷過。

答案解析

31. 這篇文章大致上討論什麼？
    (A) 西班牙有名的傳統。
    (B) 牛的比賽。
    (C) 人對於鬥牛的反應。
    (D) 瑞士兩種不同的牛隻。

    根據文章第一段「Each Spring, an unconventional contest takes place in Aproz, Switzerland, called the Battle of the Queens.」清楚說明這是一項非傳統的牛隻比賽，因此答案選擇 (B)。

32. 女王之戰跟西班牙的鬥牛比賽有什麼不同？
    (A) 女王之戰有兩隻牛會戰死。
    (B) 女王之戰的牛不大可能會是傷。
    (C) 女王之戰是由人與牛爭鬥比賽。
    (D) 女王之戰中，一次只會出現一隻牛。

    根據文章最後一段「According to records, some of the fighters have lost horns, but none have been seriously injured.」答案選擇 (B)，參賽的牛隻不會受傷。

33. 在女王之戰中可以看到什麼？
    (A) 失去牛角的牛會得獎。
    (B) 嚴重的爭鬥會造成流血事件。
    (C) 兩隻牛都會綁住牛角。
    (D) 先離開的牛隻會贏得這場比賽。

    根據文章「The cows mostly lock horns and push each with their foreheads.」可以得知牛隻彼此都綁著牛角而且用前額互推彼此，所以答案選擇 (C)。

34. 我們可以知道有關西班牙鬥牛比賽的資訊？

    (A) 在瑞士很有名。

    (B) 一直都有愛彭斯的牛。

    (C) 典型活動造成流血事件。

    (D) 這個活動相當溫馴。

根據文章「The Battle of the Queens is different from Spanish bullfighting, in which humans fight bulls in a violent ritual.」可以得知西班牙的鬥牛比賽比較殘暴而且會有流血事件發生，因此答案選擇 (C)。

背景音樂、視覺佈置還有產品樣品的結合，使商店變成一個舒適的地方。有些商人也相信舒服的味道可以增進銷售。

「香氣行銷」的觀念主要透過香氣吸引顧客。商店老闆可以使用人工香味來營造情緒或加強商店銷售品的氣味。這些味道可以用一個簡單的噴霧系統來散發出去，而鞋盒尺寸的機器存在可以讓商店非常有香氣。

馬汀‧林斯壯，也是「收買感官」這本書的作者，解釋對於 80% 的男性與 90% 的女性來說，氣味帶來強烈與情感的回憶。這是因為嗅覺的記憶被儲存在大腦裡的邊緣系統，也是情感神經系統的家。因此，如果味道可以連結到正向的回憶時，他們可以激勵顧客來買產品，或者停留在商店久一些。

然而，不是所有人都能接受使用味道來販賣產品的原則。有些商店經理人也會擔心會污染空氣，或甚至造成客人有呼吸道問題的健康狀況。但標誌、顏色還有所到之處都有音樂情況下，某些商店一定會繼續嘗試這個方法 -- 若可以跟其他商店有所不同的話。

答案解析

35. 下列敘述不是商店老闆使用香氣的目的？

    (A) 喚起情感上的回憶。

    (B) 讓客人買更多商品。

    (C) 讓客人對他們的商品印象更深刻。

    (D) 吸引更多小孩。

此文章中沒有提到吸引小孩的部分，因此答案為 (D)。

36. _____ 可能是使用香氣來增加銷售的負面影響之一。

(A) 更多的消費。

(B) 健康問題。

(C) 糟糕的回憶。

(D) 非便利性。

根據本文最後一段「Some shop managers also worry about polluting the air and even causing breathing problems for customers with medical conditions.」可以得知，香氣的行銷策略對於呼吸系統上的醫療狀況可能對空氣產生污染而對人有健康的危害，所以答案選擇 (B)。

37. 根據文章最後一段，_____。

(A) 標示、顏色還有音樂對於商店來說都很普遍。

(B) 香氣行銷不再探討。

(C) 所有人跟商店喜歡使用香氣販賣產品這個想法。

(D) 行銷策略對於企業家來說是最好的解決方法。

根據文章第一段「Background music, visual displays, and product samples work together to make a shop a pleasant place. Some businesspeople also believe that pleasant smells could help increase sales.」即清楚說明這幾種方式是吸引顧客很好的辦法，所以答案選擇 (A)。

很難想像現代人會想在他們身上注入毒藥讓他們看起來更漂亮。然而，現今全世界很多人都支付數百美元來注射肉毒桿菌毒素，這是一種被稱為「肉毒桿菌」的有毒細菌。

肉毒桿菌會弱化還有讓人們的肌肉麻痺。因此，當在臉上注入肉毒桿菌時，它會減少人們外表上的皺紋。相同地，藉由麻痺汗腺神經，注射肉毒桿菌可以解決過度流汗的問題。所以，肉毒桿菌大量被用在美容的需求，來幫助人們看起來更年輕也更有魅力。

這些益處使得肉毒桿菌越來越受歡迎。單單在 2002 年，就有一百一十萬個美國人付費接受注射肉毒桿菌。肉毒桿菌是受全世界名人支持的化學物質，同時也受到不想在舞台上拼命猛流汗的奧斯卡提名人的喜愛。

很不幸地是，肉毒桿菌的使用卻不那麼責任。通常，肉毒桿菌的注射是由美容診所來執行，甚至沒有任何醫療顧問的許可，在一些人的家裡執行這樣的醫療行為。有人將肉毒桿菌存放在冰箱，但因為觸碰到食物，會造成食物中毒。這是很危險的，要考慮到肉毒桿菌如此強大，所以常常在戰爭中被當作武器。懷孕婦女注射肉毒桿菌會危及未出生的小孩，而且對於年紀高於 65 歲的老人也非常危險。因為它的作用只持續幾個月，所以需要不斷地使用，但卻增加危險性。

鑑於這些風險，人們必須思考，粗心使用肉毒桿菌導致的危險是否勝過衰老的現象。然而，人們仍會讓外表損害健康，沉迷於神話 "青春之泉" 的世界裡。青春之毒 -- 肉毒桿菌的不當使用仍然會持續下去。

答案解析

38. 這篇文章主要探討什麼？

(A) 有關病毒的醫療新發現。

(B) 一種可以看起來更年輕的時下方法。

(C) 一個有效去除皺紋的藥丸。

(D) 一個永久保持年輕的信念。

根據文章第一句話「It is hard to imagine that people would have poisonous shots on themselves to look more beautiful.」得知全世界的人們都著迷這個可以變年輕的方法，所以答案選擇 (B)。

39. 根據這篇文章，有關肉毒桿菌是正確的？

(A) 它可以消除緊張。

(B) 它可以增強肌肉。

(C) 它大部分是由有名人注射的。

(D) 它可以協助解決過度流汗的問題。

根據文章內容「Similarly, Botox injections can solve the problem of excessive sweating by paralyzing nerves that activate the sweat glands.」，正確答案選擇 (D)。其餘的選項資訊則是錯誤的。

40. 「外表凌駕於健康」的說法是指什麼？

(A) 外表比起健康還重要。

(B) 外表次於健康。

(C) 較美的外表可以改善心智健康。

(D) 外表跟健康都很重要。

根據文章內容「In a world obsessed with the mythical "fountain of youth," however, people continue to believe that looks eclipse health. The improper use of the poison of youth, Botox, continues.」可以得知，很多人寧願漂亮捨棄健康，所以正確答案選擇 (A)。

eclipse (n.) 日（月）蝕 / (v.) 掩沒…的重要性（或優點、聲譽等）；凌駕…之上；光芒蓋過…

E.g. The economy has eclipsed all other issues during this election campaign.
 這次大選期間，經濟問題成為壓倒性的重大議題。

Reflect on your present blessings, of which every man many ,not on you past misfortunes, of which all men have some./ Charles Dickens
多想想你目前擁有的幸福，這是每人都擁有很多的。不要回想以前的不幸，這也是每個人多多少少都有一些的。（狄更斯）

Road to GEPT--Learning English with British Culture 用英倫文化學全民英檢中級

作　　者：王靜怡
企劃編輯：溫珮妤
文字編輯：江雅鈴
設計裝幀：張寶莉
發 行 人：廖文良

發 行 所：碁峰資訊股份有限公司
地　　址：台北市南港區三重路 66 號 7 樓之 6
電　　話：(02)2788-2408
傳　　真：(02)8192-4433
網　　站：www.gotop.com.tw
書　　號：ARE000900
版　　次：2018 年 10 月初版
建議售價：NT$320

國家圖書館出版品預行編目資料

Road to GEPT：Learning English with British Culture 用英倫文化學
　全民英檢中級 / 王靜怡著. -- 初版. -- 臺北市：碁峰資訊, 2018.10
　　面；　公分
　　ISBN 978-986-476-753-3(平裝)
　　1.英語　2.讀本
805.1892　　31-10710/ 5 ～代B　　　　　　107003019

讀者服務

- 感謝您購買碁峰圖書，如果您對本書的內容或表達上有不清楚的地方或其他建議，請至碁峰網站：「聯絡我們」\「圖書問題」留下您所購買之書籍及問題。(請註明購買書籍之書號及書名，以及問題頁數，以便能儘快為您處理)
http://www.gotop.com.tw

- 售後服務僅限書籍本身內容，若是軟、硬體問題，請您直接與軟、硬體廠商聯絡。

- 若於購買書籍後發現有破損、缺頁、裝訂錯誤之問題，請直接將書寄回更換，並註明您的姓名、連絡電話及地址，將有專人與您連絡補寄商品。

- 歡迎至碁峰購物網
http://shopping.gotop.com.tw
選購所需產品。